WAR
OF THE
WITCHES

THE CLAN OF THE WOLF

MAITE CARRANZA

Translated by Noël Baca Castex

WAR
OF THE
WITCHES

THE CLAN OF THE WOLF

BLOOMSBURY

LONDON BERLIN NEW YORK

Bloomsbury Publishing, London, Berlin and New York

First published in Great Britain in 2009 by Bloomsbury Publishing Plc
36 Soho Square, London, W1D 3QY

Originally published in Spain by Edebé in 2005
Paseo de San Juan Bosco, 62
08017 Barcelona (SPAIN)
www.edebe.com

A CIP catalogue record of this book is available from the British Library

ISBN 978 0 7475 8853 5

The paper this book is printed on is certified independently in
accordance with the rules of the FSC. It is ancient-forest friendly.
The printer holds chain of custody.

FSC
Mixed Sources
Product group from well-managed
forests and other controlled sources
Cert no. SGS - COC - 2061
www.fsc.org
© 1996 Forest Stewardship Council

Typeset in the United States by Westchester Book Composition
Printed in Great Britain by Clays Ltd, St Ives Plc

1 3 5 7 9 10 8 6 4 2

www.bloomsbury.com

THE PROPHECY OF O

And the chosen one, Om's descendant, will arrive one day.

She'll have fire in her hair,
Wings and scales on her skin,
A howl in her throat,
And death in her eyes.

She will ride the sun
And brandish the moon.

CHAPTER I

ꟾELENE'S DISAPPEARANCE

The girl slept in a bedroom with high ceilings and walls that had been whitewashed a thousand times. It was a cheerful room in a small-town house that smelled of firewood and freshly boiled sweet milk. The window shutters were green, as were the geometric shapes on the Turkish rug covering the hardwood floor; the valleys in the paintings on the wall; and the spines of various children's books crammed on the shelves next to many others that were red, yellow, orange, and blue. An abundance of color spread boldly on the pillows, quilt, puzzle boxes, and the abandoned slippers under the bed. But these colors of childhood clashed now with the absence of dolls, relegated to the back of the closet, and the serious desk covered not with simple drawings but a state-of-the-art computer.

Perhaps the girl was not a child anymore. Even if she was still a child, she didn't know that she would cease being one that morning.

The bright sun filtered through the openings of the poorly closed shutters while Anaíd—that was the girl's name—moved restlessly and shouted in her sleep. A ray of sunlight slithered down her quilt, reaching her hand, slowly but tenaciously climbed her neck, then her nose, her cheek, and finally, brushed against her closed eyelids, waking her up.

Anaíd screamed and opened her eyes, confused. Still in a state of light sleep, unable to tell dreams apart from reality, she was out of breath and found the intense light invading her room rather strange.

In an incredibly vivid nightmare, she had run through a storm, looking for shelter in a forest of oak trees. Amid the roar of thunder, she could hear her mother's voice screaming, "Stop!" but she didn't pay any attention. Thousands of lightning bolts were falling all around her, dazzling her, blinding her, flooding the forest with a rain of fire, until one struck her and she suddenly fell dead.

Anaíd blinked and smiled, relieved. The playful ray of light that had filtered through the window shutters was to blame for everything.

There was no trace now of the electric storm that had lashed the valley the night before. The strong wind had swept away the clouds and the clear skies shone like the purple waters of the lake.

And that intense light—was it so late? Why hadn't her mother woken her up for school yet?

Anaíd jumped out of bed and suppressed a shudder when her bare feet touched the rug. She got dressed as usual, not spending more than a second on her outfit, and searched for her watch. Nine o'clock! She'd already missed her first class. And her mother? Why wasn't she up yet? Had something happened to her? She always woke Anaíd up at eight.

"Mother?" whispered Anaíd, pushing open the door to the adjacent room. The fear from her nightmare was creeping up on her, but she pushed it down.

"Mom?" she repeated anxiously, when she realized that there was no one else in the room except for her and the icy northern air coming through the wide-open window.

"Mother!" she shouted angrily, adopting the tone she used

whenever her mother pulled a prank on her. But this time Selene didn't jump out from behind the curtain laughing recklessly, or tackle Anaíd onto the half-made bed.

Anaíd took one, then two deep breaths and wished that the wind hadn't blown away the jasmine scent she liked so much. Shivering, she closed the window. Even though it was mid-May and the first spring buds had already appeared, it had snowed the night before. In the background, the dark-slate bell tower of Urt's monastery appeared sprinkled with white like a custard tart. This was a bad omen—it was a leap year—and she crossed her fingers like her grandmother, Deméter, had taught her.

"Mom?" Anaíd repeated once more in the kitchen.

Everything was as they had left it the night before, after the argument and before the storm and the nightmare. Anaíd searched meticulously. There were no traces of a stealthily drank cup of coffee, a nibbled biscuit, or a glass of water sipped at an unusual time. Her mother had not set foot in the kitchen. That was for sure.

"Mother!" insisted Anaíd, ever more nervous.

Her voice resonated in the garden, on the porch, and it even reached the old barn they used as a garage. Anaíd stopped for a moment in the rickety wooden doorway, struggling to adjust to the semidarkness inside the barn. The old car was still there, covered with dust, the keys in the ignition. Without it, Selene couldn't have gone far. Urt was out of the way and in the middle of nowhere. You needed a car to go to the city, the train station, the ski slopes, the mountains, the lakes, and even the supermarket on the outskirts of town. So, if she hadn't taken the car . . .

Anaíd had a sinking feeling. She returned to the house and rummaged around thoroughly. Her mother's belongings were still there. She couldn't have left the house without her coat, purse, keys, and shoes.

Anaíd was starting to feel déjà vu, remembering the morning her grandmother died. It was ridiculous, but everything seemed to indicate that her mother had vanished with what she was wearing, without so much as a hairpin, half-naked and barefoot.

Her heart pounding, Anaíd yanked her down jacket from the hall's coatrack and put it on as best as she could. She made sure her keys were in her pocket; then she closed the door behind her and started running. The freezing wind crept into the alley, whistling and zigzagging through the narrow corridor formed by the thick-walled houses built to withstand the northern wind.

Urt, with its stone houses and slate rooftops, stood at the head of the Istaín Valley, under the Pyrenees, and was surrounded by high mountain peaks and glacial lakes. In the town's square stood a Romanic church, which faced east so that its altar would receive the first ray of morning light. Up high, looming over the valley and at the beginning of the mountain pass, stood the ruins of a large fortified tower, now inhabited by crows and bats. In the past, a guard would stand watch day and night with only one task: to keep alive the torch that would light the bonfire if he saw an enemy approach. The signal from Urt's lookout tower could be seen from six different towns. And legend said that it was Urt's bonfire, in an anonymous and ignored feat, that stopped the relentless advance of the Saracen troops through the Pyrenees in the eighth century.

Anaíd was fairly protected from the wind until she crossed the ruins of Urt's old city walls. Once in the open, the north wind whipped at her face. Two big teardrops slid down her cheeks, but she still wasn't afraid. Facing the gale, she took the road to the forest without stopping even once.

. . .

The old oak grove looked pitiful early in the morning. Torn-off branches, charred ancient tree trunks, fallen leaves, scorched underbrush . . . The storm had left scars that only time would be able to heal. Little by little, and with the help of a stick, Anaíd cleared the muddy blanket covering the ground. She was terrified of finding what she was looking for. She told herself over and over again that it wasn't possible. But nonetheless she kept working carefully. She walked through every inch of the forest, checking every corner.

She was looking for Selene's body.

Anaíd would never forget the morning her grandmother had disappeared, or the night before her death. Deméter, a midwife, had died in the forest on a stormy night less than a year ago, on her way back from attending a birth. Just thinking of it, Anaíd could taste the salty tears she had cried all over again.

That morning, after a torrential storm, a discolored fog had covered the sky. Anaíd's mother was worried because Deméter had not slept in her bed, and Anaíd felt a vague fear. Selene didn't let her come to the forest with her—she wanted to do it alone— and when she returned, numb with cold, her eyes clouded with pain, she could barely speak the few words to tell Anaíd about her grandmother's death. It was not necessary, though, because Anaíd already knew. She had felt the bitter taste of death coming up her throat when she awoke. Selene choked out that she had found Deméter's body in the woods, and then fell silent. Usually a chatterbox, now she wouldn't answer any of Anaíd's questions.

On the days that followed, the house was full of distant relatives from all over the world. They received hundreds of letters, phone calls, and e-mails, but nobody dared say anything about Deméter's cause of death. In the end, they concluded she had been struck by lightning, and the forensic doctor—a specialist who flew in from Athens—confirmed it. Anaíd couldn't kiss her grandmother before she was put in the coffin; her body was charred, unrecognizable.

People in town spoke at length about the lightning bolt that struck Anaíd's grandmother the night of the electric storm, though no one ever understood what Deméter was doing in the oak grove at that time of night. Her car was found on the road, parked by the gutter, with the driver's window open, the headlights on, and the blinker flashing stubbornly.

Anaíd stopped in her tracks as reality flashed back through the oak trees. Her stick had touched something, a hard object covered by fallen leaves. Her hands trembled insistently, she couldn't help it. She remembered Deméter's advice for overcoming fear when panic took over. She quieted her mind, then removed the leaves with her boots and held her breath: before her was a still-warm body. It wasn't human . . . it was . . . it was . . . a wolf, or better said, a female wolf, for Anaíd could clearly see its mammary glands swollen with milk. Its cubs couldn't be too far. The poor things, they would starve to death without their mother's milk. Anaíd hoped that they were old enough to survive with the help of their pack. She studied the animal. It was beautiful. Its fur, despite being dirty with mud, was pearl gray, soft and silky to the touch. She felt sorry for the young she-wolf and covered its body again with dried leaves, branches, and stones to prevent it from becoming food for scavengers. The wolf was far from the mountains; it had descended to the valley, ventured into human territory, and found death. Why would this wild creature come down to the valley?

Anaíd checked her watch. It was noon. She thought it best to go back home and make sure everything was still the same. Sometimes, things changed unexpectedly and what seemed terrible earlier suddenly wasn't so bad anymore.

Counting on the remote possibility that she might find her mother at home, Anaíd took the road back and, unfortunately, ran into her classmates coming out of school. The last thing she needed at that moment was to have to explain herself or answer their annoying questions. She wasn't in the mood to put up with their taunting, either, so she turned around and darted in the opposite direction, walking toward the bridge. But when she turned her head to see if she'd managed to avoid them, she lost her balance. She didn't see the blue Land Rover coming down the hill; she only felt a strong blow to her leg and the screeching of brakes. Then a cry. And then nothing.

Anaíd was lying on the ground in a daze, unable to move. The driver, a blond, blue-eyed female tourist in casual attire, with a slight foreign accent, was kneeling over her, muttering and checking her body.

"Poor girl, don't move. I'll call an ambulance. What's your name?"

Before Anaíd could open her mouth, a chorus of voices replied for her.

"Anaíd Tsinoulis."

"The know-it-all midget."

"The nerd."

Anaíd wished she could melt and refused to open her eyes. She'd heard the voice of Marion, the most beautiful girl in class, the one who threw the best parties and never invited her. And she'd also heard Roc, Elena's son, who'd played with her when they were younger but now didn't speak to her, or look at her, or even notice her . . . She wanted to die.

She assumed all the class's vultures were standing around, pointing fingers, relishing in her misfortune, and making fun of her accident . . .

She was mortified.

Ever since the other girls in her class began growing taller and taller, leaving her behind and laughing at her small size, Anaíd felt as if she'd come from another planet. Neither Marion nor the other girls invited her to their birthday parties or on their nights out in the city. They didn't share their secrets or exchange outfits and CDs with her. And it wasn't because they were mad at her or envied her for getting better grades, but because they didn't even notice her. Anaíd's big problem was that despite being fourteen years old, she was only as tall as an eleven-year-old.

Invisible, she went unnoticed everywhere, except in the classroom. In class she shined with her own light, and that was her small tragedy. She understood everything quickly and got the best grades, so when she answered questions in class or got As on her exams, her classmates called her "the know-it-all midget." To make things worse, her intelligence also bothered some teachers, and more than once, she had regretted not shutting her mouth in time. Lately, she refrained from raising her hand and always tried to make a few mistakes in order to get lower grades. But it didn't matter; she was still the know-it-all midget. And that hurt; it hurt a lot.

Still on the ground, Anaíd wanted only for the kids to go away and leave her alone, to stop staring at her with their cruel, mocking eyes.

"You kids, get out of here!" the foreigner reprimanded them.

The same sweet and steady voice that had tended to Anaíd had become harsh and inflexible. Her classmates did as they were told and scattered. Anaíd, sprawled in the middle of the road, heard the soles of their shoes resonate as they ran down the cobblestone streets to spread the news of her accident.

"They are gone, Anaíd," murmured the beautiful foreigner.

Anaíd opened her eyes and immediately felt comforted. A knowing smile and a pair of eyes as deep blue as a lake awaited her—a heartwarming welcome.

"I think I'm okay," said Anaíd, suddenly optimistic, touching her injured leg.

"No, wait! Don't get up." The tourist tried to stop her.

But Anaíd had already jumped to her feet and was gingerly moving first her knee, then her ankle. She seemed okay.

"I can't believe it," whispered the foreigner, lifting Anaíd's pant leg and searching for a fracture.

"Really, I'm fine, it was just a scratch," said Anaíd, showing her leg and feeling the soft caress of a delicate, fair-skinned hand on her knee.

"Get in, I'll drive you to the doctor myself," the woman insisted. She took Anaíd's hand to help her get in the car.

"No, no, no. I can't go to the doctor," Anaíd refused.

The woman seemed to hesitate.

"I can't leave you, they need to take X-rays, tests."

Anaíd begged vehemently. "I really can't. I need to go home."

"So, I will go with you and talk to your mother."

"No thanks!" shouted Anaíd, already running down the street, completely recovered from her fall.

"Wait!" shouted the beautiful woman in confusion. She didn't know what to do.

But Anaíd had disappeared through the first alley on the left and, at that precise moment, was opening the door to her house.

But the house was still empty. Despite the good omen Anaíd had felt in the forest when she found the dead wolf, Selene hadn't returned.

Anaíd sat down in the rocking chair that once had been reserved for Deméter and rocked herself for a long time. The repetitive motion of her body going back and forth, swaying her sadness, calming her anxiety, soothed her and relaxed her mind. She couldn't rush; she needed to do things methodically, one after another. Her mother was out there somewhere, and if Anaíd couldn't get in touch with her, she might as well try to track her down.

Before going to anyone for help, Anaíd printed out every message sent or received from her mother's e-mail account during the past month. She wrote down the numbers of the last fifty phone calls in the answering machine's memory and checked her mother's bank account transactions to see if she had withdrawn any money in the past week or made any strange payments in the last month.

She also gathered her mother's correspondence, mostly about her work or from the bank, and flipped through her calendar, where she jotted down meetings, engagements, and names. Glancing over the information, she realized that the most repeated number in the dialed and received phone calls was from Jaca, the city closest to Urt, where they shopped frequently.

Without hesitating, Anaíd dialed the number. On the other end, a male voice answered, "Hi, I'm Max. I'm not home right now, but please leave a message." Anaíd hung up. Who was Max? Why had Selene never mentioned him? Was he a friend? More than a friend? There was no trace of him in her e-mail or calendar. The only interesting thing Anaíd found was some increasingly intimate and frequent correspondence with an admirer who said she was an avid reader of Selene's comics and suggested they meet in person.

Her e-mails were signed simply *S*.

. . .

Gaya was grading exams by the fire. Sometimes, like that afternoon, she lit it only for the simple pleasure of bringing her hands near the flames and enjoying its caresses. She regretted having accepted the position as a teacher in Urt. She had too many students, winter lasted ten months, and she had no time or energy left for her music. She'd thought the town would be a quiet destination and that the isolation would allow her to compose, but she was wrong. Interruptions occurred one after another, and the miserably cold air made the notes of her music perish, frozen before they were born.

She had been deceived and wound up in the eye of the storm. Right then, the bell rang, and Gaya knew from the anxiety that invaded her that the worst hadn't happened yet.

It was none other than Anaíd, Selene's daughter, who hadn't been at school that day. Gaya had actually just graded her exam. A good exam—too good. That's why she had lowered her grade by one point, claiming that her handwriting was too pointy. It wasn't that she didn't like the girl . . . Anaíd was awkward and shy, but she wasn't annoying. What bothered Gaya was that Selene took credit for her daughter's merits, and an A was excessive for the arrogance of that narcissistic redhead.

"What's the matter, Anaíd?"

Anaíd's eyes were red and she seemed scared. Before she could answer, she burst into sobs. Gaya lost her patience and made Anaíd blow her nose and drink some cold water. Anaíd splattered her sweater with water. She wasn't ugly looking. Her eyes, a magnetic cobalt blue, had always fascinated Gaya. But the poor thing was so ungainly, so skinny in those huge sweaters. With her few sparse, short hairs jutting out from under those woolen hats, she looked even worse. Gaya had never understood Selene's poor taste in dressing her daughter and cutting her hair that way. Nobody who saw them together would guess that such an attractive and provocative redhead was the mother of that scrawny teenager. Finally, Anaíd seemed to snap out of it.

"My mother has disappeared."

Gaya grew agitated.

"When?"

Gaya noticed that Anaíd was guiltily avoiding her eyes.

"When I woke up this morning, she wasn't there, that's why I didn't go to school. I've been waiting and waiting, but she hasn't come back."

Gaya considered the possibility that Anaíd was confused.

"She's probably at Melendres's office, discussing her last installment of *Zarco*."

Anaíd shook her head. Melendres was the editor of her mother's comics, and the two of them fought like cat and dog even though Selene's character, Zarco, was beginning to do quite well.

"She hasn't gone to the city; her car is in the barn."

"Perhaps—" Gaya tried to interrupt.

But Anaíd was sure.

"I've checked her shoes and coats, nothing is missing. And her purse with her keys, wallet, and credit cards is hanging from the coatrack."

Gaya turned pale and picked up the phone, barely paying attention to Anaíd. As she dialed, she was overcome with rage. If Selene was in front of her, she would slap her, yank her hair until she'd pulled it all out. She would step on those feet of hers squeezed into those flashy stiletto boots. Why? Why didn't she follow her advice? She had been seeking her own downfall for a year, ever since Deméter's death.

"Elena? It's Gaya. Anaíd is here, and she says that Selene has disappeared."

Gaya seemed taken aback by Elena's words.

"An accident?" She turned to Anaíd. "Elena says you had an accident, that you were hit by a car this morning."

Anaíd cursed all her classmates, especially Roc and Marion.

"It was nothing. The car barely touched me."

"Did you hear her? Okay, we'll be waiting for you."

Gaya replaced the receiver and stared at Anaíd. She felt sorry for her. She was alone and had been through one tragedy after another . . . But Gaya wasn't willing to pay for Selene's mistakes. Anaíd was Selene's daughter, not hers. She glanced at the exams, then at the fire, and couldn't help feeling irritated by all the trouble she'd have to go through no matter what decision she made.

"Elena is on her way, and she'll take you home with her."

Anaíd's eyes widened in surprise. "We have to go to the police."

"No!" cried Gaya instantly. Then, when she saw the counter-productive effect her words had had on Anaíd, she corrected, "What if she's run off with . . . someone? It would be a scandal. We'll look for her ourselves."

"But—"

"Your mother isn't always completely together; she does stupid things sometimes. Do you want people to point fingers at you, on top of everything else?"

Anaíd fell silent. She knew that despite being her mother's friend, Gaya envied Selene. She envied her curly red mane, her long legs, her congeniality and self-confidence. You didn't need to be very bright to realize that the self-righteous teacher would have sold her soul to the devil to be like Selene.

. . .

Elena, the town's librarian, who had provided all of Anaíd's children's books, came in panting. Anaíd was usually embarrassed in her presence as she could never tell when Elena was pregnant, had just given birth, or neither. She reckoned that Elena must have seven children, if she hadn't missed anyone. Roc was the eldest and was just like his father, the town's blacksmith—strong, sarcastic, with dark skin and hair. She and Roc had played in the forest and swum in the river when they were kids. Now Roc owned a motorcycle, wore flashy jeans, had his ear pierced, and went to the city on Saturdays . . . And if he ran into her, he looked away like everyone else.

Unlike Gaya, Elena was affectionate, and the first thing she did was hug Anaíd and smother her with kisses.

"Tell me what happened, honey."

"She doesn't know anything," interrupted Gaya.

"She must be able to give us a clue, something we don't know about . . ."

But Gaya was furious.

"We all knew it. We knew it would happen sooner or later."

"You're jumping to conclusions."

"What did Selene expect, with her short skirts and that long red hair, all curly and flamboyant, blowing in the wind? What did she expect with those articles on the Internet, being interviewed and photographed in her house, making those controversial statements, and daring to criticize public figures? Not to mention her constant speeding tickets! And her much-talked-about drinking."

Startled, Elena interrupted her.

"Gaya, please, Anaíd is here. Behave yourself."

But Gaya had felt like exploding for too long and couldn't hold back one last jab.

"Her ego has betrayed her."

Anaíd felt compelled to defend her mother.

"She is special, different . . . I love her."

Gaya's hard words made Anaíd brave, but also cautious. Anaíd decided not to share the information she'd gathered about her mother's last movements.

Gaya sighed. She despised Selene, so narcissistic and in love with herself, and she couldn't believe that the poor girl Selene had overshadowed and neglected like an old piece of furniture was now defending her.

"I'm sorry, Anaíd. I have nothing against your mother, only against her lack of judgment. It seems she is . . . looking for enemies, for attention, you know?"

"Are you saying that she's missing because of an interview on the Internet?" Anaíd asked sarcastically.

Gaya wished she had shut up minutes before.

"No, no, I . . . Well, I, forget it. But, just so you know, I really admired your grandmother Deméter. She was a real lady."

Elena took Anaíd's hands.

"Anaíd, did you hear anything last night, or sense anything was wrong like when—"

"My mother is not dead." Anaíd was abrupt, sharp. She didn't even question where the strength that urged her to reply so confidently was coming from.

Gaya and Elena exhaled, relieved. Anaíd's certainty left no room for doubts.

"How do you know that?"

"I know it and that's it."

Elena sat on a chair and was deep in thought for a moment before speaking.

"We'll do something, Anaíd. The two of us will help you find Selene, but you must help us, too. First of all, we must ask for something that will be very hard for a curious girl like you."

"What?"

"That you don't ask any questions."

Anaíd swallowed. She needed just one reason to be sure that complying would help them find Selene.

"Is she in trouble?"

Elena and Gaya looked at each other and nodded.

"Okay, I won't ask any more questions. What else?"

"That you don't speak to anyone about this. *Anyone*. Understood?"

Anaíd needed to take in Elena's words, to believe that there was a reasonable explanation for Selene's disappearance. And there was one.

Anaíd nodded. "What should I say to people in town?"

"We'll say . . . we'll say that she's out of town. In Berlin. Do you like Berlin?"

Anaíd nodded. "And in the meantime?"

"In the meantime, I will take care of you," said Elena.

"Where will I sleep?"

"Well, with . . ."

"I can't sleep in Roc's room!" Anaíd shouted with a hint of desperation.

"Why not? You are friends."

Anaíd thought she would faint. The worst thing that could happen to her was not her mother's disappearance but to be subjected to the most terrible embarrassment of her life—sharing a room with Roc. The possibility of living under the same roof felt like torture.

"No, we're not friends."

"So . . . you can make up. What do you think?"

"I think it's awful."

Elena sighed and brought her hand to her stomach. Anaíd noticed. Did it move? Elena's big belly shook restlessly. She must be pregnant again.

Gaya stroked Anaíd's hair with a tense hand, a gesture that, coming from her, meant a great deal.

"Come on, I'll go home with you to pick up your stuff, but you must eat something first. I'm sure you haven't had a bite all day."

Gaya brought out some cold chicken and vegetables to warm up on the stove. Anaíd hadn't had anything to eat since the night before, and despite hating vegetables, she was grateful.

CHAPTER 2

____

AUNT CRISELDA

Anaíd chewed the fritter slowly, praying it would last for hours. She didn't dare look up from the plate and face the nine pairs of eyes staring at her.

She was a novelty, an object of curiosity and attention for Elena's seven children. Elena's husband wouldn't stop talking about her like she was a newly discovered species of chimpanzee.

"See how Anaíd eats? Chewing slowly, not speaking with a full mouth, or burping, or wiping her greasy fingers on her shirt. She's the perfect example of a well-mannered girl."

Anaíd wanted to melt with embarrassment.

Elena tried to distract them.

"Oh, leave her alone. Roc, have you decided on a costume for Marion's party?"

Roc replied halfheartedly, "It's a secret. I can't talk about it."

Anaíd hadn't been invited, and when she remembered that, her fritter turned into a ball and got stuck in her throat. She began to get nervous. It was more than obvious that Roc didn't want to mention the costume because she was there. Was Elena dumb? Didn't she realize that she and Roc were like oil and water? And she still tried to be a matchmaker!

Try as she might, Anaíd couldn't swallow the fritter stuck in her throat. Without looking up, she grabbed her glass and took a sip.

"Anaíd hasn't wiped her mouth!" teased one of the brats.

Anaíd eyed him through the glass, which deformed him horribly, and shot him a dirty look. He was a toothless twin with a huge bump on his forehead.

His father tried to lighten things up. "It's okay, her mouth was clean."

"No, it had fritter all over it," attacked the other twin, who had a black eye. They must attack in pairs, thought Anaíd, who didn't know whether to wipe her lips with a napkin, throw water in the twins' faces, or run away. Elena saved her.

"Can you please leave her alone? Anaíd is just like you."

"No, she's a girl!"

"And girls have boobs."

"But Anaíd doesn't!"

"Enough!"

Anaíd turned red as a beet. The little monsters didn't let anything go. Right now they were probably sizing her up and making notes of their differences to spit out mercilessly later.

"Can I go out tonight?"

It was Roc, asking his father for permission.

"With Anaíd?" asked Elena.

"With Anaíd!" Roc exclaimed, surprised. "Why do you want me to go out with Anaíd?"

Anaíd knew that Roc was embarrassed to go out with her.

But Elena insisted, "She's our guest."

"I've already made plans with other people, and they won't like it if I show up with her."

Somehow Anaíd gathered the strength to speak up. "Actually, I have to stop by my house to print out a social studies assignment."

She said it in one breath. It was the only thing she had uttered during dinner, and she did it to bail out Roc and herself. But Roc didn't even have the decency to thank her.

Once on the street, she ran and ran and ran, but she didn't head home. She took shelter in a place only she knew. The same place where, alone, she'd cried over Deméter's death—her cave in the forest.

Before she died, Deméter used to take Anaíd to the oak grove. From a very young age, Anaíd helped her grandmother gather mandrake roots, belladonna leaves, thorn apple flowers, white henbane stems, and other medicinal plants. From Deméter, Anaíd learned about the forest. She learned to be wary of the hallucinogenic properties of the amanitas mushrooms growing under the lush oaks, and the poisonous leaves of yews and wild hemlocks.

With Deméter, she celebrated the winter solstice in the quiet of the night, facing north together and opening themselves to inspiration. During the spring solstice they faced the sun, born in the East, and prepared for wisdom. For the summer solstice, they looked south in the middle of the day and celebrated their dreams. When the autumn equinox arrived, and the sun hid in the West, it was time to harvest fruit and prepare for the rebirth of a new cycle.

Sometimes, Anaíd grew tired of Deméter's lessons and hid behind the bushes to avoid her calls. That's how she discovered her cave—she had crawled into a small crack in the rock and slid down a tunnel, which ended in a wonderful hollow with wide ceilings. As she explored, mesmerized by delicate stalactites and ponds and subterranean grottoes, she knew that it would always be her shelter from the world. A small place—comfortable and solitary—that had chosen her and not the other way around. From that moment on, she would hide there whenever she was scared.

That night, she wasn't afraid to cross the dark forest, to hear the owl's lonely cry, or to let herself slide down the tunnel to the depths of her cave. There, alone, with only the light of an oil lamp, she meticulously carved two pieces of black stone into the shape of teardrops, just as she had when her grandmother Deméter died. The stone came from a meteorite that had fallen in the woods the previous summer. It had the right polish and hardness Anaíd needed. For the second time, she hung a teardrop around her neck and buried the other at the cave's entrance. There was no one to give her directions, no one to explain the meaning of the ritual. But Anaíd found comfort in it still. It was her primitive way of marking her grief and expressing her pain to the world. Now two teardrops hung from her neck, one for each woman who had loved her and abandoned her.

Deméter, sensible and strict, but fair.

Selene, wild and extravagant, but loving.

Two dramatically different mothers had created a balance for Anaíd. When Deméter died, Anaíd clung to her mother like a baby. She recognized that Selene embarrassed her quite often, that she didn't behave like the other mothers, or dress like them. But Anaíd loved her nonetheless.

And now that Selene had disappeared, Anaíd was *alone*. But she didn't want to be afraid, so she repeated to herself that her mother would be back at any moment.

Crouching at the cave's entrance, Anaíd finished burying the stone teardrop. Even though she'd have liked to stay alone with her memories, a strange rustle made her jump to her feet and focus on the darkness around her. As she shook off the mud and dead leaves that stuck to her jeans, she turned around three times, certain that a pair of eyes gazed at her through the darkness of the forest.

On her way back to town, she silently accelerated her pace as she sensed a vague restlessness behind her. Perhaps it was the product of her exhaustion and sadness, but she could have sworn that the air was thicker and that the clear radiance of the crescent moon had diminished. Without Selene, her world felt smaller and gloomier, as though someone had captured the valley of Urt in a misty crystal ball.

. . .

"Anaíd, Anaíd!"

Elena was waiting outside of school. Anaíd reluctantly raised her head.

"Your aunt Criselda has just arrived."

Anaíd was so taken aback by the news that she didn't know how to react.

"My aunt? Which aunt?"

"Your grandmother's sister. Come on, I'm sure you remember her, she was at Deméter's funeral last year."

Anaíd was astonished—she remembered Criselda perfectly well, even though she didn't look at all like Deméter. She couldn't visualize Criselda's soft, indefinite features precisely, but she remembered her lavender scent and how she'd stroked Anaíd's hair. The touch of her hand on Anaíd's head had soothed her deeply, even though Aunt Criselda was not calm herself. Small, plump, and rowdy, her mind was focused on so many things at once that something always suffered—a plate, a glass, a vase, or a poor dog.

When she hugged Criselda lovingly, Anaíd was surprised to realize that, in the brief time she'd been there, her aunt had managed to turn the kitchen upside down. Why?

"It was dirty and a real mess. The kitchen is a house's soul and it needs to be clean and tidy," Criselda explained.

Anaíd didn't think to ask who had called Criselda; how she had gotten into the house; or where she'd gotten the strange idea that the first thing she should do was empty the cabinets and the fridge, shake Deméter's jars, taste all the spices Selene cooked with, align the pots and pans, and stick her nose in the bundles of herbs festooning the ceiling's beams.

Fortunately, Aunt Criselda hadn't yet had a chance to storm through the library, the living room, or the bedrooms. Anaíd wasn't upset. She was used to such eccentricities from her mother. And Criselda was saving her from a terrible situation. She would be able to sleep in her bed again and forget the nightmarish dinners at Elena's table and sleeping in the guest bed next to Roc. If this was her aunt's way of making herself comfortable, Anaíd would accept it, but what did her arrival mean?

"Have you heard anything about Selene?"

"We'll have news soon, honey, very soon."

While she spoke, Criselda rested her hand on Anaíd's forehead and erased her worries like a balm.

Motherly Elena returned to the kitchen after a few minutes with a delicious steamy stew of beef, potatoes, chickpeas, and cabbage. Anaíd wasn't a big fan of stew, but she was so hungry she didn't think to ask who had concocted such a time-consuming dish or where the ingredients had come from. Her fridge had never had cabbage; her mother hated cabbage.

As they began to devour the food, Anaíd listened carefully to the crisscrossed and somewhat enigmatic conversation between Criselda and Elena.

She learned that Elena was pregnant for the seventh time. It was a boy again.

Criselda admitted that she knew nothing about watching children, but she was planning to stay and take care of Anaíd and locate Selene.

But when Criselda said that she had smashed and thrown away

every jar in the kitchen, including Anaíd's growth hormone medication, Anaíd was furious.

Anaíd missed Selene all the time, but when she felt the worst she also missed Karen, her doctor and her mother's friend. Anaíd wished Karen would return from Tanzania, lay her on her sweet-smelling bed, tickle her with her stethoscope, and cure her. Since she was a little girl, Anaíd had thought that Karen's stethoscope was magical and with just a touch to her chest or her back, it could heal any sickness.

"I've been taking that medicine for four years! Since I was ten and Karen noticed that I was growing so slowly . . ."

Aunt Criselda was stunned.

"You are fourteen?"

Her genuine surprise infuriated Anaíd even more. She felt utterly insulted.

Aunt Criselda opened her big mouth and asked her something only nosy aunts would ask.

"Have you gotten your period yet?"

Anaíd felt two pairs of eyes scrutinizing her. Clearly, her reply was important, and there was great expectation around it. Anaíd didn't prolong the mystery; it was obvious that her female development was a disaster.

"No."

The two women exchanged a worried look. Elena shrugged her shoulders, as if she were saying, "Sorry. I wasn't aware of that detail."

"Anaíd, did your mother ever tell you to take precautions? To be . . . prepared in case . . . ," Criselda probed.

Anaíd was hurt. Who did they think she was?

"All my friends at school have gotten their period; I know what pads and tampons are. I won't cry or be afraid, don't worry."

But Anaíd's reply didn't make Elena or Criselda feel any better; they actually grew more worried. The unspoken conversations that always seemed to occur between adults, especially when uncomfortable outsiders were present, had always fascinated Anaíd. From a young age, she had tried to decipher the signals her mother and grandmother exchanged. Now Anaíd figured they were saying something like, "Selene has played quite a dirty trick on us," but she didn't understand what they could mean, and she was still worried about her medication.

"And what will I take now? Selene was the only person who knew Karen's formula, and now Karen is working at a hospital in Tanzania."

Suddenly, Anaíd wondered how she'd learned that Karen had traveled to Tanzania. It had been very peculiar, like a revelation. She just knew it, the way she knew that Selene was alive and the way she also knew, a year ago, when she awoke abruptly at three in the morning, that her grandmother was dead.

"Don't worry; we'll take care of it. Criselda will prepare a medicine with the same prescription. I'm sure I've seen it somewhere."

Even though the word "somewhere" got lost in the immensity of the old house, Elena's maternal and practical spirit was enough to appease Anaíd, though she wouldn't completely relax until she saw with her own eyes that Aunt Criselda hadn't ravaged her special shampoo as well. Anaíd had such horrible hair that if she didn't use a hair fortifier and wash her hair with vitamin shampoo, it fell out in handfuls.

Why was Selene tall and slim with beautiful hair? Next to her, Anaíd felt like an ugly duckling. But despite that, she missed her. Her mother was so worldly and self-confident, so chatty, friendly, and outgoing, that just remembering her made Anaíd feel better and dream of being like her someday. She wasn't that angry about the medication; it was a combination of everything.

Aunt Criselda took her hand and looked deep into her eyes.

"I want you to explain it to me from the beginning. Tell me everything you remember from the night of Selene's disappearance. Everything."

And she whispered that "everything" so persuasively that Anaíd's memories—which she'd pushed away so they wouldn't hurt her—suddenly came pouring back.

One by one, obediently, Anaíd's memories arranged themselves single file and came out of the drawers of her mind so that Aunt Criselda could dust them off and study them carefully.

. . .

"Mother poured me some cranberry juice, which I love, and asked me to sit with her on the porch so we could name the constellations. While I searched for Andromeda and Cassiopeia, she caught me off guard, suggesting I spend my summer vacation in Sicily with Valeria, a friend of hers. She told me that Valeria had a house on Taormina Beach, at the bottom of Mount Etna, and a daughter my age. Then she showed me a plane ticket. I couldn't believe it—she had planned everything and hadn't said a word to me. I didn't react the way she thought I would; I didn't jump with happiness or kiss her or run to try on my bikini from last year. I just asked why she thought I would enjoy spending the summer by myself, in a foreign country, with a family I didn't know. She seemed nervous and angry. She even squinted—Mother always squints when she is in trouble. She didn't want me to notice that it was really important to her that I left the house. She pretended she didn't care and told me that everything had been a coincidence; that she'd thought of it when Valeria called to congratulate her on *Zarco*. During their phone conversation, it occurred to her that buying the ticket would be a great surprise for me. She said that if I didn't want to go, she would cancel it immediately, but that it would be a pity because Clodia, Valeria's daughter, was really nice and had lots of friends, and I needed to see the world and be around people my age. But I said, 'No, definitely not.' I didn't feel like it. And it wasn't that I wasn't curious or thought Sicily was boring. I would love to visit the Syracuse amphitheater and Palermo, climb Mount Etna, and dive headfirst into the Mediterranean. But no way was I going to be the laughingstock of Clodia and her *amici Italiani*. The more 'good qualities' Clodia had, the less I wanted to go. Didn't she understand my problems at all? If she had told me that poor Clodia had leprosy and couldn't leave the house because her fingers and ears were falling off, then maybe I would have accepted.

"But she just thought I was trying to annoy her and said I was stupid and irresponsible, and that I didn't know anything. She threatened me. She said that ... something bad would happen, a terrible tragedy. She said that if she went missing, if she had no choice but to leave or something happened to her ... someone should keep me company. I was so mad that she had used such a dirty trick to get away with her plan, I couldn't see the big picture. I thought she wanted to get me out of the way so she could spend time alone with someone. And that someone must be really important to her—the reason why she put on perfume, makeup, tight dresses, and went to the city on certain nights. I was convinced that my mother had a boyfriend I couldn't meet because I wasn't important enough, or because she was embarrassed of me. I refused to budge and swore I would never go to Taormina. Then I did what she hated the most—I got up without saying a word and left. She followed me to my room—trying to make me look her in the eye, begging me to talk to her, and forcing me to listen so I would calm down. But she just wanted to study me so she could aim for my weaknesses. But I refused to give in, just got into bed, turned off the light, and pretended to sleep.

"And I never saw her again.

"That night, I was woken up by lightning. The light was so bright that when I opened my eyes, I thought it was daytime. I had dreamed that I was sunbathing in Taormina, next to an Italian leper, and that Mount Etna was erupting. It was frightening to look at the sky and hear the thunder booming on the walls. Even the crows looked scared and kept flying in circles outside my window. Now that I think of it, and I remember thinking of it then, the crows were huge and deformed, and it was as if they were trying to get inside the house. One of them stared at me through the glass. It had intelligent eyes, and I felt it was talking to me, urging me to open the window and . . . for a moment, I almost did.

"Then I closed my eyes and tried to keep sleeping despite the storm.

"I didn't go to Selene's room so she wouldn't think that I was accepting her offer. I was still mad and wanted to show it. So I didn't move from my room and didn't climb into her bed, like other times. And she didn't invite me to go outside and dance in the garden under the rain until we fell in the mud, soaked and exhausted. We used to do that every time it poured, and my grandmother always scolded us at the top of her lungs.

"The following day, Selene wasn't in bed and her bedroom window was open. I thought she might be in the shower or in the kitchen. But she wasn't anywhere in the house. Nothing was missing—her sneakers, her book, her toothbrush, her hairpins—except for her. There were no signs of struggle or violence, either;

there was no blood on the floor or hair on her pillow. Everything was intact, as if Selene had vanished in her sleep, as if she had flown out the window and would come back to her bed at any moment.

"I didn't touch anything, everything stayed the way she had left it, but that morning I walked through the forest. I was afraid I would find my mother's body hit by lightning.

"But I only found a dead female wolf and, though I didn't know how, I knew that my mother was alive."

The Prophecy of Odi

She will stand out among them all,
Will be queen and succumb to temptation.

They will fight for her favor and offer her the scepter,
Scepter of destruction for the Odish,
Scepter of darkness for the Omars.

The chosen one's heart will reveal the truth.
The one will defeat the others.
Forever.

CHAPTER 3

ƧELENE

Selene lay still on a bed of straw, taking slow, rhythmic breaths. She didn't want to waste her strength, for she hadn't had anything to eat or drink in three days.

Green flies flew around the defecation box, and some of them stopped on her forehead and cheeks, but Selene didn't scare them away. Even though her body was there, her soul was floating far away from that dark fifty-square-foot hole. Absolute control over her body allowed her not to feel hunger, cold, thirst, or repulsion. Even her sense of smell had grown used to the stench of urine that had turned her stomach when she arrived.

Had her isolation not been interrupted, Selene would have probably remained detached from her surroundings. But she heard footsteps drawing near and knew that she wouldn't be able to continue numbing her senses. Again, she looked at the walls oozing dampness, the lice and bedbugs jumping all over the place, the roaches climbing the bed rails, and the mice's snouts quivering when they smelled her agony. As she let her guard down, she wrinkled her nose in disgust—she could smell blood, sweat, and fear dripping from the walls, and the filth of the yellowish, bloodstained straw mattress she was lying on. The self-control she had mastered vanished into thin air at the prospect of the door opening and the hope of a warm, clean, luminous world seeping in through that hole. As a prisoner, Selene was at the end of her rope. In a moment of weakness, she allowed herself to wish she could flee that dungeon at any price.

The door opened without the need for a key. In an effort to recover her dignity, Selene stood at full height, straightened the creases of her light nightgown, and ran her fingers through the thick red hair falling over her naked shoulders.

"Well, well, well," whispered her visitor, staring at her, "you are more beautiful than I expected."

Selene, her face blank and rigid as marble, was unaffected by her keeper's kind words.

"Your strength is admirable. You haven't asked for water, food, or warm clothes; you haven't moaned or cried; and you haven't contacted anyone."

Selene gazed at her haughtily.

"What did you expect?"

"Honestly, I thought you'd use your magic."

Selene laughed.

"I save it for more important things."

The visitor stood across from her prisoner and stared at her. She was as tall as Selene, perhaps younger, and without a doubt, as stunning as the exotic redhead, though hers was a classical beauty—oval face; slanted black eyes; jet-black hair; and snow-white, almost translucent skin. Her complexion was so fascinating that, for a moment, Selene followed the trail of the bluish veins in her face, vibrating in tune with her heartbeat; blood waterfalls anxious for rain.

. . .

Selene held her gaze fiercely. The stranger's eyes, two incandescent hot coals, pierced her flesh and wounded her mind, but despite being weak from lack of food, Selene didn't faint.

34

The visitor stopped her game before Selene blinked or showed any sign of vulnerability. She simply grew tired of it.

"You are powerful. The first Omar to resist my gaze."

Selene smiled wryly.

"You are Salma, I suppose."

"You suppose correctly."

Selene measured her words and responded with just a hint of anger.

"Our beginning has not been very promising. You lied to me."

Salma concealed her surprise.

"Are you calling me a liar?"

Selene still wasn't afraid.

"You promised you'd wait until summer."

Salma's chuckle sounded hollow, like the echo of a laugh repeated a thousand times. It was an old, worn-out laugh.

"What do two months matter, when compared with eternity?"

"A great deal. This is not what I planned. Everything happened so quickly that I had no time to erase evidence of our communication, or give a sound alibi, or leave my job properly, or close the house, or pay the bills . . ."

"So what? Nobody is essential. In a few months they'll declare you missing, and everyone will forget you, including your editor."

But Selene didn't agree.

"My friends won't give up. They'll search for me. They'll cause you trouble, you can be sure of that. They will put two and two together and get in my way . . ."

Salma thought Selene might be right.

"You'd have preferred to fake your own death . . ."

Selene nodded.

"That was the deal."

Salma shrugged.

"It was the Countess's order. I was doing things my way until she changed the dates."

Selene was speechless for a moment, but she recovered.

"I need to go back and fix everything. I still have time to stop my disappearance from causing any more commotion than is necessary."

But Salma wasn't about to allow it.

"Impossible. The Countess wants to see you."

Selene trembled. A slight tremor fluttered from the nape of her neck to her cold fingertips.

"Is she back?"

"No."

"So?" Selene asked nervously, sensing the answer.

"You'll have to appear before her. You'll come with me to the Dark World."

Selene turned pale and clung to the bed rails, undaunted by the cockroach she crushed.

"The Dark World?"

"Are you afraid?" Salma asked with scorn.

Selene wasn't embarrassed to be afraid now. Her fear wasn't unfounded.

"No Omar has ever returned," she said.

Salma laughed her hollow laugh again.

"You are not just *any* Omar."

Selene thought quickly; she couldn't make Salma or the Countess wait.

"I'll go . . . on one condition. I need to go home and erase my tracks first."

Salma smiled. "I'll do it."

"You?" exclaimed Selene, horrified.

"It will be fun," whispered Salma, suddenly acting like a naughty child. "I will mislead them."

"No, Salma. Not you. Besides, it's been three days already."

"It doesn't matter."

Selene grew angry. "I've told you not to go near my house. You'll regret it."

Salma was suddenly quiet, her silence too long for Selene to remain calm.

"Are you hiding anything?" Salma asked.

Selene shook her head.

Salma's face showed her annoyance.

"One more week here will help you recover your memory."

Selene grew desperate. Salma turned around, ready to leave again without offering her as much as a drink of water or a blanket. *No.* Selene knew that once hope takes form, it is impossible to banish. "Wait," she pleaded.

Salma paused and waited for Selene to speak.

"There's a man, Max, who lives in the city and will be waiting for me. He's crazy about me."

"And you?"

Selene bit her lip before responding. His kisses still hurt.

"I'll be able to forget him."

"Anyone else?"

"A girl."

"A girl?"

"My adopted daughter."

"A daughter?"

Selene made up her mind impulsively. "She's not mine; Deméter forced me to raise her. She was more her daughter than mine."

"An Omar?"

"No, an unattractive, somewhat awkward mortal, without any powers or special attributes . . ."

"And why is she important?"

Selene thought of a fluffy bed, a glass of fresh water, a warm bath, a cozy bedroom, a bright ray of sun. She stared at the astute Salma. She couldn't lie to her.

"She thinks I'm her mother and . . ."

"And?"

"I care for her," she admitted, lowering her head.

CHAPTER 4

ANAÍD'S AWAKENING

A telegram arrived on the same day Aunt Criselda appeared. It was addressed to Anaíd, though the writing didn't look like Selene's. Nevertheless, the telegram's words hurt her deeply. It read:

Anaíd,
Don't look for me. Max picked me up in his
car and we'll begin a new life away from
everything. It wouldn't have worked with the
three of us. I will send Elena money. You'll
forget me. Selene.

Anaíd read those words until she was sick of them. So it was true. Max was real; he was a flesh-and-blood man, her mother's lover in the city, someone Selene preferred over her. She wanted to dial Max's number again and shout a message into his voice mail, demanding that he bring Selene back to her, but that would be ridiculous. Selene loved him and by now they would be miles away.

Aunt Criselda, her glasses on, read the telegram in disbelief and drove Anaíd crazy with questions about Max and her mother's escapades. But Anaíd didn't respond, she just wanted to be left alone to cry.

Elena arrived a few hours later; she had found an envelope containing money and some bills—which she gave to Criselda—and a brief typewritten note signed by Selene, in which she begged Elena to take care of Anaíd and promised to send more funds later on.

"Where did she get the money?" Anaíd asked herself aloud.

"All her bankbooks and credit cards were in her purse and I already checked every transaction; she hasn't withdrawn any money."

Elena and Criselda looked at Anaíd, surprised.

"You said Selene didn't take anything with her."

Anaíd thought of what her eyes had seen the day after the storm.

"Everything is here: her clothes, her shoes, her coat, and her purse—"

As she spoke, Anaíd was shocked to realize that Selene's bag and her coat were both missing from the coatrack.

"But I saw them hanging there!" she protested.

Elena and Criselda exchanged a knowing glance.

"And her shoes?"

"Come see. Everything is here, even her suitcase."

But when she went upstairs and opened her mother's closet, Anaíd turned pale—it was half-empty. Only an old pair of Wellington boots with holes and two ratty moccasins were left on the floor. The spot where she kept her suitcase was now empty, and her book, her sunglasses, and her hairpins were missing from the night table. Anaíd walked cautiously to the bathroom. She couldn't believe it—there was no toothbrush, no shampoo. Even the loofah she used in the shower every morning was gone.

But that wasn't the strangest thing to happen that afternoon. When Anaíd showed Criselda and Elena her mother's e-mail in-box, to prove that she hadn't said good-bye to anyone or told her editor she was leaving, the messages had changed. In several e-mails dated before her disappearance, Selene had announced she was leaving her publishing house and canceled some appointments—a seminar, a conference on comics, and the opening of an art gallery. Anaíd compared the messages with the e-mails she had printed out three nights before. They weren't the same. Nor was there any trace of the relationship with that enthusiastic admirer, *S*, who had praised Selene so much.

Anaíd showed her printouts to Elena and Criselda, but neither deemed them important. When Criselda complained that the saved numbers had been erased from the phone's speed dial, Anaíd was shocked and decided to keep quiet.

It was more than obvious that someone had come back to wipe out her mother's tracks.

Anaíd shuddered.

How did this person get into the house?

How did he or she know which were Selene's personal belongings?

How did the phone's memory get erased?

Was it possible to write e-mails dated in the past?

There was only one explanation: Selene had done it herself.

Anaíd felt sick, really sick. Shivering, she climbed into bed.

. . .

She didn't have a fever, but she felt much worse than when she'd had pneumonia and was hospitalized with convulsions. Anaíd's whole body ached, from the roots of her hair all the way to her toenails. She felt her bones crack one by one and her insides stir.

She felt knives stabbing her tendons and a thousand needles pierce her muscles. Her skin felt so tight, Anaíd thought it would burst. It was impossible to sleep, sit up, read . . . or simply think.

For two weeks she'd felt like she was about to die. She had missed school, but that didn't matter to her. The doctor said that she was upset about her mother; she needed to rest and not worry about her studies. Anaíd was embarrassed. People were gossiping, and even though Anaíd had refused to believe it at the beginning, she'd begun to think that Selene might have left in a fit of madness. It would have been just her style—disappearing only to return one night to get her things, rewrite her e-mail, erase her phone calls, and send the telegram and the money. She had done everything without daring to face the music. Avoiding Anaíd. Anaíd wanted to hate her mother for being a coward and a liar, and for cutting Anaíd out of her life like an infected appendix. She'd have liked to stand in front of Selene and accuse her of being selfish and absolutely irresponsible, just as Deméter always had. But Anaíd also knew she needed her mother, even if she was selfish, greedy, irresponsible, or crazy . . .

What worried Anaíd the most during those days was her head, or what was inside of it; instead of a brain, she seemed to have a swarm of bees or a sawmill. The buzzing was unbearable and constant, but it became more acute in certain times and places. One afternoon, Anaíd tried to find some quiet in her shelter, but she couldn't walk all the way through the oak grove. Before reaching her cave, she had to turn around and run back. The jumble of sounds coming from the forest had heightened the buzzing to an unbearable level, and she nearly went mad.

Anaíd tried to think the way Karen would have, and even tried to ask Karen how she should behave. The answer came by means of a whisper on a sleepless night. *"Anaíd, honey, don't fight the pain and* noise. *It's your body, the sounds are part of you. Don't reject them, breathe deeply; listen to the sounds inside of you, accept them, let them be part of you."*

The voice's suggestion worked like magic. Anaíd was able to relax and the pounding in her head subsided, especially at night.

But after having slept a bit, she awoke at dawn, her eyes flying open and her heart hammering. Were the walls of her room speaking? What was that behind the curtains? She thought she could see a slender lady in an elegant dress, and an old-fashioned warrior, in armor and a helmet, standing on the rug.

These hallucinations began appearing every night, and they were always the same. The lady and the knight were bold and curious; they watched her brazenly and seemed to be on the verge of speaking at any moment. It was perhaps the most amusing aspect of everything that was happening to her.

Meanwhile, all sweet Aunt Criselda did was screw up and cause trouble. Anaíd tried to explain the symptoms of her strange illness, but after she had visited the doctor and not gotten a clear diagnosis or a helpful medication, her aunt panicked. Criselda insisted she didn't know anything about children, and forced Anaíd to drink a nauseating liquid that made her vomit. Criselda spent most of the day making phone calls or rummaging through the bookshelves and Selene's bedroom. Lately, she was concerned about their difficult financial situation—she had discovered that when Deméter died, Selene mortgaged the house and started wasting money left and right. She changed her car, bought new furniture, traveled, and bought other things on a whim. Now the debt and unpaid bills were about to drown them, and Aunt Criselda didn't know where to get money from. Melendres, Selene's editor, was a scoundrel. He refused to advance them a single penny unless Selene signed her invoices in person.

But Anaíd wasn't concerned about those things. Besides, she didn't trust Aunt Criselda. Except for Aunt Criselda's miraculous hands, which erased Anaíd's worries, Anaíd didn't look to her for help. She would never ask her to cook a potato omelet (she fried it with vinegar) or a steak (she served it raw) or to wash a sweater (she ruined it with bleach).

What she couldn't understand was why it was always assumed that adults took care of children. In her case, it was the complete opposite. On the other hand, Aunt Criselda seemed to enjoy all the lunches and dinners Anaíd prepared. Luckily Criselda would eat anything—spaghetti with carbonara sauce, spaghetti with tomato sauce, or spaghetti with pesto sauce, it was all the same to her. In that respect, Anaíd was grateful for her aunt's lack of taste. It was clear that Criselda was a very strange type of adult, and that the women in Anaíd's family weren't at all alike. With so many different personalities, they could populate a zoo.

Fifteen days after Selene's disappearance—and exactly thirteen days after Aunt Criselda's arrival—Anaíd realized that her clothes didn't fit anymore. Whether it was the spaghetti overdose, the bed rest, or her nerves, she didn't know, but her pants' zippers wouldn't go up, she couldn't button up her shirts, and she was astonished to realize that she needed a bra. Anaíd couldn't believe that, for the first time in her life, she was growing. And Selene wasn't there to celebrate it!

But she didn't want to mention any of this to Aunt Criselda. Her aunt was too indiscreet and clueless about girls. She would proclaim to the four winds that her niece needed a bra, or she'd say she had no idea about girls' underwear. So Anaíd decided to go out by herself, at dusk, when the noises died down and her head stopped fuming for a few hours. She grabbed money from the envelope in the bureau and left for the department store, praying that Eduardo wouldn't be there. They played together in the town's band: she the accordion, he the trombone. Eduardo had never looked at her, didn't even know she existed, but Anaíd often looked to her left for a glimpse at the beads of sweat on his dark forehead, and the vein that swelled in his neck as he played. Eduardo was older, he lifted weights at the gym, had a girlfriend, and was super hot, or that's what her friends said, envious that she played next to him in the band. If Eduardo was working she would be mortified. She would melt before the counter. She'd rather die before letting Eduardo sell her a bra.

But Eduardo was there.

Anaíd saw him clearly through the shop's window and turned around nervously, ready to leave. She was so distracted that she bumped into a woman and fell.

"Oh, I'm sorry," she said, feeling stupid for apologizing on top of falling.

"No, it was *my* fault," replied the woman in a slight foreign accent.

And they were both speechless when they recognized each other.

"Our fate is to crash . . . ," joked the beautiful foreigner, the same woman who had driven the blue Land Rover the morning Selene disappeared and had run into her by accident on the road that led to the bridge.

Together they burst into laughter.

"Are you all right?"

"Oh, yes. Thank you."

"Well, you won't get away today; I owe you for hitting you with my car. Would you like a croissant and a hot chocolate with whipped cream?"

Anaíd hesitated. How did she know that she loved chocolate with whipped cream? Anaíd celebrated all her birthdays in the chocolate shop with her mother, sometimes with friends or maybe by themselves, and now it had been two weeks since she'd had any chocolate. Her mouth watered. Buying (or not buying) her first bra was more than enough reason to celebrate, and Selene would have probably suggested it herself.

"I know a coffee shop close by," Anaíd said.

The beautiful foreigner smiled and extended her arm in a natural and elegant gesture. Just as naturally, Anaíd took the woman's arm and guided her through the alleys, occasionally glancing sideways at her.

She had very fair skin, ash-blond hair, deep-blue eyes the color of the ocean, and a charming smile. She was gorgeous and fascinating, foreign without a doubt, though Anaíd couldn't figure out where her accent was from. Each year, the tourists arrived at the beginning of spring and the end of the ski season. They stayed at the town's hotel and camping grounds. Some went rafting, taking advantage of the first thaws to enjoy the river's rapids. Others went hiking in the mountains, weather permitting, and dotted the valley with the colors of their bright jackets. The hikers soon gave way to daring climbers, who arrived in midsummer, when the ice had melted from the cracks on the rock. And there were also those who simply walked through the valleys and visited the lakes, enjoying the magnificent views and taking in the healthy mountain air. The polite foreigner seemed to belong to this last group.

"Is your mother waiting for you?"

A knot formed in Anaíd's throat. Her mother wasn't waiting for her. She didn't have a mother, or even a grandmother. Only a good-for-nothing aunt.

"I didn't introduce myself the other day. My name is Cristine Olav."

"I'm Anaíd."

46

"I remember. What a pretty name, Anaíd, impossible to forget. And it suits you. Did you know you are quite beautiful?"

That wasn't true. Anaíd knew she wasn't beautiful, but when Ms. Olav said it so genuinely, she believed that she was, in fact, beautiful, admired, and, above all, loved.

And so, despite her promise to Elena, she told Ms. Olav about Selene's recent disappearance and her sudden illness and even—why not?—the arrival of her aunt and her thwarted attempt to buy a bra. Anaíd told her everything. She needed someone to be interested in her, to listen to her carefully, and to smile. Ms. Olav was a bit vague about her own situation. She said she was staying at the hotel for a few days, that she was on her way somewhere else, and that she was planning to visit the lakes. Then her face lit up.

"Would you like to come with me?"

Without even blinking, Anaíd accepted. Throughout the whole meal, she hadn't felt the buzzing in her head, the constant pain in her joints, or the sadness caused by Selene's absence. Ms. Olav and hot chocolate with croissants were the best medicine she'd tried so far.

Suddenly Ms. Olav stood up and gestured that she'd be back soon. Anaíd figured she was going to the bathroom and took advantage of her absence to gobble up the second croissant and ask Rosa, the waitress, for another spoonful of whipped cream, please, because the chocolate was delicious but she'd run out of cream.

Anaíd didn't know if Ms. Olav was gone a minute or an hour, but she was gone long enough to bring back a present. With a mysterious smile, Ms. Olav handed Anaíd the gift, wrapped with paper from Eduardo's store.

Anaíd couldn't believe it. Ms. Olav had bought her the prettiest bra she'd ever seen. It had a lively pattern of striking geometric figures in green and blue on a red background. Would it fit her?

She stood up and headed to the bathroom to try it on. It was perfect, clinging to her body like a second skin, and exactly what she had wanted—fun, casual, comfortable. She'd never heard of the brand, but none of the girls at school had a bra like it, she was sure of that. She put on her sweater and ran to the table to thank the wonderful Ms. Olav for the present. But, to her surprise, she found only a box of chocolates sitting on the table.

"They're for you," said Rosa.

Anaíd wasn't hungry anymore. She picked up the chocolates while Rosa cleared the mugs and explained that the foreigner had paid and, along with the chocolates for Anaíd, she'd left a generous tip.

. . .

Elena was uncomfortable. She sat in her kitchen, next to Criselda, peeling beans and watching the stew. But no matter how she sat, the baby kept kicking her stomach with its small feet. They were dry, heavy blows, and the last one had left her out of breath.

"So it's true?" Elena asked.

Criselda nodded and put a chocolate in her mouth, tempting Elena to take one.

"Indeed. The Saturn-Jupiter alignment has already occurred. And it coincides with the prediction the astronomer, Hölder, made in her treatise about the arrival of the chosen one."

"And the alignment of the seven planets?"

"It's coming. In two or three months, perhaps," Criselda replied.

Elena turned down the chocolate and continued peeling beans.

"Take away the box; they are too good," said Elena. Then, thoughtful, she added, "Everything seems to make sense. The stars' alignment and the lunar meteorite mark the when and where."

"Here and now."

"I can't believe it. We suspected Selene was the chosen one, but there was no evidence like this."

"The Odish have known it for some time—since the incident . . . since Deméter died," said Criselda.

"Bloody strigas . . . Those bloody Odish witches almost took Anaíd, too."

Criselda shook her head with emphasis.

"Anaíd can't have seen a striga, she hasn't been initiated."

"Oh, no? Her description of the crow was certainly that of a striga. She said it was deformed and enormous, with intelligent eyes, and that it even spoke to her . . . It tried to bend her will," rebutted Elena.

"But . . . had it been a striga, Anaíd would have ended up like Selene. Nobody, let alone a girl, can resist their will," argued Criselda, stubborn as a mule.

"And what about that Max?"

"It's not worth trying to find him. He probably doesn't exist."

Elena grew nervous; the baby felt it and began his soccer practice again—one kick, two kicks. There were so many strange things going on. And she was convinced that Criselda was hiding even more from her.

"So you are saying that Anaíd was right, that the disappearance of Selene's clothes, the telegram, the money, everything that justified her departure was a trick to make us believe she'd left of her own will."

"I knew it from the beginning," said Criselda.

"So . . . Why did you let Anaíd believe her mother left her for a man?"

"What were we going to say to her?" Criselda replied, chewing another piece of chocolate.

"The truth," Elena shot back. "She has a right to know the truth."

"That should be decided by the coven."

"Fine, but until then, we have to protect her. She's fourteen— give her a protection shield," begged Elena.

"Me?" objected Criselda, nervously getting up from the table.

She was so anxious that she couldn't remain seated for five minutes and couldn't keep her hands still. She grabbed a ladle from the marble countertop. Elena insisted.

"In her sleep, without her noticing it. Do you remember the spell?"

As she encouraged Criselda, Elena was saddened to realize that she had never recited the spell, and given her bad luck of conceiving only boys, she might never have the chance. The protection shield was intended to protect teenage girls from the curse of the Odish, and prevent them from bleeding to death during the delicate passage from girlhood to womanhood. Anaíd was impulsive and needed to be protected.

Criselda was anxious. It was obvious that she had never created a protection shield for a teenager. She stirred the huge pot of stew vigorously as she spoke.

"But Anaíd looks ten years old; there's no need for one."

"No need for one? Her mother has just been abducted and she's going through the most delicate time in the life of an Omar. And you are saying that there's no need for one? What *do* we need then?" cried Elena in despair.

Criselda was an absolute disaster. Who'd had the brilliant idea to send for Criselda? Gaya, of course, to get rid of the girl and take revenge on Selene.

But Criselda was angry and waved the ladle above her head.

"My job is to find Selene. That's why I came and that's what I'm doing."

"And the girl?" inquired Elena.

"The girl can manage, I'm not a babysitter."

It was true, Criselda knew as much about girls as she did about stews—not a thing.

Elena changed her posture and questioned Criselda.

"You've been working on finding Selene for two weeks and haven't told us anything yet. Have you learned anything about the telegram and the money, huh?"

"Nothing." Criselda excused herself without hiding her embarrassment.

And although she wasn't lying with that "nothing," she was concealing the truth. That "nothing" meant a great deal. It meant suspicions around Selene. Suspicions she wouldn't voice until she was absolutely sure. But she had learned absolutely nothing new, which was not reassuring at all.

"And you are not taking care of Anaíd either."

"I'm not taking care of her? I live with her."

"I mean that you are not watching her, tending to her. You don't even know what's going through her head."

"Nonsense, that's what's going through her head. I place my hands on her head to erase the nonsense every night." Criselda defended herself with passion.

"That's all?"

"I'm looking for her mother, which is what Anaíd needs—her mother. I don't have children like you. Why didn't *you* stay with her?"

Elena felt faint. Living with Anaíd for two days had been quite complicated enough.

"We have to decide what to do with Anaíd in the next coven," said Elena, trying to find a solution to the problem once and for all.

Criselda eyed her with astonishment and pointed at her enormous belly.

"Will you be able to fly?"

"Well, of course, how else would I get there? I'm heavier, I can't communicate telepathically, but the spell works all the same."

Criselda tried the stew and burned her tongue.

"I'm not worried about Anaíd. Her safety doesn't concern me; she's very cautious. She doesn't even want to leave the house."

Elena felt she had to warn Criselda, who didn't know Anaíd.

"She's very clever."

"I've noticed."

"Two years ago, she finished reading all the books from the children's library. Selene brought her books from the city."

"A reader."

"She speaks and writes five languages perfectly."

"Okay."

"She can play any instrument you put in front of her."

Criselda was running out of excuses.

"What are trying to tell me?"

"That I will never understand why Selene didn't initiate her at the right age."

Elena watched Criselda react and held her breath when Criselda leaned on the pot and it wobbled.

"Watch out!" Elena screamed, too late.

Criselda grabbed the pot but tripped and held on to the window's curtain, which came down with the pot, making a huge racket. A mess of chicken, bacon, celery, carrots, onions, and potatoes splattered the floor.

Elena inhaled once . . . twice; the little kicker was nervous too.

Would she make it two more months until delivery with this soccer player going at her from within and Criselda making her life miserable outside? After the uproar, the kitchen filled with boys coming from all parts of the house.

"Where's the bomb?"

"What happened?"

"What's for dinner?"

"Out! Everybody, get out of here!" shouted Elena, on the verge of tears.

Criselda, however, seemed to float, oblivious to everything and everyone. She blindly stared at the mess in front of her as if she couldn't see it at all. Something was slowly dawning on her.

"Are you saying that Selene had a reason not to initiate Anaíd? Perhaps the girl is not an Omar? Perhaps she is a mere mortal?"

And from the floor, picking up pieces of bacon, Elena smiled through her tears. At the very least something had turned out right on that doomed day. Rowdy Criselda finally understood that Selene was hiding more things from them than they had ever suspected, and Anaíd was one of them.

CHAPTER 5

The Clan of the She-Wolf

Anaíd awoke with a start and opened her eyes. She could swear she'd heard a wolf howling, and she couldn't get back to sleep. Something urged her to get up—restlessness, or perhaps the light. It was excessively bright for the middle of the night.

Opening the shutters, she saw a majestic full moon crowning the mountains. She gazed at it with her elbows on the windowsill. The night was quite warm. She relaxed and let the rays of moonlight caress her. But the spring night air didn't honor the cloudless sky. The atmosphere seemed murky. Since Selene's disappearance, the light had stopped brightening the day and tinting the night with the same intensity. The earth's dome seemed dirty without it.

Would you like a moonlight bath? Selene would ask her. On summer nights, they would lie on the grass together, letting the fading light lull them to sleep, and smile knowingly when, from the mountains in the distance, they heard the wolves' first howls. The wolves howled at their friend the moon and communicated with one another. Mother and daughter danced to the sound of their musical calls. Calls of love and passion, longing and melancholy.

Everything that night reminded Anaíd of Selene. Where was she? Why hadn't she said anything? She missed her so much.

Again, Anaíd heard a long, insistent howl. As she listened, goose bumps formed along the nape of her neck. And just as naturally, a sad response emerged from deep in her throat. Anaíd howled and related her sadness to the wolves, her friends, her mother's friends. Then she stood still and spontaneously covered her mouth with her hand, as surprised as someone who's just been unintentionally mischievous. But she had not had time to think about it. The mother wolf replied and Anaíd, even more surprised, understood her answer: *"They have taken her, they have her; they are powerful and yet vulnerable."*

She moved away from the window with her legs shaking. It was ridiculous, totally ridiculous, but she had howled and understood the she-wolf's answer. How did she know it was a female wolf? She knew it, period. No, it didn't make any sense. People and wolves didn't communicate; they didn't understand each other. But she'd understood, though the message was cryptic. Who were *they*? Who were the ones who had taken her mother? Hadn't she left with Max?

She made sure her arms weren't becoming hairy and glanced stealthily at herself in the mirror. No, she wasn't turning into a wolf-girl. It was all so strange . . . Nonsense—it had all been an illusion. Nonetheless, she needed to tell someone about it. Someone who could convince her that she wasn't losing her mind just as Selene had. Without hesitating, she made her way to Criselda's room.

The bed was intact, the room empty, and the window open. Anaíd was astonished. The clock marked two in the morning, and there was no sign of Criselda. Where was she? Had she disappeared like Selene? Had she been hit by lightning like Deméter? That at least was unlikely—the sky was covered with murky stars and the moon swayed over the mountain pass.

With restless eyes, Anaíd studied every object in Criselda's room. She was searching for a clue, a sign. Beside a book on the night table sat an open lotion container. She was enticed by its scent, so much like her mother's. It was the same lotion Selene had used. Anaíd put some on her index finger, inhaled the vanilla scent and notes of jasmine that reminded her of Selene, and without thinking twice, rubbed her face and hands with it, the way she'd seen her mother do some nights. She inhaled once, twice, and noticed that, little by little, a pleasant sensation washed over her.

A light tingling began running up her legs and she felt faint. Her limbs felt weak, inert, and overtaken by an intense lethargy. She plopped down on Aunt Criselda's bed and her reckless fall caused the book on the night table to land next to her, open on one page at random, or perhaps it wasn't random, since the page was wrinkled and as if the book tended to open always on that page.

A moonbeam lit the page and invited Anaíd to read it. And Anaíd, a slave to the coincidences lining up before her, instinctively read the strange language. To her surprise, she was even pronouncing the grave sounds of the words. And despite not knowing them, she understood their meaning.

The more she read, the more convinced she became that she had recited them before, pronounced them with someone, knowing perfectly well the rhythm and melody of each word.

A powerful warmth invaded her body, making her blood flow rapidly through the arteries of her numb limbs. Her blood pulsed in every single pore of her skin and Anaíd felt as if she were overflowing with life. Then fog clouded her eyes and she fell asleep, even as her weightless, ethereal body melted into the night and floated away with the wind.

. . .

The forest clearing, traversed by a creek and flanked by the eastern side of the mountain, was unusually crowded that full-moon night. Four women formed a circle, and after intoning some chants, danced together. Then, the oldest one placed and lit candles in the five points that interrupted the circle, giving it the geometric strength of the pentagon.

Criselda, overweight and devoid of charm, let her long hair loose and raised her face to the moon. Her eyes sparkled, enhancing her features. The three officiants, imitating their leader's gesture, let down their hair, turned their faces to the moon, and joined hands. Then, in the language of the she-wolves of their clan, they howled.

They were calling Selene, the missing one.

A few minutes later, they received an answer. Someone was replying to their call, but it wasn't Selene. The howling was musical but imprecise. They were taken aback; there were no other members of the she-wolf's clan in the valley. But they had no chance to voice their surprise, for then they clearly heard, some of them for the first time, the mother wolf's reply: *"They have taken her, they have her; they are powerful and yet vulnerable."*

Elena, Gaya, Criselda, and Karen, who had returned for the occasion, plopped down on the ground, psychically exhausted and somewhat disappointed. No one had fully expressed the fear and doubts Selene's abduction had caused in them. Least of all Criselda. They all knew that the telepathic power they had unleashed was enough for Selene to be able to hear and reply, unless she was shielding herself from their calls.

"So? What do we do now?" Elena asked Criselda.

The intuitive Elena had realized more than once that Criselda wasn't sharing all her doubts.

"I'm working on something, but I need more time."

Criselda knew she couldn't conceal her suspicions much longer.

They all fell silent, immersed in their own thoughts, and implicitly granted her the time she needed.

Criselda seized the moment to voice a different concern.

"In the meantime, who will be in charge of Anaíd and her training?"

Criselda had no desire to accept that honor, despite being Anaíd's closest relative.

"Training?" asked Karen. "Does that mean you are planning to initiate her?"

Criselda wiped her sweat-beaded forehead. She was in the middle of the chalk circle, the candles had started to flicker and the power of the circle was waning.

"That's what Elena and I discussed. She's already fourteen years old."

Karen had come from far away, and her ideas were very clear.

"I am her doctor and can guarantee that the girl has no intuition or any aptitudes, despite being Selene's daughter."

Gaya interrupted her, indignant.

"No matter how much you imply it, Selene is not the chosen one."

Karen glared at her.

"I'm not implying it, I'm confirming it. Selene is the prophecy's chosen one."

Criselda redirected the conversation.

"We are not questioning the prophecy or whether Selene is the chosen or not; we are talking about Anaíd and her future."

"And her present," pointed out Elena. "And I beg you to hurry up, because my sleeping spell usually fades at three in the morning. If my husband wakes up and realizes I'm not home, there will be trouble."

Karen was baffled.

"He doesn't know?"

"How would he know?"

"If I had a husband, I would tell him."

"Oh, yeah? And how many boyfriends have you told?"

Karen fell silent as Elena drove the point home.

"Try telling him, and your boyfriend will be gone in the time it takes me to finish a flan with cream."

Criselda took advantage of Karen's perplexity to confront her.

"So your diagnosis as a doctor is that Anaíd has no aptitudes."

"Exactly," said Karen. "I am willing to take care of her, though. I know Selene would do the same for a daughter of mine."

Gaya and Criselda breathed calmly. Karen had offered to watch the girl and the responsibility wouldn't fall on their shoulders.

"Well, we've reached an agreement. We can leave now," concluded Gaya resolutely.

But Elena refused.

"I don't think it should be Karen. We have to initiate Anaíd. That girl hides great potential."

"Her intelligence has nothing to do with her power," complained Karen, offended. "Remember, I am her doctor."

"Her doctor, her teacher . . . The experts on Anaíd! Good move, Gaya, making poor Karen come from Tanzania to take revenge on Selene. So like you," said Elena, annoyed.

"I didn't make her come," complained Gaya.

"It wasn't you?" asked Karen surprised, turning to Elena.

"Me?" exclaimed Elena, holding her huge belly. "You know I can't make telepathic calls while I'm pregnant."

Karen needed an explanation for her rushed trip.

"Then who called me? I clearly felt the call and came back, that's why I'm here."

Nobody answered and Karen was confused. Elena confronted Criselda.

"And what do you think, Criselda?"

Criselda hesitated. She barely knew Anaíd, but refusing to initiate her felt like betraying her dead sister.

"All the women in the Tsinoulis family, including me, have been initiated as girls. There hasn't been anyone who didn't show any abilities, unless—"

She glanced at Elena. Her doubts about Anaíd's origin and the possibility that she wasn't Selene's daughter hadn't abandoned her. Only that could explain her lack of aptitudes.

Gaya stomped one foot on the floor.

"I knew it; you favor your own house, your own lineage. With Deméter dead and Selene missing, you were sent to lead us . . . In the end, you'll expect the girl to rule us."

Criselda, sick and tired of Gaya's hostility, refused to ignore the attack.

"Don't force me to conjure up an obedience spell."

Gaya lashed back like a lioness pinned to the ground.

"You don't know how, because the Tsinoulises are a fraud. Selene is not the chosen one, and Anaíd is not good enough and will never be. It's as clear as the fact that this is my hand and this is my foot."

No sooner had Gaya pronounced those words, than she realized silence reigned around her and all the women's faces were turned toward the sky, eyes bulging, mouths open. Gaya followed their gaze and saw, above their heads, Anaíd's figure suspended among the oak branches. She was looking for a gap to slowly descend to the clearing, into the center of the coven's circle. Gaya swallowed. It was an admirable maneuver and the most perfect flight she had witnessed in her life.

Anaíd's feet grazed the ground. She opened her eyes, looked at the four women, and exclaimed, "How did I get here?"

Gaya was the only one who replied. "I don't believe it! I don't believe it! I don't believe a single word of this little act you are putting on. This has to do with Criselda. She planned it."

Anaíd didn't understand Gaya's indignation. She felt dizzy and out of place. Aunt Criselda took her hand.

"Anaíd, honey, you've never done this before?"

Anaíd vaguely remembered her dream. She had flown in dreams, but how on earth had she wound up in the forest's clearing?

"What?"

"What you've just done, flying here."

"Flying? Do you mean that . . ."

Karen caressed her cheek.

"Are you sure that Selene or Deméter never taught you how?"

Anaíd shook her head, totally confused. She could hear what the four women were saying, but she didn't understand a thing.

Elena smiled, pleased. She had won her bet.

"See?"

Gaya refused to admit it.

"It's not possible; it took me six years . . . Impossible."

Karen couldn't believe it either.

"Where did you get the ointment from?"

Anaíd thought for a moment; she remembered that clearly.

"I put on some of Aunt Criselda's lotion. She left the jar on the night table."

"And the spell?" Criselda asked impulsively.

"What spell?"

"You said some words aloud, didn't you?"

"I read a book that fell into my hands."

Gaya was indignant again.

"Yeah, and pigs fly, too! Tell us the truth. Selene initiated you in witchcraft when you were in kindergarten."

61

Gaya's fierce words were like a slap on Anaíd's face.

"Witch—witchcraft?" she stammered incredulously.

"Don't play dumb—you are a witch just as I am, and these women, and your mother and grandmother."

Suddenly, all the loose pieces in Anaíd's puzzle took shape, but the word "witchcraft" was too much. Anaíd turned pale. Criselda took hold of her before she could fall. The sincere expression of horror coming from the girl's blue eyes didn't look feigned at all.

"A . . . witch?"

Nobody denied it. Anaíd turned to her teacher.

"Did you say I'm a witch?"

Gaya confirmed it without words, but Anaíd just shook her head.

"It's not true. This is a joke," she murmured.

Four pairs of eyes stared at her, not confirming or denying anything. Anaíd looked at them one by one, glanced at her surroundings, absorbed the strength of the magical circle they formed, and . . . accepted it.

It was no joke.

She was a witch.

Then, she collapsed in her aunt's arms.

THE PROPHECY OF OMA

One day, the chosen one will end the sisters' quarrels.

The sky's fairy will comb her silver hair to receive her.
The moon will cry a tear to present her an offering.
Father and son will dance together in the water's dwelling.
The seven gods in line will salute her throning.

And the war will begin,
Cruel and gory.
The war of the witches.

Hers will be the victory,
Hers will be the scepter,
Hers will be the pain,
Hers the blood
And the will.

CHAPTER 6

THE LEGEND OF OD AND OM

In the beginning of times, O, the mother witch, ruled all tribes with the help of magic, imposing peace on warriors; blessing the earth's fruit; and favoring their union with fire, water, and air.

O was respected by men and animals, and her reign was fair. She was wise and knew the secrets to heal the ill and foretell what had not yet occurred. Communicating with the spirits of the dead, with the animals and the plants of the forest, O lived in harmony with nature and mankind, and was loved by everyone. Two beautiful daughters were born to O—Od and Om, to whom she passed down her knowledge.

Om wished to learn from her mother the healing properties of plants and roots. And through her work alleviating mortals' suffering, she was able to understand death and its compassion.

Od wished to learn from her mother the art of communicating with the spirits in the afterlife. But in hearing the laments of troubled souls, those who never found peace, she began to fear death.

Om loved the world, for she was not afraid of dying.

Od wished to live forever, and so she was afraid of the world.

Soon, a daughter called Omi was born to Om, but Od, who refused to go through the pain of labor, stole her one night while Om slept.

Od renamed the child Odi and brought the child to her mother to be acknowledged.

Not wanting her daughters to fight, O accepted Od's lie with tremendous pain in her heart, for Om was more generous than her sister. Though Od promised to raise and look after Odi as her own daughter, Om grieved for the loss of Omi, but soon conceived another daughter, Oma, and forgave her sister.

. . .

Oma and Odi played together as children. They learned from their mothers' teachings and shared their discoveries with each other. Thanks to Odi, Oma was introduced to the divine arts and learned to communicate with the spirits. Thanks to Oma, Odi learned about the properties of plants, roots, and stones, and how to make potions and brews.

Then one day, Oma discovered that the dead had shared with her aunt Od the secret to immortality. Frightened, Oma told her mother, Om, about this.

Om doubted her sister's intentions and decided to spy on her. And she learned that Od was planning to sacrifice Oma, who was about to become a woman, in order to drink her blood and reach immortality.

That was the secret Od had stolen from the dead.

Om was furious and cursed her sister, the daughter she'd let her keep, and the land she inhabited. Then Om took young Oma and, without bidding farewell to their mother, ran far away to take refuge in a cave.

While Om hid in the cave with her daughter, the earth stopped bearing fruit. Snow covered the ground, freezing the crops, drying the leaves on the trees, and bringing misery to Od's dwelling.

Mother O had wished to pass down her power to one of her daughters. But she was tired of their fighting, and so refused to give her scepter to either one.

Meanwhile, the tribes' warriors were eager for war but had been forced to comply with the peace imposed by O. When they learned that the mother witch was old, her power weakening, they blamed her for the hunger, cold, and long winter that had lashed their lives.

The warriors met secretly and decided that it was time for men to rule. Men would finally break free from women's wisdom and magic and return to the power of weapons and force.

Resentful of her old mother, who'd refused to give *her* the power, Od joined forces with the warriors and helped them devise a scheme to remove O from the kingdom.

O was overthrown. But the men joined forces and refused to let Od replace her. A devious wizard named Shh stole the mother witch's knowledge and wisdom and made himself their ruler.

Furious that she would not be allowed to reign, Od demanded that Shh marry her daughter, Odi, and that they give her all their children as a tribute.

. . .

O cried and cried, and her warm tears melted the snow, allowing the buds of life to emerge from the ground again. Om left the cave with her daughter, Oma, now a woman, and abundance reigned again. The sun warmed the earth, plants became green again, animals reproduced, and fruit matured. Nature had made up for its long lethargy.

But, encouraged by Od, Shh turned the ceremonies of rebirth and life into ceremonies of war and death, which Od officiated. All of Odi's sons were sacrificed upon birth, except for one, the firstborn, who was destined to reign. Their blood was consumed by Od. Odi's many daughters, the Odish, were taught to fear death and hate men as much as they hated their first cousins—the Omars.

Od revealed to them the secret to immortality and made them swear they'd be loyal to her and pursue one mission: stealing Oma's teenage daughters to feed on their blood.

Seeing so much hatred and sorrow around her, Om decided to punish her sister with winter and famine once more.

At long last, O died of grief, cursing her daughter Od. Before dying, however, she hurled her scepter into the bowels of the earth, so no one could have it, and wrote in her own blood the prophecy of the red-haired witch who would put an end to the battle between the sisters.

Having lost so many sons, Odi died in great pain, her body weakened from so many deliveries. Since she had been betrayed by her own daughters, the Odish, she also wrote in her own blood the verses that pointed to the chosen one's betrayal.

Om died surrounded by her daughters and granddaughters, whom she encouraged to wait for the arrival of the red-haired witch who would avenge them and their descendants.

Both the Odish and Omars searched for the scepter of power, hidden in the bowels of the earth, but neither ever found it.

· · ·

After O's death, women on earth were separated from the counsels, ceremonies, houses of worship, public places, and even from the bedsides of the ill. The warriors relegated women to their homes, deprived them of music, dance, the knowledge of books, and nature's wisdom. Women were forbidden to go near the weapons or they'd be sentenced to death. They were forced to cover their bodies and heads. If they didn't abide by men's rules, women were insulted and punished in public. A law was issued to punish those who practiced magic and disobeyed Shh.

Odi's daughters, the Odish, also suffered the disdain, reclusion, and persecution by their own father and brother. As a result, the Odish poisoned Shh and sent their brother to his death at the hands of a greedy warrior.

Countless wars, betrayals, and persecutions followed.

. . .

Oma and her many daughters, the Omars, remained hidden and secretly used their healing arts to relieve the pain of the suffering. They found refuge in forests, caves, valleys, and crossroads, where they gathered whatever gifts nature offered them. The Omars prepared potions and medicines for the body's aches and used their minds and their white magic spells to soothe the pains of the soul. Used to being persecuted, they hid during the day and gathered herbs at night in forest clearings, where they celebrated their ceremonies with dances and chants that had been forbidden to them. They found shelter in the power of the moon, which controls the feminine cycle, makes the land bear fruit, and regulates the tides. They promised to help one another using telepathy and their ancient language to protect themselves from the envious Odish and distrustful men.

Oma's daughters founded the Omar tribes, and her granddaughters chose their clans among the animals on earth. They learned much from animals' totems, wisdom, virtues, language, and spirit. Om's numerous great-granddaughters founded the clans of the hen, the female hare, bear, wolf, eagle, orca, snake, seal, rat, and many others. They perpetuated their lineages and scattered around the world. The Omars were welcome wherever

they went, for they offered love and wisdom. Some became oracles, others musicians, poetesses, midwives, herbalists, and healers.
All of them were fertile, wise, and sensual, and they passed down
their knowledge from mothers to daughters, hiding their real
nature from their husbands and lovers in order to protect themselves.

In the dark times of persecutions and executions, many per-
ished at the stake; but others, the ones left behind, have longed for
the prophecy of O to come true and the chosen one to arrive—the
red-haired witch who would destroy the Odish and put an end to
the war of the witches.

According to the constellations, that time was near.

CHAPTER 7

The Revelation

"My mother is the prophecy's chosen one?" Anaíd couldn't believe it.

Criselda beamed with pride as she savored a delicious truffle from the box of chocolates Anaíd had brought home.

"The stars have confirmed it. The comet announced her arrival, the meteor fell in the valley, and the planets are almost in alignment. Her red hair and power are unmistakable signs."

"I always knew she was different, very different . . . ," Anaíd thought out loud.

"I'm the chosen one's aunt and you are her daughter. It's an honor to belong to her tribe, her clan, her lineage."

In an effort to believe it, Anaíd repeated what she had just learned: "I'm Anaíd, Selene's daughter and Deméter's grand-daughter. I belong to the Scythian tribe, the she-wolf's clan, and the Tsinoulis lineage."

It was all so new that it was hard to accept it.

"If your mother could see you . . . ," whispered Aunt Criselda, moved, but a veil of sadness quickly covered her eyes.

Anaíd noticed this.

"So . . . my mother didn't run off with Max?" she asked.

"Max probably doesn't exist."

"Actually, he does exist. I have his phone number."

"Do you know him?"

"No. Selene didn't *tell* me about him."

Anaíd and Criselda looked at each other without daring to voice their doubts. Anaíd wondered why Selene hid Max from her. Could he know anything about Selene?

"Where's my mother now? What's going to happen to her?"

Criselda took a deep breath. Anaíd was very intelligent and it would be hard to lie to her, but she could at least conceal part of her emotions and try to confuse her. She would never tell Anaíd that she feared Selene had betrayed the Omars.

"We don't know where she is. The Odish have abducted her."

Anaíd already suspected this, so she kept probing.

"Will they kill her?" she asked in a timid voice.

Criselda took some time before responding. Did the girl understand what that question entailed?

"Not her."

Anaíd caught the hint immediately, though in part. She was horrified.

"Are you saying that *they* killed my grandmother?"

A tear rolled down Criselda's cheek. In fact, Deméter, the Tsinoulis matriarch, had fought tooth and nail to save Selene from the hands of the Odish. Criselda knew her sister—she was as hard as a rock. Defeating the great matriarch must have exhausted the Odish, so they retreated to recover their strength and attack again a year later.

"That fight kept them away for a while. Your grandmother was very powerful and her protection spell lasted a long time."

Anaíd couldn't stop thinking, putting two and two together.

"So, if my mother was in danger after my grandmother died, why didn't she run away? Why didn't she hide?"

71

Criselda began to perspire. Anaíd was drawing nearer to the question with no answer. She would try to mislead her.

"Selene was so brave that she thought she could defeat them. That's why she wasn't intimidated."

"But—"

Criselda thought about casting a silence spell. She couldn't bear so many questions that she could not answer

Anaíd insisted. Bloody girl!

"But it wasn't courage . . . My mother changed; she drew attention to herself on purpose—she gave interviews on the Internet and on the radio, and . . . she drove drunk. At school they said she had lost her mind."

Criselda sighed, relieved.

"You've said it. Selene turned a bit . . . crazy."

Anaíd thought for a moment about Selene's eccentricities—some of them delicious, others disconcerting, most of them disturbing.

"Now I understand it: my grandmother's death really affected her. I probably would have gone crazy too."

Criselda was surprised. Did Anaíd know more than she let on?

"What do you mean?"

"How can you keep on living knowing that your mother died to protect you?" Anaíd concluded, wisely.

Criselda was so happy she could have kissed her. The girl was a gem. By herself, without anyone's help, she had arrived at a conclusion an experienced witch like Criselda had been trying to reach for two weeks.

Guilt had driven Selene crazy. Of course! The huge weight of carrying the Omars' future on her shoulders, plus her own mother's death, had made her feel disoriented, lost, and scared. That's why she had acted so irresponsibly despite the warnings of the coven.

Criselda recalled that when the matriarch died and a crowd attended her funeral, Selene still put up her hair and behaved somewhat discreetly; *somewhat* discreetly, because she was always passionate and impulsive. Back then, the possibility that she was the chosen one was merely a rumor. Not many people knew her, or about her; Selene was only the daughter of Deméter, the Tsinoulis matriarch, the great witch. Now, everything indicated that she might be the chosen one. The comet had announced her arrival years before. A meteor had fallen the year of Deméter's death, and the time was coming for the seven planets to align, which studies announced as the beginning of the chosen one's reign. The prophecy was coming true.

Anaíd interrupted Criselda's thoughts.

"Do you know what the worst part was for her?"

Criselda shook her head no.

"She found my grandmother's body."

Criselda covered her mouth to stifle a scream. Selene hadn't told her that. It must have been awful! The Odish disfigure their victims, leaving their bodies as monstrosities. When they were young, Criselda and Deméter had once broken the rules and disobeyed their parents. They wanted to see their best friend for the last time. Leda had been bled to death by the Odish before having been initiated and, therefore, had not been able to defend herself. Even though their mother had forbidden it, the girls went to the cemetery one night. Holding hands, they'd descended to the crypt where Leda's remains rested, and would never forget what they saw. They wished they'd never done it.

Leda was a monster—a freak.

Leda had no hair, was swollen, pale, covered in pustules; her eye sockets were empty; her finger- and toenails had been pulled out. Leda, beautiful Leda, had been turned into something horrible.

As long as she lived, Criselda would never forget Leda.

She felt sorry for Selene. The Omar forensic doctors were always discreetly involved in the cases of Odish victims. They tried to come up with logical explanations so as not to arouse the suspicions of the police. They usually attributed these deaths to falls, car accidents, fires, or drowning, and, as a result, avoided investigations.

"They didn't let me see her," Anaíd whispered, snapping Criselda out of her reverie.

The poor girl had learned too many things at once. No wonder she couldn't accept them.

"I miss them so much," Anaíd mumbled, on the verge of tears.

Criselda missed them too; they were her only family. Unable to contain herself, she hugged Anaíd, who was nestled in her lap like a puppy. Criselda stroked her forehead softly to erase her fears, her torments.

"Do you think Selene is suffering?"

"She is very strong and powerful; she knows how to protect herself."

"I want to look for my mother."

"First you'll have to learn many things."

"I'll learn them; I'll be initiated as an Omar and rescue Selene from the Odish. Will you help me?"

"Of course."

"Can we start now?"

"Tomorrow. Now sleep, little one. You need to rest."

Anaíd wrapped herself in her aunt's arms. Then she put her arm around old Criselda's neck and kissed her cheek.

"I love you, Auntie."

Criselda felt a strange tingling sensation on her skin. How long had it been since someone had kissed her? When was the last time someone had whispered *I love you* in her ear?

74

Wistfully reminiscing a distant youth when she'd known love, Criselda cradled her sister's granddaughter and realized that changing one's mind was sometimes wise. She might know nothing about children, she might not be able to cook, she might have no patience, she might not be good enough, but she wouldn't leave Anaíd; she wouldn't entrust her education to another witch.

She would stay.

It was the least she could do for the Tsinoulises.

· · ·

Look and not see; *listen* and not hear. Learn how to *read* nature and life with your intuition.

That's what Anaíd practiced day and night since Aunt Criselda decided to teach her the basics of witchcraft. She wouldn't be able to recite spells or use her birchwood wand for incantations until she'd mastered those two principles.

Anaíd was excited about the wand. She felt safe with it, and she loved to wave it in the air and draw original signs, like she did on solstice nights with a bright sparkler by the bonfire.

She'd gone to the river to pick her wand with Aunt Criselda. Before choosing the right branch and testing its frequency, Criselda showed her how to ask the old birch tree for permission. Anaíd listened and clearly heard the tree answer, offering its cooperation, but she realized that her aunt hadn't heard anything. Was she deaf? She didn't say a word though, because soon she realized that Aunt Criselda hadn't heard the complaints from the black beetle climbing the branch either.

Anaíd continued *listening* and heard more things, too many, in fact. The noise, the horrible buzzing sound that one day appeared in her head, had turned into audible signals, simple animal languages she could understand without difficulty. She could comprehend the voices of dogs, cats, hummingbirds, and ants. It was amazing the number of voices that converged within a fifty-square-foot area. She preferred to keep her discoveries secret, though, in case she'd gotten ahead of her lessons. Just like it happened at school, she'd learned too quickly and needed to bite her tongue. Anaíd had experience in that kind of trick. She knew perfectly well how to play dumb.

Anaíd was also able to *see* several signs she'd missed before. She saw messages in the shape of the clouds, the birds' flight, and the creases in her bedsheets. She learned how to *read* what she saw and to interpret dreams and premonitions using her intuition.

Aunt Criselda congratulated her on her progress the day Anaíd read her tea leaves correctly. They had predicted an unexpected visit, which actually happened minutes later. The mailman delivered a package to Criselda, a birthday gift, from Criselda's friend Leonora, which Criselda opened with trembling hands. Inside was a small kitten. Leonora's note explained that he was from the litter of her own cat Amanda, which Criselda had given her years before.

Anaíd petted the kitten and whispered in its ear. She was rewarded with a long meow, which she interpreted as, *"I want my momma."*

Anaíd's heart broke. She and the kitten had more in common than a girl and a cat could have. They had both been separated from their mothers and were at the mercy of Aunt Criselda. Anaíd appointed herself protector of the house's new tenant.

"His name will be Apollo."

"Apollo?"

"I bet he is brave like Apollo."

Aunt Criselda allowed her to take care of the cat; she was actually relieved. If a girl was a lot of work, imagine adding a meowing kitten that needed milk every three hours.

Anaíd now had Apollo's company; she had the birchwood

wand; she knew how to listen, observe, read, and interpret. But Criselda refused to teach her any spells yet.

"The technique shows you the *how*, but if you don't have the *what*, you will never be able to succeed. The *what* is your job. It means shaping your spirit, having inner peace, balance, and confidence."

Aunt Criselda repeated that over and over.

"Do you mean that I'm not at peace?"

"Only you can know that, but you must also love yourself. You must find your own balance."

"Gaya has none of that."

"That's precisely why she's such a mediocre witch. Her only talent is music. When she plays the flute and composes her melodies, she finds what she's usually lacking."

Anaíd couldn't wait. She felt an insatiable curiosity and wished she could move forward faster.

Aunt Criselda was unusually calm, however. She was developing a lethargic routine that often involved sitting by the window and gazing numbly at the fading sunsets, which were turning increasingly gloomy and murky, while she sipped tea and munched on chocolate. Anaíd suspected that age was playing a dirty trick on Criselda. Her aunt was becoming more and more forgetful. On certain nights, she wandered around the house and sometimes even asked Anaíd where she was.

Impatient and eager to learn, Anaíd went crazy when she saw her in that state. The last thing she needed was for Aunt Criselda to lose her mind too!

So Anaíd decided she could do without Criselda. Strength was flowing through her in torrents, giving her a certain confidence, which encouraged her to explore the hidden corners of her mother's and grandmother's bookcase. After a thorough search, Anaíd found what she was looking for.

Now she didn't need Aunt Criselda; she had the books of spells written in the ancient language Deméter had taught her, the language in which she'd pronounced the first spell of her life— the flying spell from Criselda's book.

Without her aunt noticing, Anaíd took the books one by one to her cave. There, with only Apollo for company, she learned how to cast spells by herself.

CHAPTER 8

THE COUNTESS

In the Dark World, Selene was kept prisoner. Away from time and contrasts, one could live eternally forgotten in this realm.

A mirror of the real world, a negative of its forests, lakes, caves, and unknown corners, the Dark World was absurdly identical to itself; like its own before and after.

The subtle movement of the river flow, the whimsical inclination of the oaks' treetops, and the different arrangement of the mountain peaks confused the mind and convinced visitors that memories had no room in this strange world without hours, minutes, or color.

Selene wandered around the woods and let herself be lulled by the mocking voices of the troublesome little men known as the Trentis, but she didn't listen to their words—she was immune to their lies and tricks. Neither was she vulnerable to the singing of the Anjanas, those beautiful maidens who perpetually combed their hair. They didn't captivate Selene anymore with their sweet voices and the love legends they told over and over again, without ever growing bored. She was no longer mesmerized by their reflection in the water.

Selene wasn't sure how long she'd been in the Dark World before the Countess received her. All she knew was that this was a place for oblivion and madness, and she almost succumbed to its spell.

As Salma guided her through the deep underground galleries full of stalactites and stalagmites, Selene dared to unblock her senses, which the Trentis and Anjanas had been fighting to steal from her, and finally speak. That's what it was all about—overcoming the tests put in her way. She'd resisted the emptiness and the deprivations she was subjected to. What else could she expect now?

The Countess sat waiting for her in the darkness. Selene felt her immense strength upon entering the gallery.

"Here she is, Countess," Salma greeted her from a distance.

The imperious voice didn't admit delays. It was a voice used to being in power.

"Come closer, Selene," ordered the Countess.

Selene did as told and something cold touched her skin, searching for an opening to sneak into her mind. Horrified, Selene noticed something sinuous penetrating her body through the air she was breathing. It was disgusting, as if an enormous cockroach were slithering through her mouth and walking down her throat, poking at her insides with its legs. Selene fought the repulsion and fear with a spell. This time she did put up a fight—she blocked her senses again and raised a protection wall, stoically resisting the thorough scrutiny she was being subjected to. The torture came to an end when the Countess's tentacle came out through one of her nostrils.

"Welcome, Selene, the chosen one."

The Countess's voice was metallic, devoid of any human warmth. *And her face?* Selene wondered—but, unfortunately, the Countess didn't reveal herself. She remained hidden in the darkness.

Despite her obvious inferiority, Selene kept her head high.

"Here I am, Countess, in the place from where no Omars have ever returned," she said.

Salma laughed her hollow laugh and pointed at Selene, glad to be able to mock her.

"She was afraid of coming, of meeting you," she said to the Countess.

Selene felt the Countess's curiosity settling in her hair, the pores of her skin. Now she was sniffing her body like a hound, but Selene wasn't afraid.

"Salma is right. Aren't you known as 'the bloody Countess'?"

The Countess sighed.

"That was long ago."

"Four hundred years," murmured Selene. "According to literature, you slaughtered more than six hundred young girls in your Hungarian castle."

"Six hundred and twelve. All of them virgins. Their blood has allowed me to survive until the present."

Selene shuddered.

"And you haven't returned to the world since then?"

"I was waiting for you."

Selene grew worried.

"Me?"

"I've been recovering my strength and studying the stars and prophecies. That's why we've been able to beat the Omars— we've been alert to all the signs following the comet's appearance."

"That was so long ago," said Selene, turning pale.

"Exactly, almost fifteen years ago, when you rejected the Omars and ran away. Is that when you also realized you were the chosen one?"

Selene narrowed her eyes. She was remembering that dark time in her life.

"Yes, I discovered my fate. Until then, I'd thought the prophecies were just a fraud."

"We don't choose our fate, Selene; it chooses us. We can't avoid it."

Selene remained silent. The Countess was right.

"So, you know about my relationship with an . . . Odish? Did *she* tell you?"

"We've heard rumors, but they weren't enough. The meteor was the sign we needed to be sure."

"The lunar meteor," said Selene. "I thought it had gone unnoticed."

"Perhaps it did for the Omars, but we knew that the meteor falling right before the alignment indicated the exact place where the chosen one would reveal herself. And it happened in the valley of Urt. It was simple. Your lineage, your strength, your hair, and, above all, your past pointed at you."

Selene held back a tear.

"That was a year ago, when Deméter died."

"You are not going to get sentimental, are you?" Salma mocked her.

Selene stood tall.

"She was my mother! You killed her!"

Salma laughed heartily.

"Oh, Omars' feelings . . . You'll lose them. You'll forget about them, like it happens with age and wrinkles."

The Countess watched Selene in silence.

"I don't understand you, Selene, you and your mother had a fight. She never forgave you for escaping and betraying the Omars."

Selene nodded.

"But she was my mother. I owe respect to her memory."

"That's stupid." Salma couldn't contain herself.

"Shut up, Salma," the Countess reproached her. "Listen to the chosen one. Perhaps what we need in order to last is feelings. We might need to learn one last lesson to survive. How many are we? Few and antagonized. The chosen one will guide us and, in our new path, she might suggest that we overcome our prejudice . . . Feelings . . . that might be our new challenge. Right, Selene?"

Selene had listened to the Countess without blinking.

"I don't know what your path is, and I don't think it's the same as mine. You have persistently searched for me and you have tested me—first the mistreatment and deprivations, then the madness of the Dark World. I'm here now, I've passed the tests, but I still don't know what you're going to offer me or what you want from me."

"What have you done to her, Salma?" the Countess thundered.

Salma took a step back. "I tried the dungeon, solitary confinement, and deprivations; she passed them all. Then I abandoned her in the Dark World and she didn't go mad."

"You are an idiot!"

Salma pointed her finger at Selene.

"I had to do it before bringing her here. She's no one, just a vehicle. We must consider her a prisoner, or else she will end up ruling us all."

"And what do you suggest? Eliminating her?" the Countess shot back, indignant.

Salma thought about it.

"Why not? It would be another way . . . The planets haven't aligned completely. The prophecy hasn't occurred yet. If we could get ahead of it . . ."

"Remember that Jupiter and Saturn have reigned together in heaven . . . ," said the Countess.

Selene broke her silence and took a step toward Salma, looking at her with pity.

"You can't do anything to me; you can't even threaten me."

"Oh, no?" asked Salma.

Selene gazed at her disdainfully.

"Ask the Countess. You are in my hands. Without me, her return will be unlikely, if not impossible. Only *I* can help her recover her strength . . . and the same goes for you and the others."

Furious, Salma cast a quick spell, but Selene closed her eyes, stuck out her palms with rage, and rejected it. Salma's magic bounced off the gallery's walls and knocked down a column. Salma was astounded.

"Your magic is powerful, very powerful. Who taught you how to fight against an Odish?" inquired the Countess.

"Deméter."

"And . . . ?"

It was hard for Selene to reply, but why deny it?

"An Odish."

"What do you want?" the Countess demanded harshly.

Selene imposed her authority with arrogance.

"I don't know, *I* didn't look for you . . . though I do know what I *don't* want."

"Tell me."

Selene felt her legs tremble. Even though she was hiding behind confusing rhetoric, she needed to be sure of the reason why she'd agreed to embark on this journey. She was afraid to take this last step.

"If Deméter could hear me, she would be embarrassed."

"But she's dead."

"Deméter taught me about austerity and self-sacrifice, but I . . . was more ambitious . . . that's why I ran away."

"We know that. We know you were curious, that you didn't settle. We know you turned your back against the Omars and stopped talking to them."

"But I came back to my mother."

"With your tail between your legs," the Countess blurted out. "Unable to make your dream come true. What was your dream, Selene? Fame? Eternal love? Power? Money? Adventure?"

Selene sighed for the dreams that had slipped through her fingers during those years.

"I had so many . . ."

Selene hesitated; the words fought to come out in torrents, but shame prevented her from pronouncing them. The Countess noticed her struggle and decided to help her.

"I suspect that you want to be rich, very rich."

"I haven't said that."

"I can see your ring. I know about your weaknesses, and your debt."

Selene brought a hand to her chest and stroked her gold ring. As a child, she'd dreamed of having her fingers encrusted with diamonds so when she waved her hands, she'd shine like a star. Why deny it?

"I don't love money itself."

"No?"

"I'd like to be wealthy enough not to have to think about money ever again. I'd like to be able to forget about money, break free from its curse."

"You could have a lot more than that."

Selene didn't want to listen to her.

"I'm already beautiful; men love me."

"But you'll stop being beautiful one day."

"I'm not worried about that now; I'm concerned about work, having to struggle to make ends meet. I hate counting pennies before going to a restaurant, or buying a car or shoes."

"That's all? You just want money?"

"With money I could travel, visit the most stunning places

on earth, savor the most delicious dishes at the best restaurants, own real estate, cars, wear the best designer clothes, attend lavish parties, meet celebrities . . . What else could you offer me?"

The Countess spoke slowly, emphasizing each word.

"Eternal beauty, eternal youth, eternal life. I'm offering you immortality."

Selene held her breath. It would be absurd not to acknowledge the nature of the Countess's offer.

"I've thought of it. Actually, I've done a lot of thinking since Deméter's death."

"And?"

Selene bit her lips.

"I'm not sure I'm willing to pay the price to live eternally."

Salma showed contempt.

"She doesn't like blood."

Selene's stomach turned.

"I refuse to kill."

"You can't aspire to be immortal and not get your hands dirty," said Salma.

The Countess stirred in the shadows and Salma fell silent. "Well, Salma, I don't need to remind you that there's nothing written about the path we must take once the chosen one has the scepter of power."

"The scepter doesn't exist!" Salma shot back fervently.

Selene's eyes widened.

"The scepter of power? Are you talking about O's scepter?"

The Countess droned her chant.

". . . and O hurled her scepter into the bowels of the earth, so no one could have it, and wrote in her own blood the prophecy of the red-haired witch who would put an end to the battle between the sister witches."

Salma and Selene stared at each other in astonishment.

Selene sighed.

"And she who holds the scepter of power will dictate the destiny of the Odish and Omars, and will reign like Mother O."

The Countess cleared her throat.

"That's it; that is . . . the scepter of power."

"Where is it? Do you have it?" asked Selene.

"The prophecy of Trebora says that it will come out of the earth's bowels and find the chosen one," said the Countess. "It will look for you."

Selene took a step forward and gazed at her naked hands. She imagined them shimmering in the darkness with the power of a thousand diamonds.

"Will you refuse it?" inquired the Countess. "Will you refuse the scepter when it comes to you?"

Selene breathed in the cave's rarefied air. She needed to fill her lungs and inhale the uncertainty. But she knew she needed to make a decision. She couldn't delay the choice any longer.

Selene toyed with the idea and let it seduce her. The scepter of power would make her a queen. She would rule the world from a golden throne encrusted with sapphires, and her long fingers would dazzle like fireflies dressed in diamonds.

A shiver of pleasure moved along the nape of her neck. She was excited by the idea. A smile replaced her blank expression, the mask she had put on so well.

"In that case, if the scepter of power exists and it comes to me, as the prophecy foretells . . ." Selene glanced boldly at the shadows where the Countess was hidden. "I'll do it. I'll reject it."

The Book of Rosebuth

Very few know the secret of love.

She will feel an eternal thirst
She will feel an insatiable hunger
But she will not know that love
Melts and thaws,
Feeds and satiates
Evil's monstrous strength
That inhabits the depths
Of her chosen one's heart.

CHAPTER 9

THE SUSPICION

Imagining that she was living her dream and Anaíd was her daughter and the heir to her powers, Elena pronounced the spell in the ancient language.

Anaíd understood the words as something like, *"Cinch her waist, press her stomach, and hide her breasts."*

Then she felt a sudden warm feeling pressing her torso like a girdle, but it soon loosened and then disappeared. Only a slight reddening was left around her belly button.

Elena examined her with concern.

"Don't you feel a pressure that doesn't let you breathe?"

Anaíd shook her head.

"I did, but it's gone now."

"That's exactly what happened when I tried," exclaimed Criselda, who until now had stayed discreetly in the background.

A big weight came off Criselda's shoulders. She'd thought her mind or, worse still, her power was failing her. The truth was that she felt abnormally tired and forgetful lately, and she'd been trying to cast a protection shield for days without success. She turned to Karen who, as her doctor, was considered an expert on Anaíd.

"Would you like to try?"

But Karen was as intrigued as Elena and Criselda.

"Everything was done correctly, but it seems Anaíd's body is rejecting the spell. If it wasn't because she is not able to, I would say that Anaíd is rejecting it herself."

"Me?" asked Anaíd, a bit fed up.

She didn't enjoy trying on clothes and, even less, being a guinea pig for some frustrated wannabe mothers trying to remember old teenage spells.

Karen examined Anaíd carefully. She checked her clothes and her hair, and paused when she saw the tiny black teardrops hanging from the girl's neck.

"It might be this talisman's fault. Where did you get it?"

Anaíd held her pendant tenderly and kissed it.

"I carved them myself, in memory of Deméter."

Karen was intrigued.

"But . . . these stones . . . Look at them. Who gave them to you?"

The other women came closer and, proud of her discovery, Anaíd explained, "They're from a meteor. I found them in the woods, near . . ."

Then she stopped. She'd almost said "near the cave," but nobody—not even her mother—knew about it.

"Near the stream," she corrected herself in time. "Do you like them?"

"How do you know they're from a meteor?" Gaya asked suspiciously.

"My grandmother told me," she replied humbly, in an effort not to contradict or annoy Gaya because, after all, she was her teacher.

"If Deméter said it, it must be true. Now, take them off. We'll try the spell without the stones," said Elena. "Would you like to try this time, Gaya?"

Elena was also trying to please Gaya and maintain the peace in their reduced coven, but unfortunately, the teacher had no luck either. The spell bounced off Anaíd's body like a ball hitting a brick wall.

"And if she's protected by a more powerful spell? A radial protection ring, perhaps?" asked Gaya.

Karen carefully studied the space around Anaíd's aura with the palm of her hand.

"No," she replied, but she didn't let Anaíd go. "Wait a moment, now that I'm looking at you, you've grown and gained a lot of weight."

"Ten pounds and three and a half inches," confirmed Anaíd.

"And why didn't you tell me?"

Anaíd shrugged.

"Aunt Criselda is mad because I'm two sizes bigger."

Criselda admitted it. She had complained every time a concerned Anaíd had shown her her useless clothes.

But Karen was thrilled with the news.

"If only Selene could see you. She was so worried . . . I knew you would have a growth spurt at any moment."

Anaíd fell silent.

"Aren't you excited?" Karen asked, surprised.

"Yes, though I feel strange and I trip a lot," she said, pointing at her awkward arms and legs. "And I don't understand why I began to grow when I *stopped* taking my medication."

Anaíd said this in a somewhat reproachful tone. She certainly felt deceived. Four years blindly taking that disgusting brew, believing it had some miraculous properties and that if she stopped taking it she would be ill, and then . . . she actually grew.

Shocked, Criselda brought a hand to her mouth. She hadn't noticed the coincidence.

But it was Karen who was most surprised by her answer, if that was possible.

"What medication?"

"The syrup my mother gave me. Aunt Criselda threw it away and you weren't here to replace it," explained Anaíd.

"Are you talking about the potion for your hair?" asked Karen.

Criselda almost fell off her chair. She exchanged a quick, knowing glance with Elena—her worst fears were being confirmed.

Fortunately, Anaíd was not paying attention and did not catch the gestures Criselda and Elena were frantically making for Karen to stop talking.

Anaíd didn't take their strange behavior seriously. She was worried about something else: she had planned to bring up her biggest concern in this meeting. So she put on her best smile and addressed the four witches.

"I would like to ask you a special favor."

The four women stared at her. Aunt Criselda picked up a piece of chocolate to better digest Anaíd's words. What would she come up with this time?

"I'd like to be initiated sooner than planned. Aunt Criselda has taught me many things, but I want to learn faster."

"Why? What's the hurry?" Karen was intrigued.

"I want to find my mother."

"And how are you planning to find her?" Karen asked lovingly.

Anaíd thought about her answer carefully.

"I know she's alive, I can feel it."

"Intuition is not enough. It can mislead you sometimes. Do you have any proof?" inquired Elena.

"Now that Aunt Criselda has taught me how to listen, I can actually hear her."

Even Criselda was disconcerted by this.

"You didn't tell me that."

Anaíd realized that she hadn't told her that or many other things. If her aunt knew about the spells she'd learned and the animal voices she could understand and imitate, she would probably have a fit.

Elena glanced around her.

"Has anyone heard Selene until now?"

They all said no. Elena made an approving gesture.

"Not bad. It's more than we've been able to do."

But Gaya was extremely reticent.

"And suppose we decide to initiate you sooner and your telepathic level increases, and you are able to reach your mother . . . What will you do then?"

Anaíd didn't think twice.

"Help her escape."

"From the Odish?"

"Well, of course!"

Gaya clicked her tongue.

"What weapons will you use?"

Anaíd felt insulted, but not intimidated. Why did they treat her like she was dumb? Didn't they realize she could learn faster than they could imagine? She took her birchwood wand out of her pocket and swung it a few times with pride. She drew the letter *S* in the air and stopped a fly in midflight. The insect was suspended in the air until Anaíd traced the *S* she had drawn seconds before backward. Baffled, the poor fly continued flying and Anaíd heard it clearly say, *"Bloody witches!"*

Gaya looked at Anaíd sideways; Karen and Elena looked at Criselda, who had turned pale.

"Where did you learn that?"

Criselda felt frustrated. She was responsible for Anaíd, and she couldn't allow her apprentice to learn spells without her consent.

But instead of concealing her defiance, Anaíd bragged about it.

"I've learned it on my own. And I can learn more."

"In due t-time," Criselda stammered.

"There is no time!" complained Anaíd.

"Time is not your problem," said Gaya.

"Oh, no? Well, you are wrong. I'm the only one who can reach Selene and help her."

"You?"

Anaíd decided to stop pretending.

"I've read the prophecies and found the Book of Rosebuth. I can read the ancient language, and Rosebuth says that only true love can pull the chosen one away from the Odish. Who else loves my mother? Who would give her life for Selene like Deméter did? At least she tried."

Anaíd gazed challengingly at the four women, who stared at her but didn't react. They were speechless.

Anaíd pointed at herself.

"I am the only one who truly loves my mother! You don't love her, you are not helping her; you are not even looking for her. Do you think I haven't noticed?"

"Enough, Anaíd," interrupted Elena. "That was not part of your request."

Criselda tried hard to sound authoritative. Anaíd had made her lose control.

"Go on . . . Take a walk and calm down."

Anaíd picked up Apollo and stormed out of her house. She debated between walking around the forest and hiding in her cave. But she didn't do either. A pleasant surprise appeared on her way—Ms. Olav in the flesh, behind the steering wheel of her fabulous four-wheel drive. She stopped by Anaíd's side, beeped, opened the passenger door, and invited her in with a charming smile.

Anaíd exhaled, relieved. It was just what she needed: a friend, someone to listen to her and cheer her up.

Suddenly, it occurred to Anaíd that, perhaps, the four women were now deciding her fate and that she should try to use her telepathic skills to eavesdrop on their conversation. But the thought lasted just a moment.

. . .

Criselda poured herself a cup of hot tea with trembling hands. She stirred in a lump of sugar slowly, took a long sip, and studied the inside of the cup. She didn't need to be an expert in fortune-telling: great difficulties awaited her, and the complications had just begun.

The three other women were in the same foul mood as Criselda. No one was speaking. Anaíd had laid several pressing issues on the table, and the witches faced a big dilemma.

Anaíd had accused them of delaying Selene's search.

And they all knew the girl was right.

Criselda, the one in charge of the investigation, had gotten sidetracked over and over again, and her research had reached no conclusions. The time had come to move into action. It was a delicate situation, for they couldn't let Anaíd, who hadn't been initiated, disrespect them and disobey their orders.

Criselda put a piece of chocolate in her mouth. Elena took another piece and decided to break the ice.

"So, Criselda . . . Do you have anything to tell us about Selene? What have you found out?"

Criselda placed the teacup on the table. The evidence had been piling up. There was increasing proof against Selene's innocence, and she couldn't defend her any longer. Unable to remain seated, Criselda stood. With her head bowed, she began to speak softly.

"I wish I was wrong; I wish I hadn't arrived at this conclusion, but I suspect that Selene hasn't been the victim of an abduction."

The women held their breath. Criselda continued speaking in a grave voice.

"Selene didn't defend herself from the alleged Odish attack. There was no struggle or resistance from her. She didn't leave any clues for us to follow her, and she immediately broke telepathic contact. Selene didn't cast a protection spell around her house like her mother did before dying. She destroyed all evidence of her previous contact with the Odish, which the tribe knew about, and she herself—or someone else—came back to the house and tried to make her disappearance look like a romantic escapade."

The women remained expectantly silent. Criselda didn't dare to continue. She nervously pulled on a wool thread from her frayed sweater.

"I'm almost sure that Selene opened the window to the strigas and flew away with them of her own will."

This confession caught Karen off guard.

"Selene, a traitor?"

Silence reigned again, and the women let their imaginations fly in search of evidence. There was too much. Gaya was the first one to point it out.

"Don't you remember how discreet and obedient Selene was when she lived with Deméter? And how reckless and daring she became after her mother died? It's crystal clear. She couldn't give herself to the Odish before because her mother prevented it. The protection spell the Tsinoulis matriarch conjured was very powerful. It lasted for a year after her death, but then lost strength. Selene tested it with her constant provocations. Every time she drank, every time she got in trouble . . . Do you remember the arguments? Her arrogant remarks? And how she laughed when we warned her? She made fun of us. She had already made a deal with the Odish and was just waiting for the right time to run away with them."

Criselda lowered her head, embarrassed; she wouldn't mention Selene's debt, her shopping sprees, or the mortgage on her house. Perhaps Gaya was right, but there was still more, much more. She didn't need to expose it all at once.

Meanwhile, Karen, Selene's best friend, refused to believe any of it.

"That's ridiculous. Yes, she was irresponsible and passionate, a little selfish, too, but she was always an Omar, the daughter of a clan's chief, the officiant of a coven, and the mother of another Omar."

Elena brought to the light the most delicate aspect of Selene's dubious behavior.

"But she prevented Anaíd from developing her powers."

"You mean she didn't initiate her at the right time," Karen corrected her.

"No," said Criselda, her heart broken. "The potion Selene prepared for Anaíd was a powerful blocker. For some reason, Anaíd thinks you prescribed it."

"Are you saying that Selene purposely blocked her daughter's powers?" Karen thought back and began to change her mind. "That was the reason for the delayed growth!"

Elena confirmed it.

"Since she stopped taking the potion, Anaíd has become a real time bomb."

"She's always been one," Gaya pointed out; she couldn't separate Anaíd from her mother.

Criselda seized the opportunity to express her concern.

"She can't control her powers; they've come to her too suddenly. She needs our help and support. Just like her body, her powers are increasing in size each month."

Even though she acknowledged the evidence, Karen couldn't accept the motives.

"But why? Why would Selene block her own daughter's powers?"

The answer was so obvious that all Elena needed to do was verbalize what was on everyone's mind.

"To avoid having to fight against her."

Karen sighed.

"So she protected her."

Then Gaya dropped a depth bomb.

"Or she protected herself from her daughter."

Elena organized the confusing ideas she'd been gathering for the past few days.

"Selene always knew she was the chosen one. Her mother, the Tsinoulis matriarch, did too, that's why she kept it a secret and carefully prepared her for her role as the Omars' savior. But Selene's fragile and passionate nature couldn't resist the Odish temptations. They offer a great deal: eternal pleasure, youth, wealth, and infinite power. You all knew Selene. Unlike her mother, she was hotblooded, impulsive, and not very sensible. There was a dark time in her life that she and Deméter never discussed. Selene was gone for some time . . . I'm sure Selene and the Odish made a deal for the scepter, plotting her betrayal long ago. Criselda might know more about Selene's past."

Criselda was forced to speak.

"Deméter never talked about the time when Selene was gone,

but she made her daughter suffer for it. I know Deméter concealed something awful, but I can't give you any details—my sister was proud and she didn't want to cry on my shoulder."

"This is very serious." Karen's words echoed the collective sentiment.

"Yes, it is," said Elena, "and we must present a plan to the tribes. They are expecting our report."

"We haven't heard anything from the tribes."

"Now that you mention it . . ."

"That's alarming as well."

"It must be a protective measure."

"Or a measure of preventive isolation."

Criselda was glad that her sister was dead. At least she was avoiding this painful episode.

"So, do we have enough evidence to think that Selene is a traitor?"

They all nodded. Criselda looked at them one by one.

"Is any of us defending her?"

They all remained silent.

"In that case, if Selene is the chosen one, something we are also sure about—"

"Actually, I'm not," Gaya objected.

"Well, all of us except Gaya," said Criselda, "believe that Selene, the chosen one, has decided to abandon our mortal condition and embrace the Odish's immortality. The prophecy announces that the chosen one will be tempted and either Omars or Odish will perish at her hand."

Criselda glanced around. They were all speechless.

"The prophecy of Odi said it, and it is coming true. Selene has been tempted . . . and, if she succeeds, she will be the most powerful Odish to ever exist. She will destroy the Omars."

Criselda's words hit them like a hammer.

"Is there time to save her from her own weakness?"

"No," said Gaya, "not now. Selene is very dangerous; she knows us and our limitations. We can't run that risk. We have to destroy her so she won't destroy us."

Criselda had a knot in her throat that was turning increasingly bitter. Not even the sweet chocolate she was eating could help dissolve it.

"Anaíd spoke about the Book of Rosebuth. I had forgotten about it, but Rosebuth did say that only 'she who loved the chosen one' would be able to make her come back to the tribe. Who better fits that description than Anaíd?"

Karen was horrified.

"She's a child, she has no resources, or strength, or enough power. If it's true that Selene is . . . an Odish now . . . she will destroy her own daughter."

Karen burst into sobs, refusing to imagine her friend killing her daughter. She couldn't conceive of it and yet . . .

"Before that happened, one of us would stop her," objected Elena, "because Anaíd wouldn't be alone. Criselda? What do you say about that?"

Elena was trying to give her hope, and Criselda clung to that possibility.

"Anaíd is intuitive and strong, but she's emotionally fragile. Her strength resides in her love for her mother. If she suspected what could happen if Selene was an Odish . . ."

Elena got Criselda's point immediately.

"Anaíd should embark on this mission without knowing the truth. We'll have to lie to her; it's the only way to protect her innocence."

But Gaya rubbed salt into the wound.

"There's no need to lie to anyone, or risk anything. Let's get rid of Selene."

Criselda stood firm and spoke: "In the event that Selene is one of them, and attacks her daughter instead of surrendering to her love . . . then, yes . . . we would have to—"

But she didn't have the courage to say the word.

"Destroy her," Karen finished, with pain.

"It would be our duty," said Elena.

"Before she becomes too powerful," concluded Karen.

Criselda was afraid of taking the next step, but it was her turn.

"Who will be responsible for this? Who will go with Anaíd and destroy Selene in the worst-case scenario?"

All eyes fell on her.

And Criselda knew she couldn't refuse to carry out this task; it was her moral duty. She owed it to her sister Deméter and to the Tsinoulis lineage.

She accepted, even though the success or failure of her mission didn't depend on her.

It depended on a girl.

Anaíd.

CHAPTER 10

———

THE FIRST SPELL

"How did it go?" asked Ms. Olav once Anaíd was inside the car again.

"Terrible," muttered Anaíd, slamming the door. "He doesn't know anything about her and he didn't believe I'm her daughter. My mother never told him about me."

"And that bothers you?"

"How could it not bother me?!" Anaíd exploded. "My mother hides from me that she has a stupid boyfriend named Max, and she hides from Max that she has a daughter."

"Why is Max stupid?"

Anaíd covered her face with her hands.

"He said that . . . we don't look anything alike."

"And that hurts you?"

"Of course it does."

Ms. Olav smiled tenderly.

"Nobody understands you."

"How do you know?"

"I was your age once, too."

Anaíd sighed. That's the kind of answer her mother would have given her.

Selene, the great liar.

Was her mother really as she remembered her? Or had she idealized Selene?

Anaíd had always wanted to believe that she had a young, affectionate, fun, and playful mother, who acted more like an older sister. But there was another Selene who argued with Deméter at the top of her lungs, who disappeared for days, who was a compulsive shopper, who was in love with her image in the mirror, and . . . who had secret lovers whom she didn't tell she had a daughter. Who was her mother really?

The Land Rover took the main road, exiting the town of Jaca.

Anaíd didn't want to think of Selene or Max. She had suddenly wanted to visit him, meet him, to check if her mother had actually run off with him. She had called, asking him for an appointment—that simple. Ms. Olav drove her to the café where they'd agreed to meet and waited in the car for the half hour the meeting lasted. Max was interested in hearing about Selene but wasn't thrilled about the fact that she had a daughter. Coincidentally, he had also received a telegram the same day as Anaíd. Selene told him that she was going far away and asked him not to look for her.

Anaíd was nervous.

In addition to that strange meeting, a few hours before, she'd had to confront her aunt and her mother's friends. She was indignant about their indifference and lack of interest in finding Selene.

"I think they really don't want to find my mother!"

"That's possible," said Ms. Olav.

"They don't care whether she's dead or alive . . ."

"That's normal, Anaíd. They don't love her like you do."

"I know, I've told them!"

"You said that to them?"

103

"They act so distant, as if they don't care about anything, as if they live in a bubble. None of them has tried to contact Max to find out if Selene has been in touch with him. And it was really easy."

"Watch out!" shouted Ms. Olav.

She swerved sharply and ran over something. Anaíd bumped her head against the windshield. She had been in a hurry and had forgotten to buckle her seat belt.

Anaíd felt her forehead. A big bump was forming there. Holding the wheel tightly, Ms. Olav apologized.

"I'm sorry, a rabbit ran into the road. I couldn't avoid it."

Anaíd didn't know whether it was the blow, the rabbit, or her grief, but she suddenly burst into tears. Ms. Olav turned on the hazard lights immediately and pulled over onto the shoulder of the road.

"It's okay, it's okay. It was nothing."

And she cradled Anaíd to her chest, stroking her temples with her soft hands.

"Is the rabbit the only thing you're crying about?" she asked Anaíd, gently massaging the painful area.

"No."

"Of course, it's a combination of everything—your mother, Max, the party . . ."

"What party?" asked Anaíd, surprised.

"That girl Marion's, the one you told me about. The one who never invites you to her parties."

Anaíd hadn't thought about it, but it was true, Marion's party was there, hovering in her mind and bothering her every once in a while like a buzzing mosquito.

"I'm not surprised, she's really beautiful," admitted Anaíd, sniffing.

"And you think you are not? Look at yourself in the mirror. You are gorgeous. I'm sure all the girls in your class envy your blue eyes."

"No way!" said Anaíd. "They don't even look at me. They don't know I exist."

Ms. Olav clicked her tongue.

"Well, it is time they start looking at you now. Don't you agree?"

"How?"

"That girl, Marion, might be very beautiful, but you are smart."

"And how is being smart useful?"

"Think about it and you'll find out."

Ms. Olav had the ability to always make Anaíd feel good and forget her worries. By her side, everything seemed easy.

"Will a bracelet and a hamburger put you in a good mood again?"

Cheering up, Anaíd wiped her last tears with the back of her hand. How did Ms. Olav know that, behind Deméter's back, Selene always took her out for burgers and then bought her costume jewelry?

Anaíd had probably told Ms. Olav herself.

When Anaíd checked herself in the rearview mirror to fix her hair, she was amazed—the bump had disappeared and . . . she did look beautiful.

. . .

The hamburger was delicious, the bracelet was perfect for her, and, since Ms. Olav had complimented her on her eyes and intelligence, Anaíd had regained her confidence.

And she'd also remembered the thorny subject of Marion's birthday party. But she now saw it from another perspective.

Marion's birthday party fell on the day of the summer solstice, and in the last few weeks it was all people talked about at school. To make things more interesting, Marion invited her friends one by one. The chosen ones would exhale, "Phew!" when she walked over and whispered the invitation in their ears.

Obviously, those who were not so lucky had a terrible time, all the way up to the last minute. Each time flirtatious Marion walked by, they prayed that she would tilt her head slightly and hand them the key to happiness.

Anaíd, who had naively thought she'd be invited for the past four years, hoped in vain that the two events that had altered her life—her mother's disappearance and her new bra—might have made Marion change her mind. But that didn't happen.

Would she continue to let Marion ignore her?

She said good-bye to Ms. Olav and thanked her for her support with a kiss. She would have gladly stayed with her instead of returning to clumsy Criselda's company. Her aunt probably wouldn't have dinner ready or remember that, at fourteen, you are usually ravenous three or four times a day.

. . .

Aunt Criselda was waiting on the living room sofa. She ate chocolate with a blank expression on her face and didn't even ask Anaíd where she'd been. No, it wasn't worth mentioning Max. Criselda wouldn't care.

"Anaíd, sit down, please."

Anaíd obeyed without complaining. The grave tone in which her aunt spoke indicated that this was more important than a scolding.

"Anaíd, the coven has accepted your offer to look for your mother and rescue her," she announced solemnly.

"Are you kidding?" was the only thing Anaíd was able to utter.

"If Rosebuth is not mistaken, you are probably the only one who can reach Selene and give her the strength she needs to defeat the Odish."

. . .

Was it really that easy? That simple? Anaíd couldn't sleep all night. She tossed and turned in bed, thinking of a thousand crazy ways to look for Selene and fight against the Odish. But everything she envisioned acquired a grotesque, surreal tone, like the thick lines with which her mother drew the characters in her comics.

Anaíd tried to think seriously about finding her mother, but other things distracted her from this new and enormous responsibility.

If she was an Omar with the power to penetrate hell itself and rescue her mother from the claws of the Odish, why did she have to put up with Marion's contempt? Why couldn't she go to her party?

So Anaíd made this her goal.

After all, she was a witch.

And she wasn't so unattractive.

And she was smart.

After class that day, she sneaked into her cave and searched her mother's books until she found a seduction spell that would be perfect for her plan.

It was slightly different from the "love filter." It wasn't a potion; it didn't alter the blood or quicken the heartbeat or breathing. This one was a pleasant spell that worked by contact and proximity. With the right words and a simple touch of her wand, the veil of

107

invisibility that concealed her from Marion's eyes would vanish and her classmate would discover her.

The next morning at school, she tried to sit as close to Marion as possible. Roberta agreed to switch places in exchange for a pack of gum, and Anaíd managed to sit right behind her victim's desk. When she was sure no one was watching, she took her wand from her backpack and hid it under her social studies book. She had waited for Mr. Corbarán's class—the social studies teacher never noticed anything. And while Mr. Corbarán went on and on, indifferent to whether anyone listened or not, Anaíd pronounced her spell through parted lips, pointed her wand in Marion's direction, and grazed her hair.

Perfect! Marion had reacted to Anaíd's touch and was leaning her head to one side. After a moment, Marion raised her hand and scratched herself distractedly.

Anaíd held her breath. It was working. Marion was responding to the seduction spell. And she must have felt a soft tingling sensation, hence the scratching. An impulse should follow; she should now turn her head and find Anaíd. Then, she would remember her name, smile, and invite her to the party.

Everything should happen just like the spell predicted.

Anaíd waited one, two, three minutes—which seemed an eternity—and then . . . Marion turned her head and found her. But she didn't smile; she laughed. She laughed hysterically, as if watching a comedy or listening to a really funny joke. She laughed in Anaíd's face and said something like, "Well, well, well . . . the know-it-all midget has grown boobs and gotten pimples."

Anaíd wanted to die. No, dying wouldn't be enough. Marion's joke was probably heard as far as Urt's watchtower, she thought, and then echoed by all the idiots in her class, the crows in the tower, and the tourists rafting down the river. The whole world had witnessed Marion's insult.

The first one to laugh, though, was Roc, Elena's son and Marion's current boyfriend. Anaíd heard that and made a mental note.

Anaíd kept her cool as best as she could and then, without asking Mr. Corbarán for permission—he wouldn't notice anyway—she ran to the bathroom, where she could cry in peace.

While she sobbed, Anaíd gazed at herself in the mirror and realized that she did, in fact, have a tiny zit on her nose. And she decided to take revenge on Marion. At this point, nothing—herself, her reputation, her honor—could look any worse.

She walked out of the bathroom with her head high and her plan thought out. The bell had just rung and everyone was at recess, stretching their legs, chattering, and munching sandwiches. Marion and Roc liked to have a snack in the café by the park, Cokes in hand and their gang around. And that's where Anaíd headed, with her wand under her sleeve.

Anaíd might have changed her mind if Marion had simply ignored her as usual, but the spell had made Marion focus all her attention on Anaíd, as if she were an irresistible magnet.

When Anaíd reached the café, Marion sensed her presence. She turned her head, piercing her with her eyes, and charged again.

"Look who's here, little Anaíd. Should we order you a bottle or do you prefer baby food?"

Anaíd walked over to Marion.

"Didn't you say I had pimples?"

"Oh, right . . . You are a teenager now."

And that's when Anaíd risked everything.

Sliding her wand imperceptibly from under her sleeve, she touched her pimple and then brushed Marion's face.

"But mine is nothing compared to yours! How many zits do you have, Marion? A dozen? Two dozen? Three dozen?"

And as Anaíd said the numbers, Marion's face and neck lost their smoothness and were covered with infected blackheads.

Shouts erupted all around them, and Anaíd, emboldened, did more than she had planned.

"Ha! Your boyfriend doesn't fall far behind," she said, brushing Roc's face, which was instantly covered in acne.

Marion couldn't see herself, but she saw the effect her face had caused among her friends, and she screamed when she saw Roc.

"How disgusting!" she shouted.

And she immediately realized that she must look the same way, for everyone around them was pulling away and wrinkling their noses. Marion touched her face in disbelief and, when she felt the horrible bumps, she covered her face with her hands and shouted loudly, "Witch! Bloody witch!"

Only then did Anaíd realize what she had done.

Worst of all, she didn't know the antidote to the spell, so she quickly turned around and ran away.

. . .

Criselda couldn't believe the words coming out of Elena's mouth. Not only had Anaíd disobeyed her, casting spells without permission, but nothing could be worse—she had cast a revenge spell in public and been called a witch.

The girl would give her a heart attack.

"Have you lost your mind?" Criselda yelled at her.

Anaíd endured the reprimand stoically, even though she was smashed to pieces inside.

"Do you realize that you have put all of us in danger? And yourself more than anyone?"

Elena hadn't lost it like Criselda, but she was concerned.

"Omar witches never cast revenge spells."

Criselda interrogated her, already recovered from her initial panic.

"They are strictly forbidden. Who taught you how to create one?"

Anaíd didn't know. It had come from within her and worked.

"I only wanted Marion to invite me to her party," Anaíd defended herself.

"How? By covering her with pimples?"

"No, first I used a seduction spell for Marion to notice me, but she noticed me so much that she insulted me in front of everyone."

Criselda and Elena brought their hands to their heads at the same time.

"Oh, no!"

Anaíd realized that the worst mistake had been done at the beginning.

"What did I do wrong?"

"Everything."

"You have no common sense."

"You can't satisfy a feeling with a spell."

"No Omar should ever obtain friendship or love with a potion or spell."

"That's what an Odish would do."

"Where did you get the idea from?"

Anaíd had been slowly shrinking, until she was curled up like a ball. Then she began to sob. She was hurt by the flood of accusations Elena and Criselda had unloaded on her. She'd never seen them so angry. Everything she did was wrong. She was good for nothing—girl or witch.

Anaíd took pleasure in her tears. She had turned into a confirmed crybaby. Growing up, she realized, involved a voracious hunger and a terrible need to cry.

Elena and Criselda sat silently by her side. Criselda touched her forehead while Elena stroked her hair. They comforted her until the spasms stopped.

Anaíd sniffed, rubbed her eyes, and wiped her cheeks, ready to continue listening to her elders.

Elena and Criselda resumed their speech, trying to use a gentler tone.

"Your power and magic should be at the service of the common good, never your individual well-being. Will you keep that in mind?"

"An Omar witch should never use spells for her own purposes."

"You have committed two very serious infractions."

"Three."

"Many."

"But one can also learn from mistakes."

"We, Omar witches, are human and mortal. We live next to humans and can't use magic to obtain love, friendship, respect, power . . . or wealth."

"If an Omar uses magic for her own purposes, or for revenge, she will be expelled from her clan and the tribe, and deprived of her powers."

"Do you understand?"

"Anaíd, our power must be limited."

"We have to cook, work, shop . . . Imagine if we didn't have to make any efforts for that."

Anaíd kept nodding and repeating, "Yes," "yes," "aha." Finally, she couldn't take it any longer and, with one last melodramatic sob, asked the question that was torturing her: "Are you saying I'm evil?"

Elena and Criselda exchanged a surprised look. Neither one had raised a young witch. Perhaps what had happened to Anaíd—her excessive self-confidence, the improper use of her powers—was common among young witches.

Criselda decided to lighten things up.

"Why don't you go to bed. Tomorrow will be a brand-new day."

"And don't say anything at school tomorrow," Elena reminded her. "I've had no choice but to give Roc, Marion, and their friends a forgetting potion. Everything that's happened in the last twenty-four hours has been erased from their minds. I feel badly for those who had studied for the music exam."

Anaíd got excited.

"A forgetting potion? That's fantastic! That way I could—"

"No!" Elena and Criselda shouted in unison.

Anaíd fell silent.

"You'll have to ask for forgiveness in the next coven," added Aunt Criselda. "Or you might be punished."

Anaíd remained quiet. She wasn't keen on having to apologize to Gaya, but she would have to do it.

She kissed Aunt Criselda and Elena and, crestfallen, walked to her room. As soon as she disappeared from sight, the two women looked at each other, concerned. They didn't need to explain with words what had crossed their minds.

"She's not ready yet."

"Will she ever be?"

"What if we've made a mistake?"

"Perhaps Deméter and Selene had a reason for not initiating Anaíd into witchcraft."

"And what if Anaíd is dangerous?"

These and other questions passed quickly between Criselda and Elena.

With Anaíd close by, they didn't dare talk about her aloud. But they had begun to suspect that the girl had not confessed to all of her powers.

CHAPTER 11

OBEDIENT SPIRITS

Anaíd went to bed depressed. If early that morning she'd felt like the most powerful person in the world, able to achieve whatever she wanted by fair means or foul, now she was convinced that she was the most wretched, selfish, and shameless person on earth.

She tossed and turned a thousand times, unable to sleep a wink. She fluffed out her feather pillow and tried to sleep on her right side, then on her left side. She tried covering herself, but she felt hot, so she had to remove the quilt. She took out one arm from under the sheet, then a leg, then the other leg, but she felt cold again. Frustrated, Anaíd turned on the light and jumped out of bed.

She wasn't depressed anymore. Now she was mad, mad at the whole world. Her life was terrible and everything seemed to be moving backward. She was much better off a week ago, and the month before, and so on.

Sitting on the rug by her bed was the knight, wearing full armor and a helmet. He had to move aside so Anaíd, who had jumped with momentum, didn't step on him.

The lady in the curtains gave a hint of a mocking smile when she saw how frightened the knight had been for a moment.

But Anaíd didn't even flinch. The two images were part of her imagination, creations of her own that had first appeared when she developed her powers. She wasn't afraid or uncomfortable. The lady and the knight appeared silently on certain nights and settled into their favorite spots—the knight liked to lounge on her colorful rug, and the lady usually hid behind the curtains. They always disappeared with the first rays of the sun.

That night, however, Anaíd was in the mood to fight, with either herself or someone else.

First she tried fighting with herself. She looked at her image in the mirror and stuck out her tongue. She hated herself. She was a freak—somewhere in between a scrawny girl and a pimply young woman. If she had to choose, she'd prefer herself before she'd started growing up. Weeks ago she was a midget, but what had she become now? A monster. A witch who could stop a fly in midair, speak with wolves, cover a pretty face with foul-smelling zits. And a selfish girl who preferred being invited to a birthday party rather than thinking about her mother and the best way to help her.

Anaíd couldn't forgive her mother for not telling her boyfriend about her, and she wanted revenge. How could her mother have concealed her love affair with Max?

Even worse, the reprimand she'd received from her elders still stung, and she was terrified of the mission she had insisted upon. Anaíd had taken a step forward without knowing which direction to turn; she was being a smart aleck when she offered to rescue her mother from the hands of the Odish.

How would she know where Selene was?

And what would she do if she found her?

What if her mother didn't want to be found?

And what if her spells didn't work and the ones she'd mastered were forbidden by the Omars?

That's why Anaíd had gotten sidetracked and started dreaming about being invited to Marion's party.

Pure escapism.

How could she have been so shallow?

How could she have wished to go to a stupid party with superficial people while her mother was captive, probably being tortured, and Anaíd, only Anaíd, loved her enough to save her?

The only possible explanation was that she was a shallow teenager with no feelings, who was scared to death . . . besides being ugly, of course.

"Coward!" Anaíd shouted at her image in the mirror.

In the same mirror she saw the reflection of the lady, who was standing behind her, laughing under her breath. Anaíd couldn't contain herself.

"What are you laughing about?" she spewed.

She didn't expect the lady to reply and thought she'd continue to laugh. It was obvious that the lady was laughing at her. Anaíd was so unfortunate that even her own nightmares made fun of her to her face, just like Marion, Roc, and their gang. But the lady surprised her; she pointed at the knight and shouted happily, "I'm laughing at him! *He's* the coward!"

The knight blushed but didn't respond. Anaíd was disconcerted.

"Oh, really? And why is he a coward?"

"Are you asking me?" inquired the lady.

"Yes, you."

The lady was delighted to be able to explain.

"Well, he ditched his army in the ravine, turned around, and ran away."

Anaíd wasn't expecting such a grounded accusation. Who was she speaking with?

117

"What army?"

"Count Ataúlfo's. They tried to defend the valley from the attack of al-Mansur and his troops."

Anaíd was surprised. At school she had studied that dark episode in the history of the valleys: when the evil al-Mansur-Bi-Llāh mercilessly penetrated the ravine, destroying the villages and towns on his way. And it was all the Christian army's fault, which set out to fight them but ran away, intimidated by the Saracen troops and their sharp swords.

Was her hallucination mocking her?

Anaíd turned to the knight, who looked especially glum but wasn't opening his mouth.

"Is what the lady said true?"

The knight raised his head cautiously and gazed at Anaíd.

"Are you talking to me?"

"Yes."

"Oh, precious child, thank you so much for addressing me. You can't imagine how I've longed to be able to talk and put an end to this silence. One thousand and seventeen years. It's been boring, truly boring."

"Is what the lady said true?"

The knight nodded sadly.

"Unfortunately, it is. My father, the vice-count, put me in a terrible predicament by asking me to lead the army at such a young and inexperienced age. When I heard the first shout from the Saracen army, my blood turned to ice. I must have run away, because I can't remember anything else until I fell dead."

Anaíd was speechless.

"They killed you?"

"Indeed, precious child, cowardice didn't save me from death.

A lost arrow took me away from this world, but my father's curse has kept me in it, condemning me to roam the land I lost."

And with a vague gesture, he indicated his surroundings.

Anaíd pointed at him incredulously.

"So you are . . . a spirit?"

"A lost soul, my precious child, who can be helped by your generosity."

Anaíd still couldn't believe what was happening.

"Me?"

"May I speak?" It was the lady's voice, a little impatient and jealous as the knight had taken the attention away from her.

Anaíd gave her the word.

"My sweet child, you can see us, you can hear us, and you can ask from us. In exchange, you'll have to give to us, naturally."

Anaíd considered this.

"What can I ask you? And what am I required to give you?"

The lady smiled.

"You can ask for the impossible, wishes humans can't conceive of. Wishes only the dead can make come true."

Anaíd didn't understand.

"Are you sorcerers?"

The pretty lady shook her head.

"We simply roam the world of the spirits and know all the corners forbidden to the living. There's no secret we are not aware of . . . We know it all. We know where you keep your riches, what secrets you hide, what crimes you've committed, what lies you're telling, and whom you love. We can whisper in the ears of the living, making them believe that their own voice is guiding them, and we can create remorse to undermine their morale. In essence, we can unleash tempests."

Anaíd was beginning to understand.

"And if I asked for something and you gave it to me, what would I have to give you in return?"

The knight spoke first. "Freedom!"

"Freedom?" Anaíd asked, surprised. "Aren't you free?"

The lady clicked her tongue.

"We are condemned to roam the earth, though we have already paid for our sins. How we wish for eternal rest."

Anaíd couldn't believe she was having a conversation with two tormented souls; especially the lady, who was so beautiful and cheerful.

"What are you guilty of?"

"I betrayed my love. I promised I would wait for him, and when he returned from the Crusades, I had already married the baron. He killed me, of course, and cursed me—that's why I'm here."

Anaíd was indignant.

"So he cursed you, on top of killing you?"

"He also roams the world for having murdered me," the lady clarified.

"Serves him right!" exclaimed Anaíd.

That was a fair punishment. The nerve . . . killing someone because of a broken promise.

The lady sighed.

"Oh, precious child, it's so exhausting to carry these years, decades, centuries, and millenniums of inactivity on your shoulders. The coward knight and I, the treacherous lady, we long to rest."

Anaíd was beginning to believe that the two spirits weren't a nightmare or a figment of her imagination. These were two poor ghosts willing to please her if only she would free them from their shackles.

What was she waiting for?

They'd said they knew *everything*.

Fantastic! Information was precisely what she needed.

But she decided to play hard to get.

"Well, I'm willing to help you if you promise to help me in return. What do you say?"

She got what she wanted—absolute attention. They both drank up her words.

"We are ready to listen to you and please you."

"Do you know what an Odish witch is?" Anaíd asked.

"Naturally, we communicate with Odish witches."

"*You* are an Odish witch—"

Furious, Anaíd interrupted the lady.

"How dare you say I'm an Odish?"

"Apologies, precious child, I thought . . ."

"I'm an Omar witch, from the Scythian tribe, and the clan of the she-wolf. I'm Selene's daughter and Deméter's granddaughter."

The knight and the lady looked at each other, regretting having made Anaíd angry.

"Whatever you say, precious child, daughter of Selene," said the lady.

"Granddaughter of Deméter," the knight added.

"We apologize for having thought you were an Odish. We accept your Omar condition, daughter of Selene."

"Granddaughter of Deméter," repeated the knight, as if chanting a litany.

"Okay, enough adulation," Anaíd cut them off. Their excessive submission was beginning to annoy her.

She was surprised to realize that, after her strict order, the two spirits had clammed up. Then she remembered that they couldn't talk unless she addressed them. Was it only the first time? Or did they always need permission to speak? They were obedient spirits, but not so clever. They had confused her with an Odish!

"Am I so ugly that you've confused me with an Odish?"

"Are you asking us, precious child?"

"Yes, answer me."

The knight spoke first. "I assume you don't know the Odish very well. I can assure you that they are so striking that the sun pales next to them."

Anaíd was astounded.

"So, they are not old and wrinkled, with warts on their nose and hair on their chin?"

The lady started laughing hysterically.

"I'm dying . . . I'm dying again—of laughter!"

Anaíd was hurt. It might have been a description from a children's book, but what other reference did she have? And now that she thought of it, neither Aunt Criselda nor the other witches from the coven had ever described an Odish to her.

"If you will allow me, precious child, that's nothing more than a popular myth," the knight clarified. "The Odish are the most powerful, greedy, and narcissistic beings on Earth. They worship youth, immortality, and beauty."

Anaíd felt like an idiot. The knight was absolutely right. Could there be a higher being so stupid as to carry an old and unpleasant body for all eternity?

If she looked at it from that angle, the spirits had complimented her when they confused her with an Odish; though . . . she shouldn't believe them one hundred percent.

"I'm sorry, I'm very young still and I've never seen an Odish witch."

Again, the lady laughed under her breath. Anaíd didn't like that gesture at all.

"What are you laughing about? Is everything I say funny?"

"No, my mistress, but I think you *do* know an Odish."

Anaíd turned pale.

"Who?"

This time, the lady shook her head.

"I'm sorry, but that information could be dangerous for us. The Odish don't want us to talk about them, not even among the Odish themselves."

These spirits must serve the Odish. She would have to be careful with those two.

"In that case, there's no deal."

Anaíd noticed that, despite her firm tone, neither spirit replied, bargained, or offered anything in return. They were definitely obedient.

So she opted for budging herself. She really wanted to know about something else.

"Fine, we won't talk about the Odish. I have another question."

The spirits smiled hopefully, eager to help her and, obviously, help themselves.

"Where is my mother, Selene?"

The knight and the lady looked at each other sadly.

"Precious child, you know she is with the Odish."

"Of course I know that, but where?"

The knight cleared his throat.

"We must be prudent, my mistress. We could be punished for our lack of discretion."

"Give me a clue, something."

The spirits exchanged a conniving look, but they seemed afraid.

"Do you promise to set us free?"

Anaíd didn't think twice.

"I promise."

"And do you promise not to tell anyone where you got this information?"

"I promise."

In a slightly hoarse voice, the knight whispered, "Where the waters slow down their course, mortals lose their footing, and the caverns connect the two worlds. Selene will speak to you, but you won't be allowed to see her."

"You will only see her reflection in the water," the lady added.

Anaíd arrived to a conclusion on her own. "Do you mean the dark pond? Is that it?"

To her astonishment, the knight and the lady feigned surprise.

"We don't know what you are talking about, precious child."

"How's that possible? You just told me that—"

"We?" exclaimed the lady.

"You are confused, precious child. We haven't said anything!"

Anaíd was annoyed now.

"Why are you denying you spoke?"

"Because we haven't said anything."

"It was your imagination."

"Or perhaps a dream."

"But I heard you," Anaíd shot back.

"We are very sorry, precious child."

"Daughter of Selene."

"Granddaughter of Deméter."

Anaíd was definitely angry now.

"You . . . you can go to hell!"

And to Anaíd's dismay, the two spirits vanished.

Anaíd didn't want to call them again. It was clear that they either regretted having spoken or that that was their deceitful way of not living. She would go to the dark pond the following day.

And while she tried to sleep, a thought crossed her mind over and over again, keeping her awake.

Did hell exist?

The Prophecy of Trebora

Noble gold carved with wise words,
Destined for hands as yet unborn,
Sadly exiled from the world by Mother O.

So she wished it.
So she decided it.
You will remain hidden in the depths of the earth,
Until the skies shine bright and the stars begin their journey.
Only then will the earth spit you out of its bowels,
And you will obediently seek her white hand,
And anoint it with red.

Fire and blood, inseparable,
In Mother O's scepter of power.
Fire and blood for the chosen one who will possess the scepter.
Fire and blood for the chosen who will be possessed by the scepter.

O's scepter will rule O's descendants.

CHAPTER 12

THE ROAD TO SELENE

Anaíd put on her hiking sneakers and hat. She packed a sandwich, oranges, a handful of dried fruit, and a bottle of water in her backpack. The expedition to the pond would take a few hours, but she didn't know how long she'd have to stay there before she could communicate with Selene.

Her grandmother had taught her that there's no such thing as being too cautious. The mountain captures those who are too daring. Caution is the best guide. Those who challenge the mountain, those who don't know, or don't listen to its warnings, end up paying with their lives. Deméter used to point them out when they appeared in town, with their huge backpacks and lost stares. They were men and women who'd insisted on reaching the summits and ended up blind, deaf, and mad. They suffered from "mountain madness," and in their attempt to reach the tops, lost fingers, hands, feet, and sometimes their lives. Deméter had told her stories of climbers who'd frozen, been trapped in the snow, struck by lightning, gotten lost, fallen to their deaths, and been eaten by wolves. If her grandmother were alive, she would have forced her to pack matches, a rope, a carabiner, a compass, a flare, a helmet, and a sweater. But Anaíd had to bring an unexpected item.

"Aaah!" she shouted, taken aback, when she was leaving the house.

A furry ball had jumped on her back and was clinging firmly to her backpack. It was Apollo, who didn't want to stay behind.

"Bad Apollo!" Anaíd scolded him. "You can't come with me. Get down."

But Apollo ignored her.

"Meow, meow, meeeoooow," said Anaíd with a perfect accent.

Apollo raised his small ears—he couldn't believe his owner had reprimanded him in his own language—and apologized for his reckless behavior.

"Meow, meow."

Anaíd accepted his apology with a smile and patted his head. She wasn't as surprised as the little cat—she often had to keep herself from chirping like a hummingbird, baaing like a sheep, clucking like a hen, or braying like a donkey. The previous morning, in fact, she'd asked Ms. Engracia's rooster to shut up with two loud cock-a-doodle-dos. Aunt Criselda had woken up but had no idea that her niece had been the culprit. Anaíd didn't dare tell Aunt Criselda about her newfound ability to understand animals and speak like them. *Listening*, like she was supposed to, she had realized that none of the other witches understood animals. Except for the howling of wolves, her own clan was incapable of decoding even the simple bark of a dog.

Anaíd ended up succumbing to Apollo's tender cries precisely because she could understand him. The kitten didn't want to be left alone; he didn't want Aunt Criselda to scold him. Anaíd put him in her backpack with a sigh, and meowing, made one thing clear: "You can come because you are small and light, but as soon as you gain some weight, forget about it."

She embarked on her journey, considering Apollo's presence a good omen. Now that she could interpret the signs around her, she realized that things happened for a reason. It would be good to have the cat's company; she would feel less lonely.

Unfortunately, she barely trusted anyone now. She'd lied to Aunt Criselda (saying she was going on a field trip with her class), and at school, she'd lied to Gaya (saying that Aunt Criselda needed her).

Anaíd had sensed something strange in Criselda's behavior. She had a feeling that Criselda wouldn't help her get in touch with Selene, and that she would probably undermine her plan. She didn't completely trust Elena or Karen either, and as far as Gaya was concerned, Anaíd was beginning to doubt her loyalty to the clan.

For moment, a brief second, a doubt crossed her mind.

Could Gaya be an Odish?

. . .

Anaíd crossed the bridge and slowly trudged up the shortcut that crisscrossed the eastern hillside, leading to the ravines. As she climbed up the steep slope, she confirmed that the dim light that had saddened the spring mornings—which she'd attributed to a persistent fog—was very, very strange.

Since her mother's disappearance and Aunt Criselda's arrival, Anaíd had begun to perceive changes in the surrounding landscape. Sometimes, she was short of breath; the air felt dense and scarce, devoid of freshness. Other times, the morning light seemed murky, without contrasts, as if it were passed through a gray filter. From the forest, the cave, and from town, she'd lacked perspective, but now she could swear that the valley was trapped in a surreal, phantasmagoric illusion. This was not a natural phenomenon.

As she walked on, she felt increasingly worried. She was approaching a dangerous place and didn't want to look back. She was about to reach the ravine connecting the valleys, an old smuggling route the locals traveled by mule. From inside her backpack, Apollo began to meow. He was afraid. Anaíd was too. And then, already high up, she was suddenly unable to continue walking. She suddenly couldn't move her legs. Her feet were like lead, stuck to the ground, and she couldn't lift them. Her sight became blurry, and she couldn't breathe properly. Anaíd wished she could turn around and let herself roll down the mountain like a stone. And she almost followed her impulse, but the image of Selene kept her from doing it.

In order to move forward, she needed a kind of strength she now lacked. She was using all her will to conquer the vertigo that was compelling her to jump. She couldn't give in to her weakness; she needed a little push, the confidence that she could overcome this obstacle, whatever it was.

It was the bee who solved her problem.

It hovered around Anaíd's head and then continued moving forward without hesitating. Anaíd understood the bee's message perfectly well. She was announcing her arrival to her fellow bees in the hive. There was no danger ahead.

That was exactly what Anaíd needed—to be sure that her fear was irrational and that, with courage, she could reach any place.

She made a fist, clenched her teeth, lifted one foot, raised one leg, and took a step forward. Then another one, and another one. Her steps got firmer and more determined. She moved forward thinking of Selene—Selene's hair, Selene's laughter, Selene's hands—and that made her feel alive and strong. Soon, her steps became agile strides that turned into a quick jog.

As Anaíd ran, she felt the barrier break. First, she felt a hard, cold object, the consistency of a frozen lake. She clashed with it and heard a loud crack. It was like hitting glass, but she wasn't afraid. She kept moving, her head bowed like that of a bull ready to charge, and felt something shatter around her. That encouraged her to keep going, but as she took one more step, a sharp pain shot up her left leg, making her fall to the ground.

She had succeeded! She had conquered the wall and could now feel the fresh spring air on her face, the strong scent of blooming heather, and the warm, unfiltered sunlight. The barrier that was stopping her had collapsed. Was it a spell? It had probably been cast by her clan to protect her. And she had destroyed it.

But Anaíd had done it for a good reason—to contact her mother. She tried to smile and cheer up. Apollo peered from inside the backpack and greeted her with an affectionate meow. Anaíd tenderly petted him. There was only one doubt in her mind: had the wall shattered or had she simply opened a hole in it?

Ready to find out, she got to her feet but fell again, crying with pain. Her leg! It felt as if a piece of her leg had been pulled out with barbed wire.

Anaíd rolled up her pants carefully. To her surprise, there was no wound. Her skin was intact, she wasn't bleeding, and there was no sign of the sharp knife she'd imagined lacerating her skin. Was it all in her mind? She tried to stand up, but her aching leg could barely support her. She bit her lip to stop thinking about the pain. She needed to calm down; she was desperate, and if she didn't do anything about it, she would faint.

Long ago, Deméter had explained to Anaíd that lucidity is a state of mind that occurs when one faces real danger. The body sends a warning to the brain, which activates all neural connections. Sight, hearing, smell, and touch become unbelievably sharp.

That's what must have happened to her, or perhaps Anaíd had

the rare ability to activate her senses when she really wanted to or needed to. The fact is that she was suddenly able to smell the mushrooms buried under the fallen oak leaves. Dragging herself with her arms, she dug them out. Her smell and sight had not betrayed her. Deméter had taught her how to use this type of mushroom to soothe the pain and move through the different states of mind.

The effect depended on the amount ingested. Anaíd licked the pointy head of one of the mushrooms and the anesthetic traveled rapidly through her body, giving her a pleasant tingling sensation. She cautiously licked the mushroom again and rubbed her leg, saying a chant she'd heard her grandmother use. Fortunately, her injured leg responded to the medicine and the massage. After a few minutes, the pain was completely gone.

Anaíd put the mushroom in her backpack, told Apollo not to eat it, and got ready to move on.

She looked back for a moment; nothing prevented her from going back the way she'd come. She checked her watch. It would take her about an hour to reach the pond. Should she continue? Or was she acting like those crazy climbers who, despite the northern wind awash with bad omens, continued climbing stoically only to die later, trapped in the summits?

She listened to her inner voice and let it guide her. The barrier she had broken wasn't a sign from the mountain; it had to be witchcraft, magic. She was getting near Selene and should move only forward.

. . .

The sun was already high when Anaíd reached the dark pond. Her trek had been slower and harder than expected. She was hungry and exhausted but proud of herself. She sat on a rock by some marsh plants, from where she could enjoy the magnificent view.

The pond was gloomy, its waters dark with mud and vegetation.

In this part of the valley, which led to the lakes, the river split into a thousand winding streams that invaded every corner. Under these streams, the spongy soil turned to mud, which trapped the unwary ones who fell into its claws. Anaíd wouldn't be one of them. She would be very careful about venturing into the swampy area.

Holding Apollo tight, she took out a sandwich and a bottle of water. She needed to regain some energy before completing her mission.

She ate slowly, savoring every bite, and let herself be lulled by the wind and the whispers of the marsh plants. Far away, echoing off the steep hillsides, she could hear an eagle hunting its prey. Without realizing, Anaíd spoke to the bird.

Wow! She was doing such strange things. Was she turning into a weirdo?

As she plunged into witchcraft, she certainly was.

She had been a strange child, she was turning into a strange teenager, and—without a doubt—she was a strange witch.

Anaíd decided not to dwell on it. After eating and resting, it was now time to try to contact her mother. But how? When she put the crumpled sandwich wrapping back in her backpack, she found the mushroom.

Was this a coincidence? Criselda had taught her that there are no coincidences in life. There is a reason we run into certain things, people, and circumstances. What's important is to understand the meaning of these coincidences and use them properly. *Reading* the world was a complex task. The mushroom was waiting for her. It had wound up in her backpack for a reason and was now telling her something. It was saying, "Here I am. Eat me."

Of course! The mushroom would guide her search for Selene. It wasn't about licking it cautiously now, but ingesting it.

Anaíd nibbled on a piece and waited a while, a moment that seemed suspended in time and altered her mind, giving her a different perspective and the courage to plunge into the dangers of the pond.

IT WAS HER,
BUT IT WASN'T HER.

Anaíd stood up, picked up her birchwood wand, and, with a few firm meows, ordered Apollo not to follow her. She moved cautiously, feeling the ground ahead with her wand extended. She had to find the place where, according to the spirits, the two worlds connected.

She walked from rock to rock, slowly, very slowly, abandoning her hearing, her sight, her touch. She followed her instincts and her wand, which swung in one direction and another, dragging Anaíd behind it. Then her wand stopped moving, indicating the exact point where she must remain.

Anaíd softly sang an ancient tune and waved her wand rhythmically. In that moment, she left her body and was immersed in her memories—images of Selene, Selene's voice, her deep red hair, her white smile, and the strength of her embrace. Anaíd called her, cried her name over and over with a fervent desire to see her, touch her, hear her. Suddenly, she felt near her mother.

And then . . . she fell.

There was nothing under her feet.

Anaíd was falling down, down, down.

Faster and faster. With vertiginous speed. Surrounded by silence and darkness.

Anaíd was plummeting into a bottomless abyss. Anxiety immobilized her, paralyzed her body.

She kept falling for what seemed like an eternity. And she was sinking into the void, small and insecure. She felt desperately around her for something to hold on to.

She was about to lose faith, when she heard a meow next to her. Apollo! Apollo had disobeyed her and was falling too. Oh, no! Apollo!

And just as she forgot about herself, Anaíd recovered the strength she'd lost and was able to grab the cat. It was that easy. The moment she thought of the kitten and extended her arms to stop him, the speed of her fall diminished.

It was her fear.

She had lost her fear when she'd recovered Apollo. That was it! Fear had made her fall into the abyss!

Anaíd cuddled Apollo's trembling body and rocked him in her arms, calming him down.

And she understood that finding Selene depended on her will.

She wanted to see her mother. Now she didn't fear the uncertainty, the darkness, or the void. She extended her hand firmly and called Selene again.

And there it was—a hand to hold on to.

She took it and stayed still, suspended in the void. Anaíd held her breath when she recognized the hand that had stopped her fall. It was soft and cold, but it was Selene's. She recognized her scent, though her touch and pulse had changed—this was a nervous and shaky hand, trying to withdraw every second. But the hand didn't move because Anaíd's longing for her mother was so strong, so powerful, that even Selene's hand obeyed her.

Finally, Selene spoke. Her voice was as shaky and insecure as her hand, and the space she was in. Darkness filled her voice, depriving it of the joy and freshness Anaíd remembered.

"Don't look for me, Anaíd. Go away, don't come any closer."

The strength of that sad voice and the trembling hand were more powerful than Anaíd's will, and snatched her out of that place, throwing her far, far away from the dark pit.

Apollo's howling broke her heart. The cat started falling again, and Anaíd, catapulted into the light, could do nothing to rescue him.

Then, the world dissolved and Anaíd lost consciousness.

• • •

She woke up hours later, frightened and in pain. Someone was offering her water and caressing her face.

135

"Mother," she mumbled, half-asleep.

But when she opened her eyes, she realized she wasn't in the pond but by the fountain on the road, and the hand stroking her was Ms. Olav's.

"Finally. How are you feeling, sweetheart?"

Anaíd couldn't respond right away. The thought of the hand she'd touched hours before made her shudder. It had been cold, frigid. It was her mother's hand, but without any love. Anaíd clenched her fists until her nails pierced her skin. Her mother didn't love her; Selene had rejected her. She had pushed Anaíd away and forbidden her to come near her.

"Are you cold? Let's cover you."

Ms. Olav got a blanket from her four-wheel drive. Anaíd was grateful and, protected by the blanket and Ms. Olav's presence, succumbed to her pain. She cried, softly at first.

"It's okay, sweetie, crying helps."

Anaíd didn't try to act tough. She let Ms. Olav cradle her as her sobs became stronger and more dramatic. She was crying because her mother had pushed her away, because she had lost her cat, because she felt lonely and small in a world she'd always thought was secure but now seemed extremely dangerous. She cried because it was not fair that everything always went wrong. First, her grandmother had died; then her mother had disappeared; and now the earth had swallowed her cat. She cried because she was ugly, because nobody loved her and she always made mistakes. And only when she had cried enough for all her past and future misfortunes, she began to feel better.

"Thank you," she said, grateful for Ms. Olav's affection.

It was just what she needed—a pair of warm arms to find refuge in and to melt the ice that had filled her heart.

Ms. Olav responded with a charming smile.

"Are you hungry?"

All of a sudden, Anaíd realized that it was nighttime and her aunt must be looking for her.

"I have to get back home!"

She got on her feet and, to her surprise, her leg didn't hurt anymore. Ms. Olav tried to stop her.

"Wait, you might have broken something. You must have fallen into the stream. Let me check."

And while Ms. Olav made her move her joints one by one, Anaíd noticed that her clothes were wet and torn, her body bruised.

"You're okay? It's a miracle. Come on, I'll drive you home."

Blessed Ms. Olav. She was discreet, affectionate, and cautious.

"How did you find me?"

"We had agreed to meet this afternoon, remember?"

Anaíd had completely forgotten.

"I'm sorry."

"Someone in town saw you walking toward the pond early this morning. When you hadn't come back, I got worried and came looking for you. You were lying unconscious by the trail."

Anaíd felt like telling her everything but contained herself as Ms. Olav helped her get in the car.

"Did you want to tell me anything?"

Anaíd shook her head. She wouldn't know where to begin.

"And those tears?"

"My cat. We fell together."

"Poor thing; I'll get you another one."

"He might be lost in the mountain."

"Would you like to come back tomorrow and look for him?"

Anaíd smiled with anticipation.

"Would you do that for me?"

"Of course, it'll take no time in the Land Rover. Tomorrow is Saturday; there's no school. I'll pick you up after breakfast and we can have a picnic at the lake."

Anaíd's heart swelled with joy.

"Don't bring any food. I'll take care of it."

Aunt Criselda was warm, but she couldn't be compared to Ms. Olav. In her aunt's arms, Anaíd felt tenderness, but not the support Ms. Olav gave her.

Cristine Olav gave Anaíd the security and affection she needed.

CHAPTER 13

Who Is Ms. Olav?

Anaíd opened the door to her house, humming to herself. Ms. Olav had hugged her, understood her, and made her forget the terrible desolation she'd felt after her mother's rejection.

But her feeling of peace evaporated when she bumped into four sullen women who grabbed her immediately; took her to the living room; cornered her against the wall; and closed doors, shutters, and windows behind them.

The women burst into a thousand jumbled questions. Anaíd could barely distinguish their overlapping voices.

"What did she do to you?"

"How long have you known her?"

"What did you tell her?"

"Did she promise you anything?"

"Did she ask you for anything?"

"What does she call you?"

Anaíd covered her ears. They were all speaking at once. They were excited, irritated, and, especially, worried. Anaíd thought they were scolding her for hiking to the pond.

"I was able to talk to her, but she rejected me."

"But you just got out of her car!"

Anaíd didn't understand a thing they were saying.

"What are you talking about?"

Criselda raised her voice above everyone else's.

"Cristine Olav!"

Anaíd was furious.

"Have you been spying on me?"

"We wish!" exclaimed Karen.

Anaíd thought she was going to die. The only thing that made her happy—her friendship with Ms. Olav—was to be disapproved of by her aunt and her aunt's friends.

"Look at the poor thing, you're all bruised. Where are your clothes?"

"I fell by myself; Ms. Olav wasn't there. I was in touch with Selene and . . ."

But at that moment, nobody was interested in Selene.

"How did she find you?"

"We know you have been seeing her."

"The whole town knew except for us!"

"You got out of her car!"

Anaíd was fuming.

"I don't care if you don't like Ms. Olav. I will still see her; I have a right to choose my friends, I have a right to—"

"She's an Odish, you silly girl!" interrupted Gaya.

Anaíd fell silent immediately. The speech about her rights—which she was articulating so well—was now dangling from her mouth.

No, it wasn't possible. Ms. Olav couldn't be an Odish. It was absurd. As if reading her mind, Karen took Anaíd's hands.

"Anaíd, I know that you don't believe a word from us right now, but even if it sounds ridiculous, please remember, did she give you any gifts?"

Without thinking, Anaíd showed them the bracelet Ms. Olav had given her the week before.

"Take it off," ordered Elena, "and leave it there." She gestured toward a table.

Anaíd hesitated. She refused to believe what they said. No, Ms. Olav cared for her; Ms. Olav protected her; Ms. Olav was warm and affectionate. She couldn't be an Odish. But she took off the bracelet nonetheless.

Once on the table, Elena placed her hands over the bracelet and recited a chant with her eyes half-closed. Her hands trembled as they slowly drew near the object. Suddenly they stopped, as if they'd found an obstacle. Elena let out a brief shout and showed the palms of her hands—they were burned. Anaíd was horrified. Pronouncing the same chant, Criselda, Karen, and Gaya stood beside Elena and extended their hands. Slowly, the four pairs of hands drew near the bracelet and broke the spell that had burned Elena. Anaíd noticed the enormous strength the four women had together. Without hesitating, she added her hands to the others and focused on breaking the spell, which felt hot like a piece of burning iron. It was at once similar and different from what she'd conquered that morning on the way to the pond. Seconds later, the resistance faded and the spell dissolved into nothing.

"Thank you." Elena sighed, exhausted.

Anaíd refrained from making any comments. She had a bitter taste in her mouth. She could taste the sourness of the counter-spell.

"How can you be so sure that she's an Odish?"

"Adult and initiated Omars can tell an Odish apart by just seeing her."

"But girls and uninitiated Omars can't?"

"No. That's why you need the protection shield. Not only can you not defend yourself, but you can't recognize them, either."

"And how do you recognize them?"

"By their smell."

"By the sound of their voice."

"By their look."

"You'll learn all that soon."

"They are unmistakable."

"There's no doubt about it."

Was this true? Was Ms. Olav planning to bleed her to death? Was Ms. Olav luring her in order to steal her strength? Did she want Anaíd's youth to feed her beauty and smooth complexion?

No.

She couldn't believe it. Minutes ago, she'd thought that happiness was resting her head on Ms. Olav's chest and being lulled to sleep by her voice.

Had she been in danger?

Cristine equaled affection. Anaíd wasn't afraid of her; quite the opposite—she was fascinated by her. She would have been her victim without saying a word; she would have offered herself to be sacrificed.

Was that how the Odish acted?

Well, she had been deceived. And she needed time to accept it, to reorganize her emotions and recover from the blow.

But Karen snapped her out of her thoughts.

"Can you think of anything else, Anaíd?"

"Please remember."

"Did you eat any food with her? Did she offer you anything she made?"

Anaíd smiled nervously.

"No, we've always gone to Rosa's café."

That had been smart. Deméter had taught her to never accept sweets or food from strangers. Anaíd had accepted the bracelet, but she'd turned down some candied pears Ms. Olav bought her.

142

And then she remembered it. "The box of chocolates! She gave them to me, but I wasn't hungry, so I left them."

Criselda turned pale and brought her hands to her stomach.

"I ate all of them . . ."

"Not all of them," corrected Elena. "I had a few too."

Karen and Gaya exhaled, relieved that they didn't have a sweet tooth.

Visibly disturbed, Criselda tried to forget about the chocolates and kept probing, "Did you always stay in public places? Did she ever suggest going to the woods, the lake, or any other isolated spot with her?"

Anaíd shook her head, no. But then she remembered.

"We were going to go to the lake tomorrow."

Criselda was furious.

"I was so stupid! I let Anaíd go out unsupervised and without a shield. It's my fault. And the chocolates . . ."

Anaíd was embarrassed too. She had concealed their friendship. But why? Had Ms. Olav suggested it? Of course, the same way she had encouraged Anaíd to cast a spell on Marion and to confront her aunt about her mother. Was that her tactic? Sowing discord?

"She'll come to pick me up early tomorrow morning."

Aunt Criselda hugged her.

"Actually, you and I will be far away tomorrow."

"Anaíd, have you ever seen a dagger in a dream—or better, in a nightmare—piercing your heart, causing a sharp, deep pain?"

Karen asked her the prophetic question so seriously that it sent shivers down Anaíd's spine.

But before Anaíd could reply, Criselda shook her head.

"I haven't seen a drop of blood on her clothes. I would have noticed that."

Anaíd denied it as well.

"Take off your clothes; I need to check you thoroughly. I don't like the way you look at all." Karen didn't want to waste a second.

Anaíd stripped off her shirt and pants. Pointing at her bra, it was she who screamed this time.

"She gave this to me!"

Again, the four women refused to touch it.

"Take it off and leave it on the floor."

Anaíd dropped it, her hands shaking.

"She bought it at Eduardo's shop," she added, though even she didn't believe it now.

Gaya studied the bra carefully.

"It has no tag. I've never seen this pattern before—too original for Eduardo to carry."

"Did you ever wish you had a bra like this one?" asked Criselda.

"Think. Did you ever see a similar bra that you liked? You must have."

"The Odish can reproduce our wishes."

"How?" Anaíd asked, scared.

"They use the dead for information; spirits who know everything."

Anaíd remembered that, one night in her room, she'd seen a similar style in a magazine. She closed her eyes and evoked the scene: she was lying in bed thinking of her mother, when she saw an ad with a young model wearing the bra. She'd thought that had she asked for it, Selene would have bought it for her. She had been alone, but . . . the coward knight was sitting idly on the rug and the treacherous lady smiled mockingly from behind the curtain.

That meant that the knight and the lady had been spying on her and could read her thoughts . . . and her wishes. Traitors!

"Yes," she replied, a hint of anger in her voice. "I remember liking a very similar one."

"I thought so."

Criselda took out an ashtree wand and waved it in the air, trying different formulas to undo the spell.

While Criselda and Gaya practiced different counterspells, Karen focused her attention on Anaíd. She checked her chest, her thorax, and felt her skin with the tip of her index finger, to detect any bumps or wounds, no matter how insignificant they looked. But even though Anaíd's arms and legs were covered with bruises and scratches, her chest was intact. Karen spotted a mosquito bite, but there were no openings through which blood could have been extracted from her heart.

"We caught her in time." Karen sighed, relieved. "Where did you fall?"

Anaíd was honest. "I'm not sure."

Meanwhile, Criselda and Gaya were able to undo the spell. The bra started to release a thick smoke, which made the two women cough loudly. Covering their noses with handkerchiefs, they fanned the smoke away. A smoky plain white bra hung from the tip of Criselda's wand. The one Ms. Olav had bought at Eduardo's store. The pattern was an optical illusion.

And it was Anaíd who put two and two together this time.

"The protection shield!"

"Of course!" said Elena. "Our spells weren't failing; you were simply wearing this bra."

Her face still blackened by smoke, Criselda pointed her wand at Anaíd.

"Take a deep breath and don't move."

Then she recited the spell.

Anaíd felt an intense heat and tightness around her chest,

crushing her ribs. She thought the pressure would drop after a few seconds, but it actually increased. Soon she couldn't breathe and was forced to stretch her neck in search of oxygen.

"What have you done, Criselda? She can't breathe," said Karen.

And she waved her evergreen wand, loosening the shield. But it didn't last. Gaya was trying to strengthen the spell. Anaíd felt an abrupt pull and an uncomfortable pressure on her chest again.

"This is awful. Can you loosen it up a bit?"

"No way," said Gaya. "Least of all in your case."

"Gaya is right. We've all been through it and know that wearing the shield can be very hard."

"And uncomfortable, but it is necessary."

"Please," begged Anaíd. "I can't stand it."

"You'll get used to it," whispered Karen.

"Like the many other things that happen to us women."

"And witches."

Karen walked over to the phone.

"I'm going to book a room in the valley's beach resort under a fake name. You and Criselda will leave tomorrow and hide there until Ms. Olav has disappeared."

Anaíd felt constrained by the shield and like a prisoner in her own town.

"I can't. I have to find my mother. I was able to contact her today; we must help her."

"Selene must be forgotten now."

"You are in danger and need to hide."

"You won't be able to talk to anyone."

"You won't be able to go out alone."

"You won't be able to use magic without our consent."

Anaíd had had enough. She started kicking and screaming with rage.

"I don't want it! Take this shield off! I don't want to be a witch!"

Aunt Criselda was touched.

"I said the same thing when my mother conjured a shield for me."

Elena stroked her belly.

"So did I."

Karen repressed a tear; she also recognized herself in Anaíd's furious tantrum.

"And I."

Gaya smiled a naughty smile.

"I rebelled too."

Anaíd looked at all of them, astonished; she didn't know whether to laugh or cry.

. . .

Anaíd waited until Criselda was asleep to sneak out to the cave and get her old books on witchcraft. She couldn't take them all, so she chose sensibly. There were still so many things to learn and experiment with . . . Unable to help herself, she searched for some morbid illustrations she'd sworn she'd never look at again. They were color sketches of Omars who'd been bled to death by the Odish. Disfigured girls with horror stamped on their faces; girls with pus-filled sores, pale, bloodless, without hair, their bodies horribly deformed. Anaíd forced herself to think that that's what Ms. Olav had planned to do with her, so the shield that barely let her breathe didn't feel as constricting. The shield's weight and solid texture made her feel safe; just what she needed to be able think in private, without interferences or spies.

Anaíd had been thinking about the spirits and concluded that they had limited mobility. Neither the lady nor the knight could follow her to the woods or slip into her cave. They probably remained in the places they had lived or died, or where they'd been cursed. She felt relieved.

Anaíd made up her mind. The images in the book confirmed that she needed to act with extreme caution and hide her plans from everyone.

She went back home full of a newfound courage—it wouldn't be easy to accomplish what she'd planned, but it was her only choice.

Trying not to make any noise, Anaíd entered her room on tiptoe. She grabbed her gym bag and put in it everything she thought she might need, including her ID documents, the books on witchcraft, and an envelope she took from one of the dressers' drawers. Then she took some money from Criselda's purse and waited impatiently at her desk, stealthily checking her watch and nibbling on a chocolate cookie. She began to write a letter.

It was past midnight when they appeared: first the knight, looking contrite, and minutes later, the scornful lady. Anaíd pretended not to notice them and continued writing and enjoying her cookie. The lady smiled under her breath and eyed her challengingly. She knew that Anaíd would speak to her.

"What's so funny?"

"Are you talking to me, precious child?"

"Yes, who else?"

The lady took the bull by the horns.

"Think twice before escaping," she said, gesticulating.

"How do you know I'm going to escape?" asked Anaíd, feigning innocence.

"It's obvious. You are dressed, your bag is packed, you are constantly checking your watch, and you are writing a note."

Anaíd still had some time, so she decided to mock her. The lady deserved it for being such a tattletale.

"I'm sure you ran away many nights from your husband, the baron."

The lady smiled without a hint of resentment.

"The good old times . . . I was young and passionate then." She sighed. "Centuries fly."

"May I?" The knight asked for permission to speak before the lady began babbling about her amorous encounters.

"Speak, cowardly knight," Anaíd sneered.

"I believe you are wrong, precious young one."

Anaíd licked her chocolate-covered fingers.

"Why?"

"You shouldn't leave these kind women who protect you and wish you well."

"Are you talking about Ms. Olav?"

The knight and the lady exchanged a worried look.

"You well know that we are referring to your aunt and her friends."

"So you want me to leave with Aunt Criselda in the morning for the beach resort Karen has reserved? You want me to lock myself away with my aunt in a senior citizen center and rot in sulfur waters for the rest of my life?" Anaíd asked, her hands on her hips.

"It's the most sensible choice, precious child. Your aunt and the shield will protect you."

"But I don't want to. I'm not going to any resort; I don't want to see Aunt Criselda again, and I'm not wearing this horrible shield either," she said challengingly.

The spirits looked at each other and the lady spoke on the knight's behalf.

"And where are you going, if I may ask?"

"Paris."

"Paris!" The spirits were surprised.

"I have a distant relative there; I speak French and I've always wanted to go up the Eiffel Tower. Much better than a boring beach resort, don't you think?"

"Ooh la la!" exclaimed the lady.

"Lovely," said the knight.

"Exciting," corrected the lady.

All of a sudden, the church bells chimed the hour slowly and gravely: four o'clock. Anaíd's heart shrunk when she thought that those might be the last chimes she'd hear from Urt's clock.

She'd never left home before.

She'd never traveled.

She didn't even own a suitcase.

Anaíd stood up with trembling legs and bid farewell to the spirits. Part of her plan had been accomplished.

"I have to go," she said, picking up her bag.

"Just a moment."

"You can't leave yet."

"Do you like me that much?" Anaíd asked.

The knight sighed.

"We are used to you and your absence will feel strange."

Anaíd looked at him, intrigued. His answer sounded honest, like his voice, and there was no hint of duplicity in his words.

"And something else . . . You promised to set us free," pointed out the lady.

That was Anaíd's small vengeance. She brought her hands to her head, as if remembering something.

"Right! It will have to wait until I get back from Paris."

"For sure?" the lady asked, hopeful.

"Do you give us your word?" pleaded the knight.

"You have my word. I will set you free when I get back from Paris." And saying that, she turned off the light, closed the door to her room, and slipped out of the house on tiptoe.

Once inside the barn, her heart skipped a beat. It was one thing to come up with a plan and a very different one to carry it out. Would she be able to drive Selene's car?

First, she had to start the ignition. She turned the key and stepped on the gas once, twice, but the engine died; the ignition spark was not strong enough. The car hadn't been used in days. One more time. And another one. Yes!

Trembling with excitement, Anaíd carefully put the car in reverse to exit the barn. She released the clutch, but the transmission screeched, and the car stalled. Damn! It seemed so easy when Selene did it. Her mother had taught her the mechanism, but something wasn't working. The lights! How the hell did you turn them on? No, not the blinker! This button, yes. Oh no, the horn! What a klutz! Had someone heard her? She had to leave soon. Finally!

And Selene's car sputtered down the road and away from the only house Anaíd had ever known.

Anaid was shaking, terrified to be at the wheel, but her plan was turning out perfectly. She had deceived all of them—Elena, Karen, Gaya, Criselda, Ms. Olav, and the spirits.

Nobody knew her intentions, or where she was heading.

CHAPTER 14

—————

DREAMS AND WISHES

The pale, long-fingered hands grouped the chips over the green gambling table, forming an enormous pile.

"Twenty-six black," ordered the young woman in the pink dress.

"Everything?" The casino employee wanted to be sure, his hands and voice trembling as he looked at the large amount of chips.

"Everything," confirmed the young woman, sitting calmly next to her red-haired companion.

The man pushed the bell to call the management. He was sweating profusely; he was in a jam and needed a witness to what was occurring. He hoped the director would arrive soon—the look of the woman in the pink dress was giving him the creeps. He was terrified.

"What are you waiting for?"

It wasn't impatience. Despite having risked a fortune, bet after bet, the young woman didn't look nervous at all. She hadn't been tense at any moment.

"There's a little problem. We have to wait for the director."

"What kind of problem?" she inquired coldly.

"Your bet is so high that the management needs to be present."

He would have preferred the player to look awful, to be rude, bad mannered, but that wasn't the case. It was the opposite. The young woman in the pink dress and her quiet but attractive red-haired friend were polite, beautiful, and elegant.

"What's the problem?" asked another voice, masculine and grave, in the employee's ear.

The man sighed, relieved. The director was standing in front of him with his spotless tuxedo and professional smile. At long last, he would be able to pass on this responsibility to his superior.

"They've won every bet," he whispered, referring to the two players.

The men spoke quietly, smiling, without losing their composure. Any observer would have thought they were engaged in a light, friendly conversation.

"Well, they've run out of luck. You know what you have to do."

With a linen handkerchief, the croupier wiped the tiny beads of perspiration trickling down his forehead.

"I've already done that. I've stopped it manually."

"And?"

"It didn't work."

The director glanced stealthily at the enormous pile of chips sitting in front of the two players.

"How many times did it *not* work?"

"None. That is, it failed five times."

"Did the machine get stuck?"

The croupier moved his bow tie with a finger to let in some fresh air. He was short of breath.

"No, and that's what's really strange. An hour ago, the ladies went to the bar for a drink and I activated the manual break on three different occasions and it worked."

The director was becoming annoyed.

"Are you saying that these charming ladies always manage to win even when *we* control the roulette?"

"Yes."

"Where's the trick?"

"I don't know, sir, I can't figure it out. You have to watch closely. Would you like to try?"

"Sure. Just step of the way."

The director sat in the employee's spot and gave the two women a gallant smile. A great pair—a brunette and a redhead. The redhead was more stunning, without a doubt, but the brunette was deliciously sexy, with that porcelain complexion and those delicate hands.

"Whenever you are ready, ladies."

The green-eyed redhead looked up. Her eyes sparkled and her pupils were dilated like those of an amateur placing her highest bet. She didn't look like a professional gambler, but she signaled for the game to start with a slight movement of her head—as if celebrating her victory ahead of time.

The roulette began to spin uncontrollably. A crowd of curious onlookers gathered around them. The director would have preferred discretion; he regretted that word had traveled so fast. Slyly, he activated the pedal in the position he considered the closest to "26 black." He would let it fall on "24 black" to make things more exciting.

As the wheel slowed down, a dense silence filled the room. All eyes were on the small ball, which jumped undaunted, sorting obstacles until it landed on the slot of . . . 26 black.

Turning pale, the director followed the last agonizing turns of the wheel with bulging eyes. The spectators in that room full of luxurious chandeliers and warm-colored carpets burst into cheers, and the two women hugged each other, celebrating their victory.

The director mentally calculated the required sum. There wasn't enough money on the premises, and after paying them, the casino would probably have to close its doors for a long time. That meant he would be fired . . . and his career would be over.

. . .

In the best hotel in Montecarlo, Selene sipped a glass of French champagne in her suite's jacuzzi.

The water filling the porcelain tub bubbled with foam, as did the delicious, chilled champagne she savored. She loved feeling the short-lived sputtering of its fruity flavor on the pores of her tongue.

"How many millions?" she asked, saying the word "millions" with pleasure.

"Almost five," said Salma from the adjoining room. She had stripped off her pink dress and was now leisurely enjoying some foie gras canapés. "Four million, seven hundred thirty-two thousand Euros."

"And they are . . . mine?" Selene narrowed her eyes.

"All yours."

Selene felt faint.

"And I can do whatever I want with it?"

Salma laughed her bitter laugh.

"Of course . . . you can do whatever you please. The Odish won't expel you from the community or punish you for using magic for your own purposes. That's the difference. One of the many you will discover."

Selene stretched her long legs and studied them carefully.

"You mean that I could . . ."

"Say it."

"Cast a spell for a man to fall in love with me?"

"Naturally; love filters are more effective than spells, though."

Selene blew at the soapy foam that had gathered on the back

of her hand. Tiny bubbles floated in the air and scattered around the bathroom. She sighed dreamily.

"And would he love me?"

"Madly. He would fall at your feet, adore you; he would kill for you."

Selene dismissed the idea, shaking her head and swaying her red mane.

"No, I'm not convinced."

"You don't want to try, at least?"

The redhead thought about it for a moment.

"I don't know . . . I wouldn't be able to fall in love with someone, knowing I had manipulated him with a filter."

"Of course not! Who's talking about falling in love? Falling in love is humiliating, embarrassing; it means losing your mind and losing control."

"The Odish don't fall in love?"

"We have fun. Do you want to have fun?"

"Perhaps . . . but not today. I want to enjoy my money today. Buy, invest, dream . . . Let me enjoy this feeling I've never had before."

"What would you like to buy?"

"The mortgage on my house in Urt. I'd like to pay off the debt and . . . I'd like to buy a house with a lot of land by the ocean."

"Where?"

Selene placed her empty glass on the floor. She was happy, hopeful; the room smelled of wealth and leisure. From the marble sink, a bouquet of dried violets spread its scent around the bathroom of Roman mosaics with mythological themes. The towels were as soft to the touch as silk, the linen sheets were fresh and smelled of lavender, and she had only to press a button to order any delicacy she wanted.

"The Mediterranean, Rome, Naples, Sicily . . . I was in Sicily not long ago. Those beaches are beautiful—Syracuse, Taormina, Agrigento. I have friends . . . I *had* friends . . . An estate on the island. That's my dream."

Salma stood up, put on a white bathrobe, and picked up the phone.

"Jack? Hi, it's me. Yes, please find me a one-hundred-twenty-five thousand-acre estate in Sicily. You know, a *palazzo* or another luxury building with farmland. Exactly, with a mortgage; especially one that is hard to maintain. I'll be here . . ."

While she waited for the return phone call, Salma paced around the room.

Dizzy from the champagne, Selene got to her feet as well, watching Salma's movements expectantly. She took a caviar canapé from the tray on the table.

Salma's voice snapped her out of her reverie.

"Yes? With ocean views? Fabulous. Please be very alert to anything that might force them to sell . . . Which one? I'm afraid there are locust plagues in that area; they come from the continent. Anything could happen. All right. You know, buy at the best price. Good-bye, Jack."

Selene licked her fingers in disbelief.

"What you've said doesn't make any sense. How can you predict that an estate will be for sale?"

Salma opened the closet and began to get dressed.

"Today, a huge and devastating locust plague will ravage the crops on that beautiful property. The owners will have no choice but to sell. Get it?"

Selene was astonished.

"You will summon the plague?"

Salma laughed.

"And *you* will help me."

"Me?"

"The property is for you, so you need to help."

Selene stood up.

"Where are we going?"

"First, to buy some designer clothes; we need to renew our wardrobe and accessories—Armani, Loewe, Dolce and Gabbana . . . Well, those are my favorites. Then we'll look for a quiet place to cast the spell comfortably. And tonight, if all goes well, your little dream, a really easy one to fulfill, will come true."

Selene could not believe it.

"That simple?"

"You have defined it perfectly. The life of an Odish is . . . very simple. We can have *anything* we want."

TREATISE OF HÖLDER

There's no doubt that the seven gods in line mentioned in Oma's prophecy refer
to the planetary alignment.

The seven gods in line will salute her throning.

The Sun and the Moon, unquestionably the gods of day and night, eternal
partners and impossible lovers, will be the first. The other five will be the most
noticeable, capricious and changing in the sky: Jupiter, the most
important, the god of the gods; Mars, the color of blood, the god of war; Venus,
the brightest, like love; Mercury, the closest to the Sun, the messenger
of the gods; and Saturn, the slowest, the god of time.

The alignment announced by O will occur when Mercury, Venus, Mars,
Jupiter, and Saturn, accompanied by the Sun and the Moon, become aligned
shortly before by the dance of father and son in the water.

Let's remember the other verse of the prophecy,
on which rivers of ink have been written.

Father and son will dance together in the dwelling of water.

And despite the wave of criticism caused by Otero's risky assumption, I have
decided to confirm his hypothesis in the following pages, maintaining that it is
indeed the alignment of Jupiter and Saturn in Pisces that the prophecies speak
about. I will also refer to Kepler's calculations on the subject and to his accurate
theory that both phenomena will occur in a relatively short period of time.

The time of the chosen one is very, very near.

CHAPTER 15

―――

THE ESCAPE

Dear Aunt Criselda,

I've caused you too much trouble and don't want you to worry anymore, so I've decided to free you from the responsibility of watching me. Look for my mother; as will I.

Kisses,
Anaíd

Criselda crumpled the note and hurled it on the mat of Karen's car, stomping on it with fury.

"Watch out!" Karen yelled, swerving to the left.

She had bumped into something. Behind them boomed the sound of shattering glass, but neither woman heard it.

"I'm sorry," Karen apologized.

On the passenger seat, Criselda had knocked her head against the window and was feeling her temple with a sorry look.

"Serves me right for being so foolish," she whined.

Karen didn't dare contradict her.

Two hours before, in her nightgown and bare feet, a livid Criselda had knocked on Karen's door and shown her Anaíd's note. Karen couldn't believe that a fourteen-year-old girl had decided to run away, and on top of it, she'd left driving. But that was the way it was. Anaíd was half an hour ahead of them, a gap they couldn't bridge. That meant she was going at more than sixty-five miles per hour. It was insane!

"How much longer?" Criselda was growing impatient.

"We are about to reach Huesca."

"Are you sure she was headed for the station?"

"Where else if not?" exclaimed Karen. "It seems logical considering she won't risk driving during the day, that the sun is about to rise, and that the first train to Madrid will be here soon."

"Will we get there in time?" insisted Criselda.

"You'll have to jump out of the car and board the train immediately. That's if she doesn't get away from us before."

"Leave her to me," grunted Criselda. Her bump hurt and she was upset at Anaíd.

"In your nightgown? Barefoot? And without any ID?" Karen objected.

Criselda realized she'd made a terrible mistake. In the rush, she had forgotten to grab her bag. She didn't have anything with her.

"Our only choice is to cast an illusion spell."

"Oh, no! Not in my car!"

But Criselda was already pronouncing the words and, just before Karen's Renault drove into the station's parking lot, she was sporting an elegant suit; high heels, very unlike her; and a bag with everything she needed hanging from her shoulder.

When she saw Criselda, Karen clicked her tongue.

"Couldn't you find anything better?"

"I'm sorry; it was the first thing that popped into my mind."

"I don't want to be seen with you. Nobody should know we are together."

Criselda understood that if anything happened, Karen, the town's physician—known by everyone—would be in trouble and have to relocate. Illusion spells entailed problems, for they could fade away at any second and the illusion created, a purely optical illusion, would vanish. The effort required to create them was so great that it left the Omars exhausted for hours, with no strength to cast another spell.

"Remember what happened to Brunilda," Karen warned Criselda very seriously.

Luckily, Criselda hadn't created the illusion of a balloon, like crazy Brunilda had, to gaze at the city with her lover. The Omars would always remember the poor thing's fall from over ten thousand feet in the air as the best example of how not to use illusion spells. A skeptical swallow had flown through the imaginary balloon and Brunilda and her companion had plummeted down at 125 miles per hour.

Karen stopped the car, opened the door, and pointed at Selene's car, which was perfectly parked. Her intuition had been right.

"Run!" she murmured.

The clatter of the train was already resonating on the deserted tracks. The conductor's whistles announcing his arrival to the station moved Criselda to action. Forgetting about her heels and her tight skirt, she jumped out of the car and sprinted toward the platform, blowing a kiss to Karen by way of good-bye. She had to stop at the booth for a ticket to Madrid; a precious moment wasting minutes and seconds. When she got to the platform, her heart was in her mouth. Through one of car's dirty windows, she saw a scrawny girl quickly put her gym bag in the luggage rack and jump on a seat. It was Anaíd, her little Anaíd.

Criselda ran and ran, but her high heels betrayed her—a few meters from the car's door, she tripped, lost her balance, and fell face-first in the middle of the platform. A middle-aged passenger who'd just stepped off the train came to her aid immediately, but Criselda didn't have time to thank him. To her dismay, the train had closed its doors and began moving forward.

At that exact moment, Karen's minivan was turning around to go back to Urt. There wasn't much she could do now. It was Criselda's job to argue with the girl and convince her to come back home. Yawning and dreaming of getting coffee at the next gas station, Karen wondered how a sensible, balanced, and practical witch like Deméter could have a sister as reckless as Criselda. Though, come to think of it, Deméter was dead and . . . Criselda, alive.

Through the window, Karen noticed that the morning air seemed cleaner and less oppressive than it had in the past few days. Even the sunlight was more translucent.

Lately, she'd been having some odd perceptions.

She concluded that what she needed was a cup of strong coffee.

. . .

Ms. Olav drummed her beautiful, graceful fingers on Anaíd's floral quilt.

"Paris?" she asked kindly, as if doubting her own words.

"That's what she said, beautiful mistress," whispered the lady, not daring to smile.

Cristine Olav pierced the knight with her somber eyes.

"Did you hear that too?"

"Yes, her words were clear."

163

Ms. Olav walked over to the window's closed shutters and, slowly, relishing the unhurried motion, began to open them.

"No, please," begged the lady, covering her face from the dim sunlight filtering through the cracks.

But Ms. Olav didn't stop. She kept playing with the shutters.

"It's such a beautiful day . . . The sun is shining in all its splendor; you should really enjoy it, even if it's the last time."

"My mistress, please don't be cruel."

"Me? Cruel?" exclaimed Ms. Olav, horrified. "I love that girl like a daughter, and now I've lost track of her because of you!"

The knight and the lady exchanged a worried look that was rapidly intercepted by the sharp intruder.

"My dear girl is too smart to tell you where she really planned to go, but I assume you are also intelligent enough *not* to believe her after so many years of unfulfilled promises, of everything you've been told."

Neither spirit dared contradict her. Ms. Olav wrinkled her nose.

"Evidently, I can't trust a traitor or a coward. That was my mistake. Somebody told her how to contact Selene from the pond."

"Oh, no! It wasn't us!" the knight shouted.

"That girl is extremely clever," said the lady.

Ms. Olav sighed.

"I should make you suffer as much as I'm suffering for having lost my Anaíd. Yes, that will be the best."

"What will be, my mistress?"

"Your image will disappear, and you'll roam the earth without a face. I'm sick of looking at you."

Horror was stamped on the two spirits' faces. A few seconds of silence went by before Ms. Olav's hands touched the shutters.

"No! It's not necessary," the lady shouted. "The knight and I will help you stop suffering."

Ms. Olav clapped cheerfully and sat back down on Anaíd's bed. She grabbed a doll and began to comb its hair gently.

"I'm listening . . ."

The knight stroked his mustache and replaced his helmet.

"She grabbed an envelope from the dresser drawer."

"An envelope is not interesting in itself. What was inside of it?"

"An airplane ticket."

"I like this. Go on. Where to?"

"Catania."

"Sicily? A fourteen-year-old girl bought a ticket to Italy by herself?"

"Selene bought it."

"Well, well, well. Look at how many things you knew and didn't tell me . . ."

"We didn't consider them of importance."

"Anaíd refused to go," the lady clarified.

"Where? To Catania?" asked Ms. Olav.

"To Taormina, with Valeria and her daughter Clodia."

Ms. Olav violently disentangled a knot in the doll's hair.

"On vacation?"

"That's what it seemed."

Ms. Olav pulled the doll's hair angrily until it all came off.

"Things are never what they seem, are they?"

When they saw the fit of anger the Odish was having, the knight and the lady started to shake.

"Please, calm down," begged the lady. "You'll find her."

Ms. Olav got to her feet and stood tall and threatening over the two ghosts, who shrank and shrank until they'd almost disappeared.

165

"You talked to Anaíd and schemed with her behind my back. You expected Anaíd to free you, of course. You thought because she's young, she'd be naïve, more trusting and more stupid than me."

Ms. Olav pulled off the bald doll's head with one yank.

"But Anaíd lied to you and me. That girl is not who she seems."

"We have no doubt, our mistress."

"Neither do I!" And saying this, Ms. Olav walked over to the window and opened the shutters wide.

In its morning splendor, the sun celebrated its arrival into the room. As it made its way in, the two spirits whimpered and then vanished, leaving a trail of smoke behind them.

Ms. Olav threw the decapitated doll against the bed, opened the closet, picked up a sweater, and sniffed it like a bloodhound. It was the last sweater she'd seen Anaíd wearing. Of course, the girl hadn't taken it because she thought she wouldn't need it in Sicily. The sweater smelled of Anaíd; it was impregnated with her scent. It would work for Ms. Olav's plan.

She carefully put the sweater in her bag and snuck out of the house as quickly and discreetly as she'd come in, an hour before.

. . .

Anaíd regretted not knowing how to put on makeup like her mother. Perhaps, if she had tried to look eighteen instead of fourteen, she would have avoided several problems.

The train guard probably wouldn't have asked her name and destination so many times; he wouldn't have sat by her side, bothering her with the sound of his electronic game.

That bronzed, muscular old lady on the bus to the airport probably wouldn't have made Anaíd share her cookies, her cheese sandwich, her fruit juice, her energizing peanuts, or her strawberry candy.

And at the airport, the pilot who scolded her for traveling alone probably wouldn't have shown her pictures of his family's last vacation in the Caribbean, and wouldn't have made her learn a stupid tongue twister.

Anaíd reached Air Italia's counter at Barajas Airport overwhelmed by the noise and the crowd. She wished she'd run into a rude adult who didn't like children; an adult who would do his job and issue a ticket to a fourteen-year-old without asking about her food preferences, her family, or her grades.

Why did this species of protective adults exist? Why did those adults consider themselves friendly and funny, and why were they convinced that all children had the same tastes and ideas and spoke in the same stupid way? Why didn't those protective adults buy themselves a dog and leave kids alone?

"Good morning. How can I help you?" asked the Italian airline employee without even looking at her. Finally, an adult who treated her indifferently, like he'd treat anyone else.

However, Anaíd quickly realized that a rude adult was much worse than a protective adult. A rude adult wouldn't care about anything else but what the law said, and the law in her case said that minors didn't exist without the consent of an adult.

"Don't come back unless accompanied by an older person who's responsible for you," he said, and handed her back the ticket, without having looked at her even once.

Inventing a terrible story—not much different in essence from her own—didn't help Anaíd convince the airline employee that she was a poor girl, alone in the world, and that she needed to move forward her trip to Catania, where some good friends awaited her.

"Next!" was his only and brief answer.

Not negotiable. Anaíd turned around and left the counter, hoping to find a protective adult who would be moved by her story and vouch for her.

She had no luck, though. She discovered only the cosmopolitan world of skeptical, anxious, and stressed-out adults. They were men and women who fled when they saw her approach, looking away and changing directions. Or they apologized without listening to her, with a "Sorry, I'm in a hurry."

What to do?

Anaíd was getting hungry and tired, and she was worried about where she'd spend the night in the event that she couldn't board a plane.

But she still had to face another species of adults: the repressive one. Her helplessness was obvious and attracted the attention of a security guard.

"ID please."

Anaíd couldn't help shaking. The police officer sniffed his prey like a bloodhound ready to snap his teeth.

"Come with me, please."

Anaíd regretted her bad judgment. But just as the police officer grabbed her arm with force, she heard a voice she would have despised hours ago but that now sounded heavenly.

"Anaíd!"

To her dismay, a horribly dressed Aunt Criselda—she looked like a lawyer from a TV show—came running, gasping for air, and smiled charmingly at the agent.

"Here you are, honey! Thank you so much for finding her, officer."

Anaíd found Criselda's motherly arms a thousand times better than the policeman's repressive claw. She buried her head in her aunt's red jacket, which stank of a horrible perfume that was supposed to be as elegant as her suit.

"Do you know her?"

"Of course, I'm her aunt. We are traveling together, but because of the airport's terrible signs, the poor girl got lost. I've been looking for her for hours."

Anaíd didn't deny Aunt Criselda's story, and she didn't know what did the trick—the suit, the perfume, or the hug—but the officer didn't even check up on their relationship. He turned around, but not without speaking the last word.

"You should be more careful next time."

Anaíd didn't move. She knew that the officer had walked away, that they were alone in the middle of the airport's hallway, and that her aunt was about to reprimand her harshly.

But instead, a shaky Aunt Criselda said only, "Don't ask me any questions, especially what you are thinking."

And that was worse. It made Anaíd curious; she obviously wondered what it was that she couldn't ask. What first came to mind was what she'd wondered when she first saw her—why was Aunt Criselda dressed like that?

"I can't ask anything? Not even something silly?"

Criselda covered Anaíd's mouth and dragged her to the ladies' room.

"Don't even think of it!"

But that was just what Anaíd did. She thought about it so much that a few feet from the bathroom, she heard her aunt shout, "Oh, no!"

Criselda was covered in thick white smoke for a few seconds. When the air cleared up, Criselda's suit, hairdo, shoes, and handbag were gone. To Anaíd's astonishment, her aunt was barefoot and half-naked—she had only a nightgown on—and her hair was tousled.

169

They reached the bathroom and hid inside. Fortunately, it was empty.

Anaíd was horrified.

"What happened?"

Aunt Criselda gazed dejectedly at herself in the mirror. She looked a lot worse than she'd imagined.

"You broke the spell. You didn't believe in my costume, and the enchantment vanished."

"You mean that what you were wearing was a costume?"

"Yes."

"And why did you pick such a ridiculous outfit?"

"Bloody girl! I picked whatever crossed my mind. I think it was a character from a TV show ... Because of you, I left the house with nothing on. I've been trying to find you for the last nine hours. Where were you thinking of going?"

Anaíd had no reason to conceal her plan anymore.

"Taormina."

"To Taormina? Why?"

"For three reasons—because Selene wanted me to go there, because I want to find her, and because Ms. Olav will think I'm in Paris."

"What are you talking about? Why would she think you are in Paris?"

"I told the spirits I was escaping to Paris. They were the ones who told me how to get in touch with Selene, but they betrayed me and ..."

Aunt Criselda didn't understand a word of what she was saying.

"Do you mind explaining everything from the beginning?"

Patiently, Anaíd told Criselda about her relationship with the spirits, her adventure in the ravine, her journey down the pond's abyss, and her suspicions that the lady and the knight were Ms. Olav's informants. As Anaíd recounted her experiences, her aunt grew increasingly pale. When Anaíd had finished, Criselda lowered her head over the sink, opened the faucet, and splashed her neck with water. Criselda seemed so disturbed by her confession that even Anaíd was scared.

"Are you okay?"

Criselda shook her head.

"No, I'm not okay. I just heard that you are seeing and communicating with spirits like it's nothing."

"Yes."

"And that you broke some sort of invisible barrier that prevented you from leaving the valley."

"Yes."

"And that you fell into a dark abyss after nibbling on a mushroom and were able to talk to Selene."

"Yes."

"Anything else you haven't told me?"

"I can understand animals and speak their language."

Criselda put her head under the stream of cold water again, until shivers ran down her spine. She seemed to be slowly processing the information. She took one, two, three deep breaths and then exhaled. Color returned to her cheeks and oxygen flowed through her brain again.

"How many chocolates did I eat?"

"A whole box."

"I've been numb this whole time."

"I think so."

"We'll go to Taormina, you and I. I'll never leave you alone again."

"Oh, Auntie!" Anaíd hugged her.

But Criselda refused her embrace and asked one last question.

"And, may I ask, why didn't you tell me instead of causing this mess?"

Anaíd avoided Criselda's eyes and decided to tell her aunt the truth. She needed Criselda—she needed her aunt and had to be honest with her.

"I don't completely trust you."

"What? Where did you get that nonsense from?" Criselda was indignant.

"I thought that you didn't want to find my mother, that you were afraid of finding her. Selene or I, something... scares you."

Criselda held Anaíd's accusatory glance. The girl was right.

"It was the chocolates. They've numbed my mind."

But it wasn't enough for Anaíd.

"There's something else. Something you are worried about and don't want to tell me."

Criselda looked down. Anaíd was very perceptive.

"Why wouldn't I let you go to Taormina?"

Anaíd felt unusually self-confident.

"That was Selene's plan. She wanted me to go there. Valeria probably knows things about my mother that I don't know. I'm sure Selene wanted me to be there for a reason. I'm going to find out what it was."

Overwhelmed, Criselda fell silent. Anaíd's reasoning was excellent. Her faith in Selene was admirable, and her acts weren't consistent with the teenage irresponsibility Criselda had expected. Her niece was making her nervous.

"Fine, you got away with your plan, but now you'll have to do something that will leave you as exhausted as I am. It's your only punishment for making me get up at four in the morning."

Anaíd had no idea what Criselda would come up with. And it was definitely not something she'd imagined.

"You will cast your first illusion spell today. I want to look like your aunt, and the costume has to be convincing enough for people not to doubt its authenticity. Do you understand?"

Anaíd's mouth was wide open.

"Like the bra?"

"Exactly. I will help you. You have to capture an image that contains a wish of mine and reproduce it. Remember that we need my ID, passport, and money. That should be included in the package too. It's a very delicate situation, Anaíd, and these spells don't last long."

"I know the spell."

"How?"

"Do you want me to show you?"

"No, wait . . . not yet."

But Anaíd had already grabbed her wand, pronounced the words, and dressed Aunt Criselda in a long floral dress, a pair of sandals, a large wicker basket, and a braid that covered the length of her back.

Aunt Criselda opened the basket and took out her personal documents. They were impeccable, with her exact date of birth . . . She didn't know how Anaíd could have been so quick. And this old-fashioned hippy outfit? It felt familiar and close. Of course! Criselda remembered it from a picture of her and Deméter, a picture from their youth she hadn't seen in years.

Anaíd smiled.

"I've always liked you in that picture."

A clear memory flashed back to Criselda. The memory of a

wonderful vacation she'd shared with her sister, her friends, and her first love.

And this time, Criselda hugged her niece tenderly for giving back to her, forty years later, the memory of a sunny and hopeful summer.

They needed each other.

CHAPTER 16

Sicily, at Last

Anaíd walked through the automatic doors of Catania's airport, overwhelmed by the heat, the crowd, and the loudspeakers. Criselda ran behind her, gasping and holding up her long floral dress to avoid tripping. Anaíd wanted to reach Taormina as soon as possible and, there, ask for Valeria Crocce. She hadn't done any research at home because she was being watched by the spirits.

During the trip, Criselda had told her what she knew about the Crocce family. Valeria, a marine biologist, was a charismatic matriarch and the head of the clan of the dolphins. The Crocce were powerful and had once fought against the Fattas, the other Omar family on the island, who'd disputed the dolphins' leadership and established their own—the leadership of the crows. The Sicilian witches, initially of Greek origin, belonged now to a branch of the Etruscan tribe, famous for their divinatory powers. The Etruscans were able to interpret any signs—the clouds, the winds, the ocean's currents, the birds' flight—and they were experts in reading flames and the entrails of sacrificial animals.

Anaíd wondered what Valeria would be like and whether it would be hard to reach her. If only she had a picture of her, or her phone number . . .

But it wasn't necessary. To their surprise, Valeria Crocce was waiting for them a few feet from the barrier in the crowded arrivals hall.

"Are you Anaíd? Anaíd Tsinoulis?" asked a dark-skinned, black-eyed woman who smelled of salt and algae.

Anaíd knew that she was Valeria right away.

"How did you know we were coming?"

"Are you really Valeria? You are so young . . . I can't believe it!" a confused Criselda exclaimed.

Anaíd couldn't believe it either. No one, except for Criselda and herself, knew their destination or which flight they were on. How on earth had Valeria gotten this information?

Valeria took both of them by the arm nervously and guided them to the parking lot, where her daughter waited idly, listening to blasting music in the backseat of a Nissan.

"The omens announced your arrival. Last night we interpreted that Anaíd would make it to Catania," she whispered as she glanced around to make sure nobody in a thirty-foot radius was listening.

"But . . . what about the time? And the flight number?" Anaíd was astounded.

Criselda spoke first. "Have you been waiting all day?"

From Valeria's tired face and the girl's obvious boredom, they could tell Criselda had guessed right.

"Yes, but it was worth it," said Valeria, laughing. "Anaíd, this is my daughter Clodia."

Clodia didn't seem as polite as her mother, though it was very clear that she respected her. She formally extended her hand to Criselda and gave Anaíd a forced smile.

"Welcome to Italy."

Valeria smacked Clodia in the head.

"Is that the way to receive friends in danger? Is that how you show them affection? Hospitality?"

Clodia swallowed her pride and Anaíd saw her give her mother a dark, reproachful look. Clodia kissed them coldly, and they all got in the car. Valeria sat at the wheel, and Anaíd noticed the muscles in her arms. Valeria's biceps, shiny with perspiration, swelled as she maneuvered the vehicle. She was strong.

"It's a pity we can't stop for a bite to eat or have a more relaxed first visit. We'll avoid Catania by taking the road by the shore. I won't be able to breathe until we're home."

Anaíd and Criselda looked at each other in surprise.

"What's wrong?" asked Criselda.

"That's what I'd like to know. We haven't heard from you in two months."

Criselda stirred on her seat.

"I'm confused . . ."

Valeria clicked her tongue.

"That's what I feared. So it wasn't you?"

Anaíd didn't understand a word. Criselda gasped, stunned.

"Of course. I get it now. We thought you were being cautious and that's why we weren't receiving any information."

"Can you please explain this to me?" asked Anaíd, perplexed.

Valeria said what she already knew.

"Since Selene's disappearance, you've been under the bell's mantle."

"When the Omars believe they are in danger," Criselda clarified to Anaíd, "they sometimes shelter themselves under a bell that shields them from the outside. Communication is impossible and nobody can get in or out of it unless the spell is broken. But, in this case, none of us created the bell."

Valeria confirmed their suspicions.

"And neither did we, which means it was done by an Odish, and she must have done it very well."

Anaíd brought a hand to her head.

"The bell! Of course! I broke it when I left the valley."

Valeria gave her a sidelong glance.

"It was you?"

Criselda confirmed it.

"Nobody told her how, but she was so determined to leave ..."

Valeria whistled with admiration.

"And what about the Odish?" she asked immediately.

"We discovered her in time." She sighed, relieved. "She went by 'Cristine Olav' and was after Anaíd."

Valeria's expression relaxed and she turned toward Criselda, who was sitting in the passenger seat.

"The augury didn't announce your arrival."

Criselda felt old and exhausted after that hectic day.

"*I* don't even know how I ended up here."

Valeria inquired curiously, "Did you have any problems, Anaíd? Did you need Criselda?"

Anaíd recognized that, without her aunt, she would have never been able to board the plane.

"Yes, they wouldn't let me change the date of the flight."

"That's why Criselda followed you—to facilitate your arrival."

"Are you saying that my destiny was to come here?"

"Exactly."

"And that Aunt Criselda has helped my destiny come true?"

"Wow!" said Criselda with sarcasm, "I'm part of my niece's destiny. What a nice role I have!"

"Sorry, I didn't mean ... ," Anaíd began to apologize.

But she couldn't finish apologizing because she saw something spectacular through the car's window—a grayish blue blanket calmly covering the earth as far as the eye could see. It looked like a meadow full of little blue flowers swaying in the wind. It was the ocean. Anaíd had never seen it before.

"The ocean!" she shouted, unable to control herself.

And she opened the window to gaze at it better. She was overwhelmed by a strong salty smell and the cackling of seagulls, those sea rats that flew over the masts of the small ships anchored in the harbor and fought over the fishermen's carrion. Anaíd could understand their squabbles but preferred to ignore them and enjoy the view without interference.

"You've never seen the sea before?" asked Clodia in disbelief.

Anaíd was embarrassed. She must be the only person on the whole planet who had never seen it. What she knew about geography, she had learned from books, the television, and the Internet. It dawned on her that she'd never left Urt, a remote corner surrounded by mountains. Her mother and grandmother had never allowed her to travel with them.

Anaíd had never seen the color of the ocean; or heard the sound of the waves crashing against the rocks at dusk; or taken in the aroma of salt and sand mixed with lavender, thyme, and broom. She welcomed these deep and intense Mediterranean scents, gazed at the pine and evergreen trees, warm in the late afternoon, and wished she could stroll around those fragrant forests brimming with life.

Valeria called her, gesturing toward the ocean again, to show her a rare spectacle through the car's windows.

"Do you see those small islands?"

Anaíd could see them well; they were only a few feet from the shore.

"They are the rocks hurled by Polyphemus, the Cyclops, who was furious at Ulysses when he realized that he'd escaped from his cave."

Excited, Anaíd looked up at the mountains. The dark cracks indicated hideouts, caves.

"If we have time, I'll show you the mythical Scylla and Charybdis channel in the Strait of Messina."

"And that fortress on the horizon?" Anaíd asked, pointing to the old building.

"Clodia, why don't you tell her about the spots we are driving past?"

Clodia took her mother's suggestion as if she'd been asked to walk on burning coals. Anaíd was uncomfortable. Valeria was favoring her, as if her life depended on it, and seemed to disapprove of Clodia's every word and gesture. Clodia eyed Anaíd with indifference and said, "The first Greek settlers arrived on this coast and founded the city of Naxos, very near Taormina. Our house is on the coast, but Taormina, famous for its Greek amphitheater at the bottom of Mount Etna, was built on a hill and was originally a Sicilian town called Tauromenium."

Her tone was so indifferent, so very unpleasant, that Anaíd would have rather she stopped talking.

"Thanks for the information, but I'm so tired. I think I'm going to sleep for a while."

Trying to make herself comfortable, Anaíd closed her eyes and realized that she'd done Clodia a favor. Dark skinned like her mother, but with curly hair and fingers covered with rings, Clodia simply turned on her MP3 player and, humming to herself, forgot about her guest.

It saddened Anaíd to realize she'd been right to worry when she first heard Selene rave about Clodia. People her age never liked her. She tried to sleep but couldn't, so Anaíd pretended to sleep and listened carefully as Valeria chatted softly with Criselda.

"They are becoming more and more daring. The situation is very disturbing...," said Valeria. "Since Selene's disappearance, the number amounts to seven girls and three babies."

"And Salma? Is it true that she's back?"

Valeria nodded.

"She has been seen in four different places. I was told this morning she is here on the island."

Criselda shuddered.

"So she wasn't burned at the stake?"

"No. She misled everyone. Only Omars died."

"Where has she been all these years? Why is she coming out now?"

"It's her moment. It's more than clear. She's been waiting for centuries."

"The only one immune to the bell was Anaíd." Criselda's voice was hoarse. "She wasn't numbed by apathy like we were. She was able to communicate with Selene."

"What about the Odish?"

"She lured her with a seduction spell but wasn't able to numb her mind."

"That's strange."

"Anaíd twice accused us of not doing anything."

"You haven't done anything?" asked Valeria, rather harshly.

"Nothing. Two months lost," Criselda reproached herself. "And to think that Karen, Elena, and Gaya are still inside the bell . . ."

"They'll get out soon," said Valeria.

"Do you think so?" Criselda asked, skeptically.

"If the Odish were after Anaíd and Anaíd broke the barrier, they'll try to isolate us again, but we won't let them this time."

It made sense, thought Criselda, but she couldn't stop thinking about her listless attitude and felt the bitter taste of guilt.

"What have we done these past two months?" she lamented. "We haven't learned anything about Selene's location."

"Not even a clue, as insignificant as it may seem?"

"Nothing."

"That in itself is evidence . . ."

"Unfortunately, it is."

Valeria and Criselda both fell silent for a minute or so until Valeria decided to confirm her worst fear.

"Are you sure?"

"One hundred percent. It's clear that Selene didn't want us to go after her."

"You said the girl was able to contact her?"

"She was able to get into an opening between the two worlds."

"By herself?"

"And without a guide, but Selene pushed her away."

Valeria turned toward Anaíd, who pretended to sleep. But an unconscious gesture revealed she was not.

"So . . . Anaíd . . . is the key."

"For the moment, she's our only hope."

"What does she know?"

"Little, very little, but she's a quick learner."

"Very quick; she's been listening to our conversation all along. Right, Anaíd?"

Anaíd hesitated for a moment. It wasn't worth denying what was obvious. She opened her eyes and nodded.

"I'm sorry. I still don't know what I should and shouldn't listen to."

"What do you think of the situation?" Valeria blurted out unexpectedly.

"Well, if we had moved quickly in Urt to find Selene and reassure the other Omars, the Odish would have probably not dared to go this far," Anaíd answered quickly.

Criselda and Valeria were perplexed.

"Do you have any ideas?"

"We should rescue Selene as soon as possible instead of freaking out and protecting ourselves with these ridiculous shields."

Criselda burst into a coughing fit.

"I'm sorry, Valeria, sometimes she shoots her mouth off and says outrageous things."

"She asked me," Anaíd defended herself.

"You are not ready; you haven't even been initiated. How can you scheme strategies? How dare you lecture the chief of a clan?" Criselda scolded her.

Valeria stepped on the gas and shifted to fifth gear.

"Calm down, Criselda, I agree with Anaíd. There's only one problem."

Anaíd held her breath.

"Only one?"

"We have to initiate her immediately."

"Before your daughter?"

Valeria glanced at Clodia sideways, but her daughter thought only of her music.

"She's my daughter, but I'm not blind. We need Anaíd. Clodia can wait."

. . .

Anaíd was exhausted; she hadn't slept in two nights and had been through several mishaps. Even though she shared a room with Clodia and it would have been natural to chat with her briefly before going to sleep, as soon as she laid her head on the pillow, she fell into a deep slumber. In other circumstances, she would have tried to stay awake and talk, but Clodia was so blatantly hostile that she didn't feel like feigning a friendship she wasn't interested in. And she didn't feel bad about it. Above all, she needed to rest.

She slept a profound, rejuvenating sleep, which was interrupted early the following morning. She dreamed she was crashing against the invisible barrier and felt that lacerating pain all over again, tearing her flesh like a knife. A knock on the window woke her up. Confused, she opened her eyes and saw a fully dressed Clodia jumping into the room. They were on the second floor of an old detached house with thick walls. Clodia had climbed the branches of a cherry tree growing in the garden next to the window. The day was breaking, and Clodia, used to not making any noise, silently stripped off her clothes and curled up under the fresh sheets.

"Where were you?" Anaíd couldn't help asking.

Clodia was startled; she had been caught.

"Were you spying on me?"

Anaíd thought her roommate must be stupid.

"You woke me up when you came in."

"Wow, what good hearing you have!"

"Why did you come in through the window?"

"What do *you* think? My mother doesn't let me go out."

Anaíd felt compelled to warn her.

"Seven girls like us have been bled to death."

Clodia laughed.

"And you believe that?"

"I actually came here to escape from an Odish."

But Clodia didn't seem fazed by the information.

"That's what they've told you."

Anaíd wasn't intimidated by Clodia's tone.

"I'm not a tattletale, but I'm not stupid, either. We have to take precautions."

"Oh, yeah? What kind of precautions?"

"Wearing the shield and never going out alone."

Clodia seemed annoyed.

"She already knows, right?" she said unexpectedly.

"What?" asked Anaíd. Clodia's question had taken her off guard.

"About the shield. My mother asked you to watch me and tell her when I took it off."

"You took it off?"

"I'm not going to wear that orthopedic girdle all day."

Anaíd had two choices: explain to Valeria that her daughter was stupid and reckless or keep quiet. If she kept quiet, she would be responsible for Clodia's actions. If she spoke, she would always be considered a hateful tattletale.

"All right, w-whatever," she stammered, turning over to try to go to sleep again.

Clodia was curious about her comment.

"Are you going to tell the authorities?"

"No."

"So? What did you mean, if I may ask?"

"That if you want to be victim number eight, that's your problem."

And Anaíd smiled to herself. If she hadn't scared Clodia, at least she had given her food for thought.

But Clodia flipped her middle finger and turned her back to Anaíd as well.

CHAPTER 17

The Witches' Palazzo

The neoclassical palace of marble columns sat atop a hill, overlooking the Strait of Messina.

It was surrounded by romantic gardens, and Selene loved to stroll around and lose herself in the labyrinth of hedges, have a soft drink in the gazebo, submerge her hand in the pond full of brightly colored fish, or contemplate the white sculptures stolen from the many Greek necropolises on the island.

She hadn't left the confines of the palace since her arrival, to Salma's desperation, who kept asking her to go with her to the many parties that filled the Palermo nights.

Selene preferred to rest and enjoy the pleasures of her retirement in the countryside. She appreciated the fine, real-wood furniture and liked to estimate the value of the frescoes adorning the rooms, the Persian rugs covering the floors, the Syrian tapestries that hung from the dining room walls, and the Tuscan weapons that flanked the corridors and steep marble stairs. She couldn't believe that everything was hers. Hers, too, were a yacht moored in the private port on the bay, and a powerful black BMW with a driver awaiting her instructions to take her wherever she wished.

Selene wouldn't leave her sanctuary, however.

Diamonds glittered in her jewelry box, but she wore them only at night, by herself. She would turn off all the lights and, in the dark, cover her fingers with diamond rings. Then she would flutter her hands like a butterfly, like waves moved by the wind, open the windows, and gaze at the moon. Even though she missed the howling of the wolves and the clean, fresh air of the Pyrenees, her senses were slowly growing used to the warm scent released by the pine trees at dusk, the salty flavor of the ocean, the hot sand on the beach, and the suffocating midday heat, which she avoided by staying in the cool rooms with high ceilings and closed windows that prevented the sun from slipping in.

One of those afternoons, when the weather was so oppressive that even flies didn't feel like flying, she overheard a conversation.

Two girls from town, armed with buckets and rags, were chattering away while they cleaned the enormous windows.

Although they spoke in a Sicilian dialect, Selene could understand them perfectly. She perked up her ears and stood still.

"First the plague ruined our masters."

"That's not enough, Concetta."

"It only struck the duke's lands!"

"So what?"

"Where did the locusts come from? How did the cloud appear so suddenly and then vanish into thin air? It came out of nowhere, Marella, it didn't cross the strait; the locusts weren't seen on the peninsula."

"You can't say they are witches just because the locusts ate the wheat."

"What about the gardens?"

"That, I don't believe."

"I saw it with my own eyes, Marella. Look at me, I saw how

the dead grass turned into a lush, beautiful lawn—like a golf course. It happened after the dark-haired lady pronounced some magic words."

"If they are witches, why did they have the rooms painted by Grimaldi instead of using magic?"

"Because that would have been too obvious."

"You are being superstitious."

"Haven't you heard the rumors in Catania?"

"What rumors?"

"Two babies have disappeared and they found a girl bled to death."

"What are you trying to say?"

"When the women arrived . . . Listen carefully, that very night a baby disappeared, and that's not the worst."

"What is?"

"I clearly heard a baby crying in this house."

"That can't be true, are you saying that . . ."

"It was them! The dark-haired one gets them and the redhead kills them."

"Is the redhead more powerful?"

"Her hair is red, like blood. It was her."

"What do we do now? Do we tell anyone?"

The young women turned pale. The mysterious red-haired foreigner had appeared out of nowhere and was staring at them mockingly through the glass. They took a step back, fear oozing from every pore of their skin.

"Tell me, Marella. Who would you tell?"

"No one, madam."

"Concetta . . . do, you think I'm a powerful witch?"

"No, madam."

"I just heard you—I can summon locust plagues, turn dry

grass into fresh lawn, and I feed on young girls and children. Is that it?"

"No, madam. That's nonsense. We don't believe in witches."

"Good, because . . . you are about to forget everything."

"Excuse me, madam?"

"That right now, when I snap my fingers, you'll forget everything that's happened in the past few days. Now!"

Concetta and Marella blinked for an instant, and when they opened their eyes again, they saw a stunning redhead in a light floral silk gown.

They had no idea who she was.

THE PROPHECY OF TAMA

The moon will walk on the earth in her honor
And protect her dwelling
Revealing with its pale beams
The unmistakable aura of the chosen one.

A lunar meteorite,
Cold and black,
Will guard her nights
And wash away her sorrow.

The sharp lunar stone,
Slashes evil
In the lacerated skin
Returning its reflection.

CHAPTER 18

THE OCEAN

Anaíd closed her eyes to better absorb Valeria's words and enjoy the pleasant sensation of floating in the waves. No, it wasn't a dream, she was on a sailboat and the timid blue sea looked more like a lake than the ocean. With her eyes narrowed and the sun and wind softly caressing her face, Anaíd listened to Valeria's firm voice.

"Nobody knows for sure how many Odish exist. We estimate there are at least a hundred. Very few die; they make sure they prevent it. Their immortality makes them fearless and wise, for they have lived through many ages and survived all catastrophes. Only a few, you can count them on one hand, have chosen to become mothers and bear offspring. Perhaps they were curious, or just reckless, but the truth is that their powers have diminished and they've aged more than the others. The thousands of Omars scattered amongst various tribes, clans, and lineages need a common language to communicate, and signs and symbols to recognize and identify themselves. But the Odish have no trouble—they can speak multiple languages and, what's worse, they know one another very well. They are thousands of years old. Imagine the number of quarrels that have ensued over such a long time. The fights between Odish, when they happen, are fierce and gory. As for their appearance, that's what's most surprising—they remain eternally young. Many of them fake their own deaths and pretend to be their own daughters, granddaughters, and so on. They do so to avoid losing their status of power and privilege. Once wealth is achieved, it is easier to maintain it. That's why many Odish bought land and aristocratic titles and hid for centuries, protected by their status and secluded in their high castles. They've always lived close to power, to the courts, and surrounded themselves by royalty, always participating in plots and conspiracies. Stikman, a prestigious Omar from the clan of the owls, recently named the Odish responsible for the most important assassinations in old Europe. The best-known case is that of Joanna of Navarre, queen of France. It was the Odish who instigated her from the shadows, who supplied poisons, daggers, and potions. The Odish have no scruples. They buy and sell alliances with their spells; they poison their enemies with their potions; they invade the conscience of the living with the help of their allies, the waking dead. With their power and black magic they control oceans, rivers, storms, winds, earthquakes, and fires."

"So it's true?"

Anaíd, who had remained silent until now, couldn't help but interrupt Valeria's explanation.

"What is?"

"That they can conjure up storms, wind, rain, and hail."

Valeria hesitated.

"Only the most powerful Odish can do that. And they do it on few occasions, when fighting against one another or an Omar. They are not worried about human mortals at all."

Anaíd's hands trembled slightly, a painful memory coming back to her: the terrible storm on the night her grandmother Deméter died. It had been an astonishing sight. The dome of the sky had been ignited for long hours like a thousand-watt light-bulb, and the wind had uprooted two cypress trees from the cemetery's hedge. Did the Odish conjure it? Or . . . was it Deméter? Her mother's disappearance was also accompanied by a storm. Had she unleashed it?

"And can the Omars dominate the elements?"

"You really don't know?" Valeria was surprised.

Anaíd shook her head anxiously. Valeria's remark had made her feel insecure. Should she know?

"Let's see. Clodia, jog your memory and explain it to Anaíd."

Clodia had been absently silent while she helped Valeria, efficiently but without enthusiasm, to raise the sails and maneuver the boat. This way, crouching, loosening ropes, listing to port and starboard, she seemed almost normal. But as soon as her attention was needed, she turned into a real idiot. Valeria was so used to her disdainful expression that she didn't notice it, but when Anaíd saw Clodia scowl, she felt like slapping her. She wasn't interested in what that spoiled brat had to say in her mocking, monotonous drone.

"The Omars, daughters of Oma, granddaughters of Om and great-granddaughters of O, scattered around the earth fleeing from the evil Odish. The Omars and their descendants founded thirty-three tribes that divided into clans. The clans populated the realms of water, air, earth, and fire, and they were devoted to them, learning their secrets and how to control their wills. The clans took their names and wisdom from living beings, adopting their language and skills. That allowed them to blend in with them and protect themselves."

Anaíd tried to feign indifference but grudgingly drank in Clodia's words. She was envious of the basic knowledge any stupid Omar like Clodia possessed. Why had her mother and grandmother denied her that? Despite the books she'd read, she felt as ignorant as a rock. She had no choice but to ask more questions.

"If all the clans are related to an element, which one does the clan of the she-wolf belong to?"

"Earth," replied Valeria. "The she-wolves effect the harvests and forests, earthquakes and plagues . . ."

"And the dolphins belong to the water," concluded Anaíd.

"Yes, we can control the tides, conjure rain and fight against tsunamis, floods . . ."

"And what about fire? Who dominates that element?"

"The clans of the ferrets, moles, worms, snakes—the animals who live in the depths of the earth, near the magma there, where the fire that volcanoes spit out is formed."

Anaíd perked up.

"And the air is controlled by the eagles, hawks, partridges . . ."

"Correct."

"Anaíd, I'll have to teach you a few spells so you can pass your initiation," Aunt Criselda interrupted, her face pale. "You must show that you can turn the wood of your wand green and make a piece of fruit mature."

Anaíd looked disappointed.

"Is that all?"

"What did you expect?"

"Well, that I'd have to conjure an earthquake, a volcano's eruption, or . . . a storm," she lied.

Valeria let out a loud laugh. Criselda was embarrassed— Anaíd's ignorance was her fault.

"Not even the chiefs of a clan do that," Clodia corrected her in a smart-alecky tone. "The newly initiated do stupid stuff: they make a tangerine mature, set the branch of a pine tree on fire, fill a washbasin with water, make a feather float in the air. You've seen too many fantasy movies."

Anaíd made a mental note of the insult and swore to get back at her. Valeria defended her, however.

"Don't mind Clodia. Ask as much as you want."

"I have no more questions, thanks," Anaíd said drily.

"Very well, in that case, the theory class is over for today and we'll move on to practical training."

Valeria began to strip off her clothes.

"Hand me the water bottle, please," she ordered Clodia.

Clodia did so reluctantly and pointed at her watch.

"Are we having 'meeting and transformation' today?"

"Is that a problem?"

"I have plans for this afternoon; you can't do that to me."

"I told you, but you might have been asleep."

"Why? Why today? Why did *she* have to come here?"

"*She* has a name, and this is a lot more important than one afternoon in your life, trust me."

Anaíd witnessed the altercation uncomfortably; after all, she, and her presence in the sailboat, were the culprit. Valeria, considerate with her guest, perceived this from the corner of her eye. She took a long swig from her water bottle and dragged Clodia by the arm to the boat's small cabin. Anaíd appreciated Valeria's symbolic gesture. The boat's reduced space made it almost impossible not to listen to conversations, let alone loud arguments, but if she made an effort, Anaíd could disconnect herself and decode the sounds of the animals around her. She turned around and saw Aunt Criselda, pale and still, holding on to the railing. It dawned on her that her aunt hadn't uttered a word all day, and now she knew why—the poor thing was terribly seasick.

"Aunt Criselda!"

Criselda didn't have enough strength to answer. Anaíd came to her rescue; fighting against dizziness was relatively easy: she just needed to put her aunt in the right position, give her a cold compress to stimulate her circulation, and some sweetened chamomile tea—all home remedies Deméter would have given Anaíd. She took off one sock, soaked it in the ocean water, made Criselda lie down, and applied the makeshift compress to her aunt's forehead while she massaged her wrists to activate her circulation and asked her to breathe in more frequently. Soon, her cheeks regained their color. Anaíd grabbed the water bottle and offered it to Criselda, who took a long sip and then coughed.

"What is it?" she asked, wrinkling her nose.

Anaíd smelled the contents of the bottle; she'd thought it was water, but it smelled sweet, like mint tea. She took a sip. She liked it. Valeria had just had it, it couldn't hurt her. It was probably a tonic or a hydrating drink, just what Criselda needed. Anaíd offered her aunt another sip and continued massaging her wrists while she hummed a song Deméter used to sing when tending to a patient. Criselda began to feel better and sat up. She took Anaíd's hand and studied her palm, comparing it with her own.

"You have the gift."

Anaíd was taken aback.

"What gift?"

"Your grandmother's and mine, the one the Tsinoulis family has. Our hands are special. You've never noticed before?"

Anaíd shook her head.

"Deméter discovered it when she was child. She healed her dog's broken bone by placing her hands over the injury."

"And I can do that?"

"You have the ability."

Anaíd studied her hands with pride. It was true that, sometimes, she felt a tingling sensation when she petted Apollo. Was that it?

The voices coming from the cabin died down. Valeria had clearly ended the argument with her daughter, but Clodia was a tough nut to crack.

To Anaíd's surprise, Valeria appeared in a bathing suit, tanned and muscular, and without further ado, dove headfirst into the water with impeccable style. Anaíd witnessed the dive, astonished. One, two, three minutes passed . . . And no trace of Valeria. Anaíd grew worried, but Clodia remained impassive. Suddenly, Criselda gestured toward the stern. Anaíd followed her aunt's finger and bumped into a pair of round, cheerful eyes peering at her, studying her through the waves. The enormous gray fish emerged from the waters with a surprising leap and squealed a greeting. Without stopping, it appeared at the stern, at the bow, at port, and at starboard. The fish jumped, multiplying itself into four, five, repeating the same welcome squeals and ejecting water through the hole in its back. Suddenly, Anaíd realized it was a dolphin—and not just one, but a whole pod. Among them, swimming alongside and laughing, was Valeria. With her hair wet, covered in foam, and her skin sparkling with salt, Valeria looked less human than a few minutes ago.

"Don't be afraid; come closer, they want to meet you!" she shouted to Anaíd in her human voice.

Anaíd extended her arm and was ritually greeted by ten wet snouts that filled her fingers with salty water and rubbed their good mood on her.

"The females have said hello; they are the most curious ones."

"And the most affectionate ones," Anaíd added, moved.

Valeria translated her words and the female dolphins cheered Anaíd's observation with leaps and shouts. Criselda was astonished—she could barely open her mouth.

Inspired by the liveliness and effusiveness of the female

dolphins, Anaíd couldn't control herself and responded in their own tongue.

It's not easy for the human mouth to reproduce dolphins' sounds; Clodia had been trying for years but to no avail.

"How did you do that?" She turned to Anaíd, annoyed.

"I don't know, it just happened."

Anaíd realized that, perhaps, she shouldn't have let herself be carried away. But the dolphins disagreed and, once recovered from their shock, received her greeting with great joy and hushed Clodia's envious remarks with their squeals, or better said, with their questions. The female dolphins were extremely curious and terribly gossipy. They chitchatted about the little resemblance between the young she-wolf and the great red wolf. They talked about her hair, her eyes, her legs, and compared them with Selene's.

Anaíd was offended.

"If you are going to criticize me, I'm leaving."

Laughing hysterically, Valeria invited her to dive in.

"Come on, jump."

Anaíd was startled.

"I've never swum in the ocean before."

"You'll float easily. The Mediterranean is very salty."

"It's just that . . ."

"Why don't you help her, Clodia."

And Clodia, relishing the chance to pester Anaíd, gave her a good shove, and Anaíd fell into the water with what she was wearing—shorts and a T-shirt. Anaíd didn't expect it and had a good scare. She felt herself sink in the tepid waters that were so different from the icy Pyrenean lakes. The sea's thick, compact texture, like molasses, was enveloping her, swallowing her, filling her mouth, nose, and ears with salt and water. A saline taste impregnated everything and almost reached her lungs. She was drowning. She needed oxygen. She paddled like a dog and came out to the surface gasping and regretting not having taken better advantage of her swimming lessons. She knew enough to manage a few strokes, control her breathing, and duck her head underwater with her eyes open for a few seconds. Only a few seconds, though, not minutes like Valeria could. And suddenly, something soft and slippery grazed Anaíd's left arm, placed itself underneath her, and lifted her in the air, above the water. Anaíd held on instinctively and she realized that she was riding a dolphin. Valeria whispered a few words in her own mount's ear, and the two dolphins swam off, gliding over the waters like a catamaran. Anaíd missed the reigns of her horse in Urt. She didn't know where to hold on, and the aquatic race, which really lasted about half an hour, felt like an eternity. Despite the calm waters, she was afraid of slipping and falling into the immense and intimidating sea. Finally, Valeria stopped.

Anaíd didn't understand why the two of them had come this far alone. Where was Clodia? And Criselda? Valeria spoke to the female dolphins and pet them softly between the eyes.

"Thank you. You've been very careful. Go find something to eat and come back later. Anaíd, come down, please."

Anaíd didn't want to get off her mount. What did Valeria want? Were the two of them going to stay floating in the middle of the vast ocean with not even a board to hold on to? The mere thought of it made her shudder.

"No, please," she begged, refusing to release her dolphin.

Valeria laughed.

"Let her go and stand up."

And, to her surprise, Anaíd realized that she could indeed stand up—the water reached only to her knees. They were on a headland, an emerging rock, something like a small underwater islet made of porous stone, probably volcanic. That wasn't surprising. Mount Etna had been spewing out its molten lava for thousands of years in those coasts that had seen islands and sharp cliffs be born and destroyed within hours.

"Are you afraid?"

"It's just that I don't know why we've come here."

Valeria took her hands and invited her to look under the water with her.

"Open your eyes wide and then tell me what you've seen."

Anaíd did as Valeria said, but her ability to hold her breath was limited. In the few seconds that her eyes were open, she managed to see only some soft and sinuous algae floating at her feet.

"Algae."

"Are you sure? Try again."

Anaíd dove in again and studied that colony of inert algae rocked by the current.

"I'm positive."

"They are actually fish that look like algae to capture the unwary like you, who don't look well enough." Valeria laughed.

Before Valeria asked her again, Anaíd ducked underwater for a third time, brought her hand closer to the so-called colony of innocent algae, and realized that the hasty reaction of one of them was a little too quick to have come from a vegetable. Anaíd was stung on the finger, but in the fraction of a second that the rapid movement lasted, she distinguished a pair of shrewd little eyes.

"Ouch!"

"I told you."

"It bit me."

"It only tasted you. It doesn't like you."

"How do you know?"

"If it had liked you, it would have called its family, who is very greedy, and they would be having a feast now."

"How very smart."

"Smart, that's exactly what they are. The mimicry some aquatic animals have developed to survive in the ocean is amazing."

"And why does this happen in the ocean?"

"I'm a biologist, but I like to give a poetic explanation to this phenomenon. Water allows for confusion and deception. Our sight is blurred, the volume and colors distorted or lost. What humans consider objective values are not so in the ocean, especially once we leave the shore behind. As depth increases and light diminishes, sight and perception are transformed and can no longer be considered universal parameters. Do you follow me?"

"Yes," said Anaíd, remembering her dizzying fall through the dark abyss.

There, in the gap between the two worlds, she'd also realized that the earth's laws had stopped making sense. Gravity was an illusion caused by fear.

Anaíd listened to Valeria, convinced that she'd soon witness something very exciting. Why else would she have brought her here? To show her a colony of algae? She doubted it.

"The dolphins clan has inherited secret knowledge from our ancestors that we treasure zealously. We've rarely shared it with other Omars. Your mother was an exception, and she wanted you to come to Taormina so I could show you the art of transformation."

When she heard mention of her mother, Anaíd's heartbeat quickened. Had she understood correctly? Did her mother want her to witness a transformation? A transformation into what? And why?

Valeria glanced up at the sky.

"It's almost time. You must promise me that you won't be afraid, no matter what happens."

And, as she spoke, Valeria took off her bathing suit and handed it to Anaíd.

"Hold it for me and wait."

"What are you going to do?"

"Transform myself."

"Into what?"

"I don't know. Mimicry is opportunistic."

"And how will you do it?"

Valeria began to tremble slightly, her teeth chattering.

"I'll blend with my surroundings. I'll become a part of everything. I'll try to get rid of my body and look like another living being, when I find one that suits my spirit."

Anaíd noticed that Valeria's body was shining intensely, in a special way; even her eyes glistened. Valeria leaned on the waves, closed her eyes, and blended with the ocean, letting herself be carried by the current. Her hair floated around her and became tangled in the seaweed. Was this a mirage? Moments later, Anaíd realized that Valeria didn't have hair anymore but algae, and that her body was turning round and polished like bronze, blue like the ocean, and compact like rock. Anaíd brought her hands to her mouth—despite Valeria's warning, she couldn't suppress a scream.

A tuna fish.

Valeria had transformed into a huge female tuna. The fish swam around Anaíd in concentric circles as if celebrating a reunion, dancing or cornering her; then she suddenly and unexpectedly changed directions and swam away toward a dark stain that moved slowly in the distance. It was a school of tuna traveling north toward the strait. Valeria joined them and was received with great joy. Anaíd could see the fish leap in the air and hear the sound of their fins splashing in the distance.

"Come back, Valeria!" she shouted.

Her voice sounded lonely and vulnerable. It was Valeria. She was sure of it, she had transformed before Anaíd's own eyes. But . . . was she really another being now? Or had she kept her human mind? Anaíd couldn't imagine what would happen if Valeria, transformed into a tuna, crossed the strait and forgot about her. She climbed onto the highest rock—where the water lapped at her feet without swallowing her and the sun could dry her skin. It was a desolate picture; a blue blanket covered everything. If the mountains were treacherous, the ocean was unforgiving. Abandoned and alone in the middle of the Mediterranean, she wouldn't survive very long.

But Anaíd refused to be afraid.

Valeria was powerful, and it wasn't only her muscles and courage that proved it. Valeria, like Deméter, emanated power. And it wasn't common. It was never so obvious. Neither Criselda nor Gaya (or Elena or Karen) exuded the energy Anaíd felt when she was with Valeria. Did that power come with being the chief of the clan? Perhaps. But even if Valeria offered her security, the school of tuna and the dolphins had definitely disappeared. Anaíd had been left with only Valeria's word and bathing suit. She had asked Anaíd to "hold it and wait."

. . .

Anaíd waited. Sitting on the islet, she tried to move often and stay dry to avoid feeling the cold that was starting to penetrate her bones. She got rid of her wet clothes and massaged her hands and legs while she slapped herself and pinched her cheeks. A thick web of clouds had just covered the sky. The clouds were turning increasingly darker, and the wind was blowing faster as the sun began its slow descent. How long had Valeria been gone? Three hours? Four? Her thirst and hunger, the sunset, and the slowly developing storm began to worry her.

Anaíd saw the pale reflection of lightning on the fine line of the horizon and shuddered. A storm in the ocean was probably worse than in the mountains.

A large flock of seagulls flew overhead. The boldest ones moved lower and closer, inspecting her with curiosity, making sure she was alive. Anaíd shooed them away with her hands and in their own tongue; she hated those scavenging winged rats.

However, the seagulls were better company than no one. Anaíd thought of the anguish the shipwrecked must feel— besides the lack of water was the loneliness. Hours passed by slowly, inexorably, and unless she looked underwater, there were no signs of life around her. She could hear only the increasingly disturbing clapping of thunder and the whistling sound of the wind.

She couldn't spend the night there. And night was drawing nearer and nearer.

She couldn't swim back to shore.

She didn't have flares or fire or a horn to alert other boats.

The only thing Anaíd could think to do was ask the dolphins for help. She had reached the islet riding a dolphin. And, before the sun finally hid behind the horizon, Anaíd called them in their own language. She called once, twice, and with the third time, she saw a shadow slowly approach through the water. She assumed it was a dolphin but was startled—judging from its size and appearance, it could well be a shark.

Fortunately, it was the female dolphin Anaíd had ridden. Her name, in her language, was something like Flun.

Anaíd felt stupid for not thinking of this before. She tried to be polite.

"It's so good to see you. Could you please take me to shore?" she asked, trying to climb onto the dolphin's back.

But Flun avoided Anaíd, and like the tuna, swam in concentric circles around her before replying, "Valeria won't let me."

Anaíd thought she was going to faint.

"Did something happen?"

"No."

"So tell her I'm here so she can pick me up with the boat."

"Valeria knows where you are."

It was obvious. Valeria had abandoned her and knew that, by this time, Anaíd would be cold, hungry, thirsty, and terrified.

So if Valeria hadn't had any problems and didn't want the dolphins to help her . . . What did she want?

Anaíd stared at Flun. She could swear she saw a hint of sympathy in the dolphin's eyes. The female dolphin leapt elegantly out of the waters and then disappeared in the shadows of dusk.

Anaíd was terrified, and a hint of a doubt began to form in her mind. She had already succumbed to the charms of an Odish. Was Valeria an Odish too? No, she couldn't be. No way. The thought that Valeria wanted to get rid of her was ridiculous.

However . . . there had been no witnesses, no one to be held accountable. Valeria could give a thousand excuses for Anaíd's death.

The pale sunlight suddenly disappeared. The storm had reached the edges of the sun and eclipsed it. The waters turned black and flashes of lightning lit the darkness that threatened to swallow her. Anaíd held her legs close, instinctively protecting herself, and curled up into the world's oldest position. She rocked herself back and forth and hummed a song Deméter used to sing when Anaíd was a child. The rocking motion and the song's rhythm soothed her, and she opened her eyes. The outlines took shape again. The light, though dim, wasn't as frightening as before.

Everything would have looked almost familiar, considering

she'd spent long hours in that scenery, had it not been for the man. He gazed at Anaíd curiously from a few feet away. He looked at her insolently, without any qualms. He was half-submerged in the water, but the lightning revealed his curly hair, his beard, his shield, his short curved sword, and his helmet with a crest in the shape of a horse's mane.

Anaíd wasn't intimidated at all.

"Hi."

The warrior looked around, surprised. Anaíd had clearly spoken to him.

"Are you talking to me?"

"Certainly, there's no one else here."

"So . . . you can see me."

"And hear you."

"I can't believe it!"

"Neither can I, but it's true."

"You . . . you are the first person I've talked to in . . . Goodness! I've lost track of time. What year are we in?"

"If I told you, it wouldn't make a difference. Where are you from? Greece? Rome? Carthage?"

"I'm Greek, from the Italic colonies. My name is Calícrates, I was an infantry soldier who survived the siege to the city of Gela, under the great Dionysius of Syracuse."

"Wow! I think that happened in the fifth century before Christ."

"Before who?"

"Let's say that you've been wandering for about two thousand five hundred years."

"I thought it had been a long time."

"And how did you end up here, if I may ask?"

"I drowned."

Anaíd suppressed a shudder.

"You didn't know how to swim?"

"I was a soldier, not a marine."

"And now you are a wandering soul who longs to rest in peace."

"How do you know?"

"I've met others like you. Who cursed you?"

"I suppose it was my wife. I swore to her that I would return to Crotone in time to reap the harvest, but I failed her."

"So you drowned on your way home."

"I did, as a matter of fact. I fought honorably against Himilcon, the great Carthaginian general; we left with dignity but our ship sank when we reached these shores."

"And you drowned."

"No, we were picked up by another vessel, but I was thrown overboard."

"They threw you in the water?"

"All of us wouldn't fit and that ship was about to sink too, so we drew straws and I lost."

Anaíd barely heard Calícrates' last phrase. A loud thunderclap boomed.

"A rough night, it reminds me of—"

"No, please," interrupted Anaíd.

"You don't want me to describe the storm that made my ship crash against the rocks?"

Anaíd was annoyed with this jinx of a soldier.

"In case you haven't realized, I'm alive and have no desire to die. Death by drowning must be horrifying."

"It is horrible, indeed. You try to breathe but your lungs fill with water instead of air and—"

"Stop!"

The soldier fell silent. Besides being a jinx, he was sadistic. Anaíd recalled her other spirits' obedience and submission.

The storm was drawing near, bringing strong waves with it. Anaíd held her breath when the first one of them covered her completely. She had no protection, nothing to hold on to.

"I will grant you eternal rest in exchange for your help."

"Are you talking to me?"

"Yes, I'm talking to you, Calícrates. Tell me how to get out of here before a wave swallows me."

Calícrates seemed to think for a moment and looked around him.

"There must be way, but I'm not aware of it."

"What do you mean?"

"The other ones disappeared. I didn't see their drowned bodies. They went somewhere. But never during the night."

"What other ones?"

"The other girls."

Anaíd grew nervous.

"Are you saying that I'm not the first one you have found here on this rock?"

"No, but you are the first one who doesn't cry and who can see me," Calícrates added.

"How many girls have gone through this?"

"Well . . . throughout the millenniums, I'd say maybe hundreds."

Anaíd turned pale.

"That means that every five or ten years, you find a girl like me, half-naked, stranded on a rock, and the following day she's gone?"

"Exactly."

Anaíd was horrified. Who could live thousands of years

pretending to be different people? Who chased girls and drank their blood? If she was looking for confirmation to a terrible suspicion, she had found it.

"She's an Odish!"

"That's what they thought too."

"Who?"

"The other girls."

"Can you read minds?"

"Yes."

Anaíd was desperate. Time was running out. She refused to drown to death or stay there and be captured by an Odish pretending to be an Omar.

"Will you help me?"

"I'd like to. How did you get here?"

"On a dolphin."

"Nice mount."

"But it refuses to take me back to shore."

A bigger wave covered Anaíd, and this time, she slipped and was almost dragged away by the current. At the last second, though it hurt her hand, she managed to hold on to a protrusion on the rock.

The storm finally exploded and rain poured down with all its might. The evil wind raised high waves and thick drops lashed the waters. Anaíd was beginning to lose her footing and didn't know what to hold on to. She felt as if she were part of that choppy ocean, part of the water and the foam. And, as she discovered these new sensations, she saw the dolphin swimming by her side.

Anaíd closed her eyes and let herself go. She leaned over the waves and blended with the ocean.

The soldier waited one, two, three minutes and sighed.

"No, not again."

The poor girl had vanished and wouldn't be able to help him now. Once again, he was alone with eternity and his curse. The cheerful squeals of a pair of dolphins distracted him for a few seconds, but they soon swam away. And the soldier, bored like every other night, leaned over the waves to watch the lightning.

An hour later, a motorboat driven by a woman in a raincoat skillfully maneuvered around the rocks several times and made three fruitless circles, looking for something.

The soldier, knowing she couldn't see him, positioned himself on the rocks to get a better view of the brave intruder.

"Hey, you!"

Calícrates couldn't believe it.

"Me?"

"Yes, who else?"

Calícrates, who had drowned and been ignored for two thousand five hundred years, was delighted to be able to talk to a live person for the second time that night.

CHAPTER 19

Rites of Initiation

Criselda wrung her hands desperately.

"Do something! You have to do something."

Valeria pretended to be in control of the situation, but she hadn't expected this inclement weather. The wind lashed at the shutters and the rain hit the windows with fury.

"The omens said the day would be favorable."

Criselda opened the door wide; she could barely hold it open.

"Favorable? Is this favorable?"

This was the worst storm Valeria could remember in a while. She began to fear her predictions had been wrong.

"An initiation cannot be interrupted. Once begun, it must be finished."

"I care more about Anaíd's life than her initiation. If she's not initiated by a water clan, she'll be initiated by a clan of fire or air, but please get her out of there."

Valeria checked her watch.

"It will be morning in a few hours. Let's finish the ritual."

Criselda stepped out to the porch.

"If you don't do it right know, I'll tell the patrol and report her disappearance."

Valeria finally gave in to Criselda's stubbornness. She thought of Anaíd's trusting smile, her awe when she saw the ocean for the first time, her blind faith, how she'd shuddered when Selene was mentioned. That girl who had just lost her mother was now alone, abandoned in the ocean at night, at the mercy of a tempest.

It was extremely cruel.

Initiations were always hard, but the novices usually had an adjustment period. Under normal circumstances, Valeria would have left Anaíd alone in the ocean after a month of sailing and scuba diving, and after testing her resistance and skills. She would have probably checked the weather forecast instead of relying only on her interpretation of some animal entrails.

But the omens in the flames had predicted an excellent day for Anaíd's initiation. Had they been wrong? The omens never lied, but she could have misread a sign and caused a tragedy. Nobody would hold her responsible, though. Those things could happen . . .

Tragedies occurred sometimes. Valeria didn't want to recall it, but the case of Julilla, Cornelia Fatta's daughter, came to mind. The girl couldn't bear the darkness of the cave where she was captive and had died searching for a way out. She'd fallen into a deep chasm, and it took three days to find her body. Her mother accepted the accident with integrity and took comfort in the thought that Julilla's death was a minor mishap that had prevented a greater tragedy. A witch who couldn't tolerate uncertainty or control her impulses wasn't qualified to use magic. A witch who couldn't spend a night alone in the company of nature's elements couldn't be initiated. But Cornelia Fatta was never the same after that; the death of her daughter changed her forever.

Valeria remembered this as she followed Criselda, who, despite her plump legs, reached the docks where the sailboat was moored in record time. She even seemed ready to jump on the boat without waiting for Valeria.

"Wait, Criselda, wait. I'll need help!"

Valeria regretted not having woken Clodia up before running after Criselda. Criselda was an inept sailor, but how could she have been dizzy that morning when the water was so calm?

"There's no time. I'll help you," replied Criselda.

She seemed so determined, so confident in her abilities, that Valeria shrugged and got ready to cast off the line. But she was blinded by a flashlight.

"I'm sorry, but you are not allowed to leave the docks."

Valeria turned pale.

"It's just a swell."

"We have waves up to ten feet high, a fishing boat run aground, and a motorboat steered by a woman who ignored our orders and is out in the open sea. We've interrupted the rescue efforts until the storm subsides."

Valeria let the rope drop.

"I understand . . . ," she mumbled.

She imagined the ten-foot-high waves destroying the islet. She imagined Anaíd being dragged by the current, her body floating. Flun had been instructed to help her in case of danger, but . . . who could hold on to the slippery back of a dolphin riding ten-foot-high waves?

Criselda sensed Valeria's fear and guilt and felt sorry for her. Instead of accusing her, she took Valeria's hand.

"Let's call Anaíd."

"Can she respond to calls?"

"She herself called Karen and made her come back from Tanzania. She didn't know how, but she did it."

Criselda and Valeria joined hands under the hard rain and,

hiding in the darkness, loudly called Anaíd with their minds—the response was almost immediate.

She was alive.

The two women looked at each other, astounded. Anaíd's reply had come from a different body.

"A dolphin?" asked Criselda.

Valeria couldn't believe it. She nodded, unable to utter a word. There was no doubt. The mind that had replied to their call was inside the body of a dolphin. She could envision the fins and snout and understand her musical reply emitted in sound waves.

"She hasn't drunk the potion."

"What potion?"

"The one that enables the transformation."

Criselda remembered something.

"Was it in your water bottle?"

"Yes."

"She did. She took a swig."

Valeria thought quickly.

"I drank almost a full glass," added Criselda.

Despite the dire situation, Valeria couldn't suppress her laughter.

"You are kidding! So . . . you'll start flying or crawling at any second."

Criselda turned pale.

"It can't be so easy."

Valeria turned suddenly serious.

"Actually, it isn't."

"How did she do it then?"

"I don't know, Criselda. I don't know how she did it. Nobody was ever able to do it until now."

• • •

Clodia got home before sunrise, soaked to the bone. Before jumping in through the window, she made sure no one was in her room—she thought she'd seen a shadow behind the window. Valeria might have come to close the shutters and realized her daughter wasn't sleeping. Perhaps that stupid Tsinoulis girl had returned before expected and accused her of sneaking out at night. Anyway, she was freezing and her room was empty, so she slipped in, leaving a puddle of water on the hardwood floor. She groped the other bed—Anaíd wasn't there—and turned on the bedside lamp.

There were wet footprints on the floor from shoes that weren't hers. Shit. She'd been discovered. She knew she'd be discovered sooner or later—it was surprising that she hadn't already been caught. Valeria had been too busy with the responsibilities of the clan and some other problem concerning the Odish. And now, the young Tsinoulis's arrival had totally distracted her. It was perfect—there was nothing Clodia wished more those days than to go unnoticed and be able to escape her mother's oppressive watch.

She took off her dripping clothes and decided to dry her hair and body with a clean towel. When she opened the closet and stuck in her hand, she felt a strange burning sensation. The closet was hot, sweltering, as if the afternoon's warm air was trapped inside. Clodia grabbed a towel quickly and nervously closed the door. While she'd dried herself, she thought that the burning sensation could have been caused by the contrast between her frigid hands and the sudden heat. She turned off the light and put on her nightgown, but it was so thin that she continued shivering like a leaf. Even after covering herself with the light sheet, Clodia still couldn't get comfortable. Her bed linens weren't warm enough for a cool night. Though she thought she'd seen a sweater on Anaíd's bed . . . Or had it been her imagination? While she pondered whether to get up and put on the sweater, she heard the soft creaking of the closet door opening.

It wasn't her imagination. She could clearly hear the sound. Her shaking got worse. A small shadow moved toward the window. Was it a rat? A ferret?

With the agility of a fifteen-year-old, Clodia turned on the light and felt a sharp pair of eyes piercing hers. An instant, a millisecond, went by before a cat jumped out of the window, but it was enough to startle her. Clodia brought her hand to her chest to soothe the pain; she'd felt her blood freeze in her veins and block her heart. Fear was not letting her breathe.

Slowly, she calmed down, but she still couldn't stop thinking of the eyes of the cat that had hidden in her closet. They reminded her of another pair of eyes she'd seen that night at the beach; they belonged to a woman who'd also stared at her.

Clodia got up, closed the window, and looked for the sweater. She'd been right—Anaíd's sweater sat folded on her bed. And it came in very handy. She put it on and felt a strong stinging sensation as powerful heat relieved the cold that had invaded her. The sweater's warm embrace was so comforting that she didn't mind the itching so much.

She curled up under the soft blankets and fell into a deep slumber. It wasn't a pleasant or light sleep. She didn't hear anything. She didn't see anything. It wasn't until midmorning that Clodia would learn about Anaíd's return, the commotion that took over her house, the phone calls, the astonishing story Anaíd narrated. Clodia didn't even hear Anaíd's breathing, as she slept all afternoon and all night after having gone through the most extraordinary experience of her life.

Clodia dreamed that a pair of eyes peered inside her, quietly rummaging in the corners of her heart.

. . .

Anaíd still hadn't recovered from her exhaustion. Perhaps she never would. Deméter had once told her that some types of emotional fatigue lasted forever. Now she understood—hers was one of those.

Thinking she was dead when she had actually survived an ocean storm inside the body of a dolphin had made her so tired that all the hours of sleep in the world wouldn't help her.

It had been incredibly draining to discover that the woman Anaíd thought had betrayed her was, in fact, the one responsible for her initiation.

But Valeria had summoned a coven and Anaíd couldn't miss it. She was the reason for it. The recent events that were threatening the Omar community had the Etruscan clans on edge. The witches from the clans of the owl, the crow, the orca, and the snake had already announced their arrivals from Palermo, Agrigento, and Syracuse. They were all dying to meet the Tsinoulis girl—famous not only for being the chosen one's daughter, but because of her recent feat.

Even though Valeria had tried to keep it a secret, the gossipy female dolphins had shared the news and Anaíd's transformation had spread from mouth to mouth like a germ. Everyone wanted to attend her initiation and meet her face-to-face, hoping it would help them cope with the uncertainty threatening them since Selene's disappearance.

In the small east-facing cove, Anaíd was the center of everyone's stares. More and more witches kept arriving.

"Where is the young Tsinoulis wolf?" was the most repeated phrase of the night.

"She looks like Deméter."

"She doesn't remind me of Selene at all."

"Poor thing, to lose both of them."

They talked all around Anaíd, or just stared at her. Some discreetly, and some others with mature sincerity—without scorn. Anaíd could read the same question in their furrowed brows: how could that scrawny girl turn into a dolphin? Luckily, nobody asked her directly. The answer would have been disappointing, for Anaíd didn't even know how she'd done it. And she probably wouldn't have been able to return to her own body had it not been for Valeria, who came to the rock once the storm subsided, patted her wet skin, and told her step by step how to recover her human form. Anaíd didn't know if she'd be able to repeat that experience. Neither did Valeria.

Finally, when the crescent moon dimly illuminated the southern part of the cove, safely hidden from the wind and any curious eyes, Valeria lit the candles. Acting as officiant, she handed out earthen bowls to the attendees. Then she invited them to sing, dance, and drink with her.

This was Anaíd's first coven, and she found it exhilarating. Perhaps it was because she was at the center of things, or perhaps it was the feeling of being one with all those minds and voices, celebrating the joy of seeing one another, of knowing they were connected and protected by the group.

It was the joy of being an Omar.

Anaíd realized that this would also be her burden—even if she wanted to, she'd never be able to escape the community's tight control.

Her initiation was simple, a piece of cake. Just as Clodia had predicted, Anaíd had to show that she was able to suspend a feather in midair, fill an empty bowl with water, ignite a dry tree trunk, and turn the wood of her wand green. All of that in front of the other witches, and using only her will and powers. But Anaíd wasn't intimidated. She had discovered that the success of her magic depended in part on her own confidence and emotional balance. Rage, for example, could be a great stimulant, but she would never be able to embark on a magical adventure feeling it.

Finally, Anaíd was greeted by each one of the coven's attendees. Valeria offered Anaíd her pentagram, and Cornelia Fatta, the matriarch of the powerful Fatta lineage and the chief of the crow's clan, gave Anaíd her athame, a double-edged knife Anaíd would carry from now on to cut the branches, herbs, and roots needed to prepare potions; trace magical circles; and defend herself.

Old Lucrecia, who at one hundred and one still participated in the covens as the matriarch of the snakes, recited a chant as she caressed the moon stones Anaíd carried around her neck. The old snake confessed that she could feel Deméter's hands in them. Then, she took off Anaíd's clothes; anointed her with the ashes of a sacred oak tree; and invited her to take a purifying bath in the dark ocean.

When she came out of the water, Anaíd wasn't the same. Now she was a witch. An initiated witch who, despite belonging to the clan of the she-wolves, had the support of Valeria Crocce's dolphins, Cornelia Fatta's crows, and Lucrecia Lampedusa's snakes. Anaíd was now protected by the other three elements of nature: water, air, and fire.

It was all so stimulating that Anaíd felt suddenly weak. The ritual, the chants, the dancing, the gifts, and the tests had immersed her in a state of constant excitement.

The only thing missing was her dream.

Criselda, her closest relative, gave her the earthen bowl she should keep for future ceremonies and invited her to drink a potion. It tasted bitter but Anaíd drank it all nonetheless.

A few minutes later, Anaíd felt dizzy. The witches began to chant around her, and she burst into a spontaneous, rhythmic dance that slowly dragged her to other dimensions of perception. Then her body abandoned her and she fell into a restless, enlightening dream. It was the dream of the initiated.

The witches surrounded her affectionately, watched over her, and studied her facial expressions, which revealed her anxieties, fears, and happiness.

• • •

Anaíd dreamed that she had wings and was flying through the skies, her long hair rippling behind. There was light beneath her and darkness above. As she descended, the light turned to fire and the air in the sky acquired a liquid texture. Anaíd penetrated the fire and picked up a red stone with her mouth. Her skin was burning, but Anaíd didn't release the stone, and she began her return through the water. She traveled through the water in the form of a dolphin and came out to the surface as a wolf. In the forest, Anaíd howled to the moon and cried.

When she awoke, Anaíd narrated her confusing dream to the witches. It was so fresh that she felt as if she were still inside it.

Valeria listened and then interpreted her dream.

"Her journey will be long and dangerous, but the strength of her heart will help her move forward. She will be weakened by doubt. She will reach the insides of the earth, under the water, and will find the treasure she's looking for. She won't give in to pain, or avoid danger, and for that she'll have to use her skills and power. The weight of her discovery, however, will frighten her and she will cry over her lost innocence."

Cornelia Fatta read the signs Anaíd's body had left on the sand.

"Her fate follows her like a shadow, and she will be deceived. But the sacrifice won't have been in vain."

Cornelia Fatta's confusing words left all the witches thinking. A worried feeling prevailed, but Valeria didn't let pessimism alarm them.

The time had come to talk about what was happening; it was the most eagerly awaited moment of the night.

"I won't hide anything from you," Valeria began. "The Odish are attacking us with increasing frequency. You know it, I know it—we all know it. They have Selene, the one with the hair of fire, and that makes them feel powerful. The chosen one is their weapon. As long as they have her, they will harass us. That's why we've initiated her daughter, Anaíd; so she can help us."

"What about Selene's clan? What have they done so far?" asked a crow.

"The she-wolf's clan was isolated for two months by an Odish bell. An Odish numbed their minds and tempted Anaíd. Fortunately, they managed to break out of the spell and now Anaíd has been initiated. As you know, her power and knowledge are remarkable. She's the only one who's been able to communicate with Selene until now. A mother cannot reject a daughter who truly wishes to find her. That's why Anaíd, on behalf of all us, and in order to fulfill the prophecy, will embark on the difficult mission of rescuing Selene and bringing her home, to the Omars."

"She might be able to reach Selene, but how will a child defeat the Odish?" asked a bony dolphin.

Criselda decided to intervene.

"She won't be alone, I'll go with her."

"And assuming that is possible, what will happen if Selene refuses to come back? What if Selene prefers the Odish's power, immortality, and wealth to the Omars' honesty?" inquired a witty owl.

"That's impossible! My mother is not and will never be an Odish! She would never betray us!"

Anaíd's outburst was so sincere that the owl who had asked the question fell silent, embarrassed. One could never discredit a mother, or attack her morals, in front of her child unless there was evidence against her.

Anaíd realized that her impulsiveness had silenced any unformulated questions. In the end, however, they all boiled down to one thing: distrust.

"May I speak?"

Anaíd waited a few seconds until a surprised Valeria nodded her approval.

"I know I'm not as strong as Valeria, as powerful as Deméter, or as wise as Lucrecia . . . I know that, even though I'm already a witch, I am not a woman yet and my age is a hindrance for confronting the Odish. But they are chasing *me*, so, by going after them, I'll become an unusual enemy. If I were an Odish, it would never cross my mind that someone like me would be so stupid to step into the wolf's mouth."

"And if the wolf shuts its mouth?" A dolphin cut her off.

Anaíd shrugged.

"You won't lose anything if I die. I, in turn, will lose a great deal if I don't run the risk. I'll lose my past, my lineage, my family, and my dignity. I've put everything on the scale and it weighs a considerable amount. I will look for my mother in hell if I have to. And if I return with the chosen one, remember the prophecy, the Odish will be destroyed forever. You, who are losing your babies and daughters, will also win. I'm only asking for your support, nothing more."

Anaíd paused and observed the effect her words had had around her.

Valeria and Criselda were speechless. Where did that child's poise and self-confidence come from? When had she learned how to address a crowd? How had she managed to touch so many women and get their support with just a few words?

But it wasn't only Anaíd's words that did it. Her perspective and innocence had convinced the witches that they had nothing to lose. Or perhaps they did. They could lose a brave young girl who, in a few years, might become a clan chief. Anaíd had inherited her grandmother's charisma and had the power of the chosen one's daughter. There was no doubt about that.

Valeria picked up where Anaíd left off.

"Are we willing to help Anaíd, the she-wolf's clan, and the Scythian tribe in this mission?"

Cornelia was the first one to respond.

"If luck is for the daring, Anaíd will have plenty of it. Good luck, Anaíd; the crows believe in you."

"But luck is not enough," Old Lucrecia interjected. "She'll have to defend herself. Some snakes have mastered the art of fighting. My granddaughter Aurelia is the best fighter of the fire clans. She'll teach you. Come closer, Aurelia."

A young, athletic snake, with very short black hair and a flat nose, stepped closer. She stood before Anaíd, her hands on her hips.

"I'll show you the art of fighting with the mind and unfolding the body, as requested by my grandmother, the chief of the snake clan and matriarch of the Lampedusa lineage." Then she clarified, "We've never shared these arts with any earth witch; you'll be the first one."

Aurelia's offer caused a slight commotion. The witches whispered among one another. Valeria smiled from ear to ear.

"You hadn't heard about Aurelia, the great fighter?" she asked Anaíd.

Anaíd hadn't.

"She's never been defeated and, until now, she's never had a disciple. We were afraid her knowledge would die with her."

Anaíd greeted her with respect.

"Fighting? I have to learn how to fight?"

"You will need it." Aurelia was firm.

Confused, Anaíd looked at Criselda for help, but her aunt's eyes confirmed what Anaíd had expected: she couldn't refuse.

CHAPTER 20

THE OATH

Criselda couldn't swim and got terribly seasick, but she still got on Valeria's boat. In the high seas, with only the moon and its pale reflection on the water for company, the clan chiefs and Criselda met after the initiation coven to assess the latest information they'd received on Selene's whereabouts. The situation couldn't be more dire.

A rosy young crow, the owner of a fresh pasta restaurant in Messina, related the rumor.

"They arrived a few weeks ago and bought the Salieri dukes' palazzo for pennies after a strange locust plague devastated their crops."

"Are you sure it's her?"

"Red-haired, foreign, tall, with green eyes; draws in her free time, swims like a fish, collects diamond rings, and dances by herself under the moonlight."

"Selene, without a doubt," confirmed Criselda.

The crow's cheeks were flushed.

"The redhead never leaves the estate, but the other one, the brazen one with dark hair and pale skin, goes out every night and comes back by sunrise. She never sees the sun."

"Salma," muttered Valeria, suddenly nervous.

"They are immensely rich and they've been splurging left and right. In town, they say that the girls who work in the palazzo mysteriously lose their memory and don't remember the horrors they witness there."

"What horrors?"

"There's talk of babies crying and girls bled to death."

"Have you found this out yourself?"

The crow sighed.

"My informant, a girl named Concetta, lost her memory and was then fired."

The island's three matriarchs and Criselda looked at one another, shocked. Old Lucrecia broke the silence.

"I wonder why they've come here."

"To challenge us, perhaps," suggested Valeria.

"Salma is very smart. She wants to frighten us," said Cornelia.

"And undermine the Omars' morale, including Anaíd's," Criselda added.

"Or to force us to make our move before it's time," said Valeria.

"It's just their way of showing their victory. The chosen one has been tempted," concluded Lucrecia in a Sicilian accent.

"But the alignment hasn't occurred yet," objected Criselda.

"That's why. We must move fast and prepare Anaíd," said Cornelia.

"First we should be completely sure of Anaíd's powers," said Valeria.

Criselda objected.

"You don't expect Anaíd to be able to rescue Selene by herself..."

Cornelia wisely reassured her.

"I trust you completely, Criselda. But you must understand that our only hope lies in the prophecy of Rosebuth."

Lucrecia thought aloud, "We all agree that the girl can't lose her love for Selene; she can't know what's happening."

"I suggest that just as we have supported her initiation, we pass on our secrets to her; she will need them during the hard mission of returning the chosen one to the community. My clan has already shared the secret of water with her," said Valeria.

Cornelia accepted.

"We will initiate her in the secret of the air."

Lucrecia approved.

"Besides the art of fighting, we will give her the secret of fire."

"What if, despite everything, she fails?" Criselda couldn't hide her fears.

"The oath," Valeria whispered softly.

"Is it necessary?" Criselda pleaded.

The three matriarchs exchanged glances and nodded. Criselda took out her athame and made an incision on the palm of her hand. She sucked out her blood and then made the matriarchs taste the blood on her palm.

"We swear by the blood of Criselda, joining us now, that we will defend with our lives the mission entrusted to Anaíd and her mentor from the Tsinoulis lineage."

"I, Criselda, swear to act with honesty and rigor, and to execute the sentence the Omars have pronounced against Selene, the chosen traitor. If Anaíd's mission fails . . . I will have to finish Selene with my own hands."

Treatise of McColleen

*When a comet comes near the sun, its nucleus warms up and the
volatile materials evaporate. The evaporated molecules become detached
and drag with them small solid particles that form the head of the comet, which
is formed by gas and dust. The shiny tail that develops sometimes extends
for millions of miles in space.*

*Hence our certainty that the first verse of the prophecy of
Oma announces the arrival of a comet:*

"The sky's fairy will comb her silver hair to receive her."
*Recent studies conducted by American observatories on the Kohouetek and
Hyakutake comets have made me believe that the arrival of the comet
predicted by O's prophecy is near. It will be unique; it won't visit the sun
again due to the severe alteration of its original orbits, caused by the gravitational
action of the gaseous giants in the outer solar system.*

CHAPTER 21

———

THE BIRTHDAY PARTY

When Anaíd got back that night, Clodia was waiting for her in bed, pretending to read with the bedside lamp on. She looked restless.

Before going out again, Valeria kissed Clodia and apologized to her daughter.

"The next initiation will be yours, I promise."

Clodia didn't respond. She enjoyed mortifying her mother. She knew it had been hard for Valeria to initiate Anaíd before her own daughter, and she was punishing her mother with her silence.

Valeria wished them both a good night, and as soon as Valeria had closed the door, Clodia jumped out of bed. Without saying a word to her roommate, she got dressed and began to put on makeup. She was shaking like a leaf.

"Are you leaving?"

"No, I'm trying to look nice to hook up with you."

Anaíd tried to ignore her but couldn't.

"You don't need to treat your mother that way."

"Mind your own business."

But Anaíd didn't feel like it. The ceremony had filled her with so much adrenaline that she wouldn't be able to fall asleep easily.

"Where are you going?"

"To a birthday party."

Anaíd was suddenly jealous that Clodia was invited to parties and she wasn't.

But something about that didn't make any sense.

"Why are you sneaking out?"

Clodia stopped putting on lipstick for a moment.

"Do you think that if my mother let me go to parties I would have to escape?"

"She doesn't let you?"

"No, and a big part of it is your fault."

"Mine?"

"It all started with that nonsense about your mother and her abduction."

"And what does that have to do with it?"

"That the Omars have panicked and are obsessed with that story. It's called a policy of fear."

Anaíd was indignant.

"We haven't invented anything! My mother *has* disappeared."

"She must have run off with someone."

Anaíd jumped out of bed and slapped her. Clodia was shocked—she didn't know whether to laugh or cry. Anaíd regretted it immediately; Clodia was shaking so much that her teeth chattered.

"What's the matter?"

"Get away from me!" Clodia shouted. And with trembling hands, she reached for the sweater on the chair and put it on over her T-shirt. The shaking stopped immediately, and Clodia breathed, relieved.

Anaíd, however, was even more aggravated.

"What are you doing with my sweater?"

Clodia was defensive.

"Putting it on. I'm cold."

"Where did you get it from?"

"It was on your bed."

"I didn't bring it here. I didn't put it in my suitcase."

"Oh, no? And how did it get to Sicily? Swimming or flying?"

Anaíd realized that it was implausible, but she was sure she hadn't grabbed the sweater. She had decided against bringing it because it was too thick. She'd had it in her hand when she was packing, but she had put it back in her closet. She was convinced of that.

Anaíd watched Clodia finish styling her hair with mousse; she was scratching her arms often.

"Give it back to me," said Anaíd, not knowing why she was saying that.

"If I take it off now, I will ruin my curls. I'm sorry."

Clodia grabbed her bag and jumped out the window. Anaíd felt stupid watching Clodia walk away while she still had on her pajamas. But she reacted quickly—she took off her pajamas and squeezed into a pair of jeans and a sleeveless T-shirt. Seconds later, she would be secretly following Clodia.

When she turned off the bedroom light, she thought she saw two small red lights in the darkness and felt a burning sensation on her back. But she was curious and angry, so she kept going.

Even though Clodia was wearing high-heeled sandals, she ran fast. She zigzagged through the yards of the beautiful houses by the beach, their fences covered by blooming wisterias.

From far away, Anaíd heard laughter and music filling the night. Clodia approached a garden that was adorned with garlands and colored lights. What Anaíd saw made her envious.

A group of boys and girls danced, drank, and laughed, and some embraced half-hidden behind the ivy and gardenias.

Anaíd saw how they cheered as Clodia approached and received her with a round of applause.

A tall, dark-haired boy with brown eyes and a pierced nose stepped forward and trotted toward her. Clodia shouted his name—Bruno—and they blended in an embrace, kissing passionately in front of their friends.

That sequence of images flashed before Anaíd's eyes in a few seconds. The night was brimming with stars and smelled of suntan lotion, makeup, alcohol, and sweat. They were young and having fun. Clodia laughed, chatted, and sitting on her boyfriend's lap, drank from a bottle. As she talked, her phrases were interrupted by long kisses, Bruno's hand on her knee, tickling her leg.

Anaíd didn't want to see any more. She got it. She understood Clodia, though she couldn't imagine how it felt. Was that happiness? Being in love, having friends, being invited to parties?

I am a great girl, in a great world, but it doesn't mean anything to me, if you are not here with me, said the song on the stereo.

Anaíd sat on the ground by the garden's fence. She hugged her knees to her chest and let herself be lulled by the music.

"Hi."

When she raised her head, she found a boy her age facing her. He was a bit thin, a bit pimply, and a bit shy.

"Hi," she replied halfheartedly.

"Would you like a drink?" He offered the bottle he was holding.

Anaíd had never had a drink before and was embarrassed to admit it.

"No, thanks."

"A smoke?"

Worse, she would start coughing.

"No, thanks."

"Would you like to go for a walk?"

Anaíd was tense. Was he making fun of her?

"No, thanks."

"Am I bothering you? Do you want me to go inside?"

Anaíd didn't know what to say. The boy was clearly making an effort to be polite, and she, who seconds before would have given anything to be normal, was now behaving like a perfectly abnormal person.

"No, please don't go."

A satisfied expression covered the teenager's face.

"My name is Mario."

"I'm Anaíd."

Mario sat next to her and lit a cigarette. Anaíd took in the sweet smoke of the cigarette, but she also smelled something unpleasant, pungent, and she wrinkled her nose.

"What's wrong?"

"Something smells bad."

"Are you saying I smell bad?"

"No . . . it's not you . . . it's . . ."

Anaíd glanced toward the spot where the strange scent was coming from. She thought she saw a shadow, but Mario was already on his feet, offended.

"Listen, sweetheart, we are not getting anywhere like this. I'm going for a walk."

Anaíd got up.

"I'm coming with you."

Mario started walking toward the beach. Standing next to him, Anaíd realized that anyone who saw them would probably think she was a normal girl leaving the party because she wanted to be alone to kiss him.

And why not?

Of course, Mario didn't seem willing to take the initiative. It wasn't surprising after so many disappointments. So Anaíd mustered courage and took the first step.

"Do you want to kiss me?"

Mario stopped in his tracks, speechless.

"You're just going to say it like that?"

Anaíd realized she had screwed up again.

"Well, how do you want me to ask you?"

"Not so suddenly."

"Slowly?"

"That's right."

Anaíd decided to put the cards on the table.

"I'm sorry; I've never kissed anyone before."

Mario coughed, uncomfortable.

"I think . . . I'm not ready."

Anaíd hesitated. Was this a no? A postponement? A haphazard escape?

"You haven't kissed anyone either?"

"I didn't say that!"

"I think that we're in the same situation," Anaíd admitted.

"Give me a break!"

"And you are freaking out."

But Mario would have rather died than admit it.

"No, you just don't inspire me."

Anaíd felt her blood boil.

"I . . . don't inspire you?"

"Not at all; I can't be romantic when you are so unromantic."

Anaíd was expecting him to call her ugly, childish, or inexperienced, but the word "unromantic" was a lot worse. That meant it was her nature. She produced romantic repulsion. She repelled kisses, as if she were covered in a boy repellent instead of a mosquito repellent.

Indignant, she imagined Mario as a mosquito trying to bite her unsuccessfully and . . .

Mario's arms began to flutter and he moved convulsively, emitting a buzzing sound.

"What are you doing, Mario!"

"*ZZZZZZZZ!*"

Anaíd covered her mouth, horrified. Mario thought he was a mosquito.

Luckily, everyone had been drinking and wouldn't think anything of a boy strangely hopping around the beach, mimicking a flying insect.

But Anaíd wanted to die. She had just been initiated as an Omar witch, she had been appointed the leader of the good forces, and, a few hours later, she was making a poor boy think he was a mosquito because he had rejected her.

Worse, she hadn't known she was casting a spell. It had slipped, in a manner of speaking.

The good thing, on the other hand, was that she'd finally mastered the antidote to her spells.

Drooling, his arms cramped from so much flying, Mario plopped down on the sand and began to slowly move his fingers to make sure they responded. He didn't understand what had just happened.

Meanwhile, Anaíd quietly walked away.

Her first attempt at being normal had been a total disaster.

CHAPTER 22

ONE MORE TIME

"One more time."

Anaíd jumped in the air again, leaving the optical illusion of her body in front of Aurelia. Then she moved at the speed of light and surprised her contender from the right.

But this wasn't Aurelia; it was an illusion too. Aurelia was standing behind her and pressed her finger on Anaíd's jugular, paralyzing her. Anaíd screamed with pain and dropped her arms in defeat. It was impossible to catch Aurelia by surprise; she would never be able to beat her.

"One more time," said Aurelia, relentlessly.

Anaíd was exhausted. Aurelia was so strict—she wouldn't let her rest, and forced her to do the same exercises over and over again until they became automatic, mechanical. At night, when Anaíd plopped down in bed, she kept hearing "one more time," like a drum beating in her ears. And, when she heard that phrase, her body contracted and she resigned herself to lose. But this time, Anaíd rebelled.

"I can't take it anymore. I can't surprise you. I'm trying to unfold as quickly as you do, but I can't."

"One more time," replied Aurelia, impassively.

Anaíd exploded. Didn't Aurelia understand? Was she deaf?

Anaíd had been clear. She didn't have the strength or the energy to try something so ridiculous and was obviously destined to fail again.

"One more time," Aurelia insisted, her voice neutral and monotonous.

And the disciple knew that, until she'd made real progress, she would keep hearing that phrase, devoid of meaning but as terrifying as a drop of water rhythmically falling on her frayed nerves. So she did the only thing she could think of. She focused her rage toward Aurelia and thought of how nice it would be to surprise her and be able to use the same mocking tone on her. Anaíd smiled at the thought of pronouncing those stubborn words herself. "One more time," she would tell a confused Aurelia, who would look in every direction without knowing where or how she'd be attacked by the superfast Anaíd. Without hesitating, she leaped at the speed of light and completely modified her technique. She moved in the opposite direction, keeping her body in front of Aurelia while she unfolded the illusion of her body to one side.

"Look me in the eye!" shouted Aurelia.

Anaíd didn't know whether confusion or submission made her do it, but her body and not the illusion of it looked at Aurelia—and was trapped by the teacher's claws.

"Damn!" shouted Anaíd, aware of the trick now.

"*Never* listen to your opponent when you fight. One more time."

This time, Anaíd risked everything. Aurelia had taught her how to unfold the illusion of her body and move as swiftly as lightning. Aurelia could distinguish the two bodies perfectly well—the real one and the fake one. What if Anaíd tried with three bodies? The milliseconds it would take Aurelia to rule out possibilities would be enough for Anaíd to catch her off guard.

She decided to try surrounding Aurelia with illusions and attacking her head-on this time.

When three Anaíds surrounded Aurelia, she was actually disconcerted by the risky move. Before she could unfold into many Aurelias, she was neutralized by Anaíd's arm around her neck.

Defeated, Aurelia smiled for the first time in the long days of training. Anaíd even thought she looked beautiful. The smile softened her hard eyes and her captivating white teeth lit up her sun-tanned face.

"How did you do that?" asked Aurelia.

"One more time," suggested Anaíd.

And again, even though Aurelia was aware of her disciple's trick, she lost too much time trying to tell the real Anaíd apart from the others and was defeated for the second time. But Aurelia didn't lose courage. Quite the opposite, she seemed more eager to continue fighting.

"It's a new technique, and much more effective. One more time."

And Aurelia tried to imitate Anaíd and unfolded into two Aurelias, but she wasn't able to pull it off and was beaten again.

"One more time," Anaíd said again.

They continued fighting for hours until, exhausted, they realized that they were both prisoners of their opponent. They were tied.

"You've figured it out," said Anaíd. "That's great."

"What do you mean 'I've figured it out'?" protested Aurelia. "I'm your teacher. It is you who has learned how to fight."

Anaíd stood up.

"Oh, yeah? One more time."

Aurelia burst out laughing.

"Have you dreamed of me? Have I been your worst enemy? Do you want me to swallow my 'one more times' with a good dose of thorn apple?"

Anaíd blushed.

"How do you know?"

"That's what happened to me when Juno, the fighter who trained me, had me on a diet of 'one more times' for a year, until I defeated her."

"A year?" Anaíd was horrified.

They had been practicing for two weeks and it felt like an eternity.

"And how did you teach me in such a short time?"

Aurelia wiped the sweat from her forehead and offered Anaíd a sip of grapefruit juice.

"The accomplishment is not mine. I knew you were better than me."

Anaíd wanted to die. She had made another enemy. Why did she have to be so clueless and not realize that nobody liked to be second best?

"That's not true, there is so much I could never do . . ."

Aurelia was surprised to see that Anaíd was embarrassed.

"Hey, hey, hey . . . Do you think I'm jealous?"

Anaíd was mortified now.

"I don't know, I don't think so, but . . ."

Aurelia stood up and pointed at Anaíd.

"You don't even know how powerful you are."

Anaíd turned pale. What was she trying to say?

"Powerful?"

"Do you know how many dolphin witches have been able to learn the art of transformation?"

Anaíd shrugged. She thought all dolphins could do that.

"Valeria is the only one, and she doubts that Clodia will ever learn how to transform herself."

This time Anaíd choked and began to cough.

"So I'm the only one who's ever done it, besides Valeria?"

"Selene was trying to, but she had to go back to Urt."

A warm feeling invaded Anaíd when she heard her mother's name.

"It was my mother who asked Valeria to teach me," she thought out loud.

Aurelia grabbed her towel.

"Do you realize that Valeria didn't teach you anything?"

"What do you mean?"

"She transformed in front of you, but she didn't tell you *how* to do it."

Anaíd didn't want to feel different. She had never been happy feeling different. She wanted to be just another witch, not a "special" witch.

"Just as I didn't teach you how to unfold into multiple illusions. You learned it on your own."

"Actually, I did it using the same idea. It's a question of will and focus," Anaíd explained.

"And power."

Anaíd brought her hands to her head.

"You shouldn't have told me."

"You are the chosen one's daughter," Aurelia insisted. "You have inherited her power and must learn how to use it."

"But she's not here to teach me."

Aurelia sympathized with Anaíd.

"I know, but we all know that only you can help her."

"I'm really scared," she confessed.

Aurelia sat next to Anaíd and stroked her hair.

"I know it is hard to know that those who should protect you are less skilled than you. It happened to me when I was a child."

"What?"

"It was horrible . . ."

240

"What happened?"

"My sister was killed by an Odish."

Anaíd remembered the images of pale, deformed, and blood-less Omar girls in her books. She shuddered.

"I was little. We slept in the same room. I'd noticed she'd been afraid and anxious for several days. Then one night, I saw an Odish come to her bed and squeeze out the last drops of blood from her heart."

Anaíd was horrified.

"And what did you do?"

"I fought the Odish. Nobody had taught me how, but it is an ancient art among the snakes. It was instinctive."

"How brave."

"But I was a child and believed that mothers are always stronger than their daughters. So I asked my mother for help."

"And what happened?"

"My mother surrendered."

Anaíd was silent. Aurelia's story had answered many of her own questions.

"One more time . . . ," Anaíd whispered.

Aurelia wiped a tiny tear with the back of her hand.

"I swore I would never give up again and then realized that *that* was the snake's fighting technique. I knew it by instinct, but not all of us have the instinct. My mother lacked it."

"Have you ever fought another Odish again?"

Aurelia glanced around. Then she took Anaíd's hand and guided her to the showers. She opened the faucet and confessed, "Once," the sound of the water drowning out the word.

"Why are you telling me here?"

Aurelia seemed uncomfortable.

"It's forbidden."

"Fighting against the Odish is forbidden?"

"Don't you know the story of Om? Om hid her daughter Oma to prevent her sister Od from bleeding her. That's what we, the Omars, have done for thousands of years; we've hidden and avoided the fire."

"But Om didn't turn a blind eye to what was happening; she destroyed the crops and brought winter."

"Exactly. That's why we've learned how to dominate the elements."

Anaíd couldn't fully piece together the puzzle.

"But I'm an exception. I'm learning how to fight . . . A sister coven has entrusted me the mission to rescue Selene from the Odish, that's why you are teaching me how to fight."

"They're afraid, really afraid."

"Of what?"

"Of the chosen one."

"Of Selene? My mother?"

"The prophecy predicts the end of the Omars if Selene turns into an Odish."

"But that's ridiculous. My mother would never sell herself to an Odish."

"Let's hope not."

Anaíd sensed the anxiety in those words, the alarm interlaced in every syllable, the long hesitation before the word "not." Could a fighter like Aurelia be intimidated?

"Are you afraid too?" Anaíd asked.

"Salma is back."

"Salma? I heard that name from Valeria. Who is she?"

"A very cruel Odish. She's had thousands of names and appearances over the years."

Anaíd shuddered.

"What does that mean?"

"That something will happen, if it is not already happening."

"I need to hurry, don't I?"

Aurelia showed Anaíd her left foot; she was missing two toes.

"If you ever have to fight against an Odish, remember these two things—one for each toe I've lost."

Anaíd stepped closer.

"*Never* believe them, even if what they're saying seems possible, or if there is a hint of truth in their words. Don't listen to them. They will mislead you."

Anaíd engraved this golden piece of advice in her mind.

"And the second one?"

"Never look them in the eye. Their power lies in their eyes. They can freeze your mind and pierce your heart with them. Avoid looking at them. Fight always in the dark, or cover your eyes with a bandage—anything that will protect you from their gaze."

Anaíd was anxious for more.

"Anything else?"

Quietly, Aurelia walked closer.

"Yes," she whispered. "There's something extremely important."

"What?"

And she shoved Anaíd under the shower's icy stream. Anaíd screamed. Aurelia laughed.

"Always be on guard, silly girl!"

Anaíd got out of the shower dripping. She stood in front of Aurelia, her hands on her hips.

"One more time," she challenged her.

CHAPTER 23

BLOOD

The door burst open with the force of a gale. In her room, Salma opened her eyes, surprised.

"What do you want, Selene? Why didn't you knock before coming in?"

Selene looked taller, stronger, more fearsome than ever. She pointed at the baby Salma was holding.

"What does this mean?"

Salma placed the child on the bed. He was sleeping peacefully.

"What's wrong? Does this upset you? Do my pleasures bother you?"

Selene slammed the door, its echo reverberating across the room like a slap. She walked toward Salma, pointing her diamond-studded index finger in her face.

"Do you think I'm stupid?" she asked, and unleashed a storm of dust at Salma.

Salma was disconcerted, but recovered in time, freezing the particles in midair.

"What's the matter?"

Selene laughed, mimicking Salma's hollow laughter.

"The Countess will be very angry if she finds out that instead of following her orders, you're indulging your whims, disregarding the consequences of your excesses. You're defying her power and mine."

"There have been no such excesses." Salma was, of course, lying.

"Oh, no? The whole island has heard about them. There are pictures in the newspaper of the bloodless girls and missing babies; all Omars."

"Oh, right."

"Right? What's right? The alignment hasn't occurred yet, but it is about to. Do you look at the sky every night, Salma? I do, I dream of the alignment, and when that happens, I swear, Salma, that my first act of power will be to punish you. Are you trying to become more powerful than me? Do you want to displace the Countess? How much blood have you already had? Enough to live an extra hundred years? This wasn't the deal, Salma. You've played dirty."

Salma recoiled.

"I need to recover my strength."

"That's not true!" thundered Selene. "You are challenging me. Fine, Salma, from now on I order you to give me your victims for my own pleasure. You've had a feast. And look for them outside the island. This is my house; I will reign from this palace."

"Reign? Please, don't make me laugh. Where's your scepter?"

Selene took another step forward.

"It will appear soon, and when I have it in my hands you won't talk back to me anymore."

Selene picked up the baby, who was now awake and began to cry. She undressed him slowly and found the small gash Salma had opened in his chest. Slowly, she brought her mouth to the tiny incision.

Salma was fuming.

"You said you didn't agree with our methods."

Selene raised her head and glared at her.

"That was before; before I owned all of this. Why would I ruin it? I'm not as stupid as you thought."

Salma stormed out of the room, furious.

"Where are you going? Remember what I've told you," Selene warned her.

"There are exceptions to the rule," Salma replied. And she left, leaving Selene alone with the crying baby in her arms.

THE PROPHECY OF OD

Gold, blood, and immortality for the chosen one.

Beautiful as mother of pearl her skin,

Eternal moons her time,

In her dreams of surrendered loves.

Extreme ambition,
Equal parts envy and jealousy
Adds betrayal to revenge.
She will be tempted and will succumb to temptation.

CHAPTER 24

CLODIA'S SECRET

Anaíd strolled around the beach. She had graduated from her fighting lessons with honors, but instead of feeling proud, she was overwhelmed by a sudden feeling of emptiness. She might have become a warrior, but . . . would that be enough to combat her loneliness, her inability to make friends, her unattractiveness, or her orphanhood?

Back in the house, she found Clodia lying in bed. Her roommate never went to bed early, and Anaíd, convinced that this was a trick, was expecting Clodia to get up, change, put on makeup, and climb out the window.

But she stayed in bed, coughing and shaking under two blankets and a twill quilt.

"Are you sick?"

A strange silence followed. They had barely spoken during the past few weeks. They were like two strangers sharing a room, and now, Anaíd had asked a personal question.

"It's freezing," Clodia said after a while. "Aren't you cold?"

It was the middle of summer, and the temperature on the island was stifling, suffocating; especially for Anaíd, who was used to the mountain air.

"You must be sick."

"No!" Clodia shot back defensively.

Anaíd didn't say anything.

"Or maybe I am . . . ," Clodia whispered.

"Have you told Valeria?"

"Are you crazy?"

Anaíd remained silent and Clodia opened up like an oyster, slowly, painfully.

"I think I got sick the night of the storm. I caught a cold and haven't been able to shake it. I can't sleep well."

"Does anything hurt?"

"My bones, my chest when I breathe, and my head."

The mere effort of speaking gave her a coughing fit. Anaíd got up and felt Clodia's forehead. She was freezing, ice cold. How bizarre! She didn't have a fever . . . Before Anaíd could take away her hand, Clodia stopped her.

"No, please, leave it there; it makes me feel better."

Anaíd felt reassured. Clodia was asking her to heal her headache. She placed both hands on Clodia's icy forehead and absorbed the cold that enveloped her roommate. Anaíd felt how it took hold of her own body and oppressed her heart. Clodia stopped shaking and smiled. That was enough for Anaíd to continue. With renewed strength, she carefully felt Clodia's skull and her fingers stretched magically, penetrating each and every swollen nerve in Clodia's brain. With the tips of her fingers, Anaíd could feel the tensions dissolve and the blood begin to flow freely again. Clodia's breathing, agonized before, was normal again, and her face relaxed. She closed her eyes and her eyelashes fluttered unconsciously.

Anaíd observed her for some time. Asleep like this, her dark, curly hair on the pillow framing her sweet, oval face, Clodia reminded Anaíd of a classical angel. In front of her, Anaíd saw a girl who was in love and suffered because her mother kept her imprisoned. She regretted not being able to be Clodia's friend.

Back in bed, Anaíd started shivering from head to toe. She felt terribly cold and her teeth chattered. Clodia's cold had taken over her body. She opened the closet, put on her sweater, and felt immediately better. Then she plopped down in bed, exhausted, and closed her eyes.

When she awoke hours later, Anaíd was sweating profusely and felt an intense stinging sensation on her skin. The sweater's rough wool was to blame, she thought. Had she fallen asleep wearing a sweater in the middle of summer? When she tried to take it off, she felt that acrid stench again, the same one she'd smelled at Clodia's friends' party. Her instincts told her not to move.

That's when she heard Clodia moaning and crying. She seemed to be having a terrifying nightmare. But when she tried to get up to comfort her, Anaíd's body didn't respond. She felt the horror of paralysis. Even though she sent orders to her extremities, Anaíd's body was inert, deaf. Her eyes didn't respond either, they remained shut. Thinking she might be dreaming, she tried to wake herself up, but the smell was too strong and Clodia's crying was real. Anaíd was actually awake. So what was happening?

A spell. Anaíd was under a spell.

Focusing all her energy on her eyelids, she made a desperate attempt to break free from her paralysis. That had been one of Criselda's lessons—when panic distorts your feelings, concentrate your strength on only one point.

Her eyelids were as heavy as a cart full of rocks; opening them would require the strength of a hundred men. Up, up, up . . .

She'd done it! The room was in semidarkness, and Clodia's

dolls and plush toys lined up on her shelves cast ghastly shadows on the wall. Anaíd blinked. Slowly and with effort, she turned her head and was able to get a glimpse of Clodia's bed. Sitting on it was a shadow as grotesque and surreal as the ones on the wall—the silhouette of a slender woman with long fingers, who was rummaging in Clodia's chest.

Anaíd wanted to scare her away, but she must have made a noise because the woman, alerted by the movement, pierced her with her eyes. Anaíd sank into a terrible nightmare.

· · ·

Anaíd was sweating. The kitchen was burning, the midday sun was burning, and, most of all, her face was burning with embarrassment for what she was about to do.

"I don't want you to think I go around telling on what other people are doing; but listen, Clodia is pale, she coughs a lot, and she has dark circles under her eyes. Her head hurts and she's been having nightmares."

Valeria listened as she checked the roast in the oven.

"Yes, I noticed. I've prepared her an energizing potion. She has a bad cold."

Anaíd nodded.

"Her chest hurts and she has nightmares."

"What about her bones? Do they hurt too?"

"Yes."

"That's what I thought; she has the flu."

Anaíd wrung her hands uncomfortably.

"I think I saw a shadow in her room last night."

Valeria, who had been paying more attention to the roast than to Anaíd's words, paused and immediately slammed the oven door shut.

251

"Speak clearly, I don't like hints."

"I think that an Odish is bleeding her."

"In this house?" Valeria was speechless.

"Yes."

"My own daughter?"

"Yes."

"How?"

"She takes advantage of the fact that you're not paying much attention."

Valeria, usually calm, was now furious. Anaíd took a step back.

"You'd better watch it, Anaíd. The fact that I treat you like a daughter doesn't give you the right to judge how I take care of my family. Got it? If I've neglected Clodia, it's been because of you. Remember that."

"I didn't mean to insult you, but—"

"You should apologize to me."

"I'm sorry."

"And I don't want to hear another word about this nonsense. No Odish would dare bleed my daughter under my nose."

Anaíd brought her hands to her cheeks, even more embarrassed—if that was possible—than at the beginning of the conversation. She had made a mistake, both in form and in content. She didn't have the courage to tell Valeria about Clodia's frequent escapes at night, her secret boyfriend, or the fact Clodia usually got rid of the protection shield at night. If Valeria heard that, she would probably take Anaíd's suspicions more seriously. But saying more would only make her look like a miserable tattletale.

That afternoon, they began preparing for the divination ceremony. They lit some firewood and went looking for a rabbit.

Anaíd noticed that Clodia was distant. She walked away if Anaíd got close, and pretended not to hear her. She was the same old unpleasant Clodia again.

Valeria, however, was a lot more attentive and deferential with her daughter. She offered Clodia her athame to officiate the ritual and held the rabbit tight for her. With determination and a firm hand, Clodia chopped off the animal's head in a single blow. Anaíd was used to the sacrifices of pigs, hens, and rabbits, but in Urt, no girl Clodia's age would dare to take the knife and use it with such precision. Valeria placed the silver basin on the ground so that the animal's blood could drip into it, splattering the beautiful metal with red.

Then Clodia gave the athame to Valeria, who, with a clean cut, opened the rabbit from top to bottom and took out its warm entrails. Mother and daughter spread the naked, labyrinthine remnants of pulsating life, full of corners and mysteries, on the surface of a silver tray.

Moving their heads silently, Clodia and Valeria began to distinguish the signs they saw in the color, texture, and shape of the rabbit's liver and intestines. They acted with such complicity that Anaíd felt suddenly excluded and regretted having opened her mouth.

She would never learn how to bite her tongue in time. Anyway, what did she care about that conceited liar?

Clodia took the initiative and pronounced the augury.

"The right place for you to communicate with Selene is the stone quarries, in Syracuse."

"The stone quarries?" Anaíd asked, intrigued. "What are the stone quarries?"

And, after posing the question, she eyed Clodia sideways, expecting a sarcastic response to her ignorance. But Clodia, pale, with dark rings under her eyes, remained silent. This was a much more sophisticated form of condescension—Anaíd didn't exist for her. Valeria spoke for both of them.

"The stone quarries are caverns excavated in the old limestone mines. The most beautiful buildings in Syracuse were erected with the stone extracted from them: the temple of Jupiter, for instance, the theater, the fortress of Ortygia. Seven thousand Athenians were kept prisoner in the stone quarries during the war against Athens, and then they were sold as slaves."

"And I will be able to communicate with my mother there?"

"That's what the omens say."

They were interrupted by Criselda. She'd entered the room holding a tray with a pitcher and glasses and tripped when she slipped on some spilled drops of blood. Poor Criselda, she was so clumsy that even though she tried to hold the glasses, they fell one by one to the ground and shattered. Valeria and Clodia stared motionlessly at the damage. Criselda apologized as best as she could and crouched to pick up the pieces, but she stopped when Valeria and Clodia screamed in unison.

"Nooo!"

They were both horrified.

"What's the matter?" asked Criselda.

"Don't touch anything! We should create a spell to counteract the bad omen."

"What omen?"

Clodia couldn't believe what she was hearing.

"Can't you see it?"

As she deciphered the message in the glass scattered on the honey-colored tiles, Criselda took her hands to her mouth too. Clodia pointed at the floor.

"I see a death in the near future. A terrible, awful death."

Valeria held Clodia's arm.

"I see a devastating fire that will destroy the land and put our lives in danger."

Clodia covered her eyes.

"I see pain, tears cried from sadness and suffering."

Anaíd glanced at Criselda, who stood small and distressed as she listened to Clodia's and Valeria's threatening words. The reputation of the Etruscan oracles was enough for her to take the bad omen of death and desolation they announced seriously. Anaíd agreed with Criselda—the imminence of a terrible event floated in the air. Both Criselda and Anaíd looked at each other, astonished, when they realized they were communicating telepathically.

Nobody that night had the stomach to taste the rabbit stew.

Anaíd decided to create a protection shield for the bedroom she shared with Clodia, but she had to wait until Clodia got in bed. Then she stayed awake, vigilant. Clodia breathed heavily.

"Do you want me to give you a massage so you can sleep better?"

Clodia's reply was hostile.

"Don't touch me, big mouth."

Anaíd cowered in her bed. It wasn't fair; she was trying to protect her. Now Clodia was angry at her instead of blaming Valeria or the Odish.

Clodia's sleep was intermittent, full of rasping breaths and abrupt starts. She said she couldn't breathe, walked toward the open window, took in the light breeze, and then returned to bed.

The acrid stench that had invaded the garden days ago now overlapped with the scent of the gardenias and wisterias.

Anaíd was alert.

A presence in the garden was causing Clodia's uncontrollable anxiety. An Odish witch was outside, but she couldn't get into the

house or cast a spell without the power of her stare. She was calling Clodia insistently, like a cow calling her calf, and Clodia was
eager to please her. Suddenly, Clodia got up, ready to put on her
clothes.

"Where are you going?"

Anaíd stood between Clodia and her clothes. Clodia's hands
tried to reach for her jeans.

"Bruno is sick. He needs me."

Anaíd turned on the light.

"How do you know?"

"I know it. I'm a witch, just like you. It's that death omen. It
announced Bruno's death."

"You are wrong."

"Shut up."

But Anaíd didn't want to shut up. She switched off the light,
took Clodia's hand, and guided her to the window. The shape of a
woman was perfectly silhouetted among the garden's shadows.

"Do you see her?"

"Of course I see her. She's Bruno's cousin. She's come to pick
me up."

"You're crazy! She's an Odish. She's bleeding you, that's why
you are so pale and sick, why you moan in dreams and have that
pain in your heart. Open your shirt and I'll show you the wound."

"Leave me alone, don't touch me."

Anaíd withdrew her hands. Clodia, clearly nervous, coughed
and had difficulty breathing.

"Why can't I leave this room?"

Anaíd couldn't lie to her.

"I've created a spell so no one can harm you."

Clodia put her hand on her chest; she was incredibly agitated.
She paced around the small room for a few minutes, like a lion in

a cage, and then stopped in front of the window. She seemed to mull something over, then sat down and lowered her head to her chest.

"So Bruno's cousin is actually an Odish, and she's bleeding me?"

Anaíd let down her guard. Clodia was finally beginning to accept the situation.

"I saw her last night in this room, by your bed."

"And that's why you talked to my mother; you wanted to protect me."

Anaíd nodded. Clodia brought her hands to her head.

"I've been so stupid! I understand now. You just wanted to help me."

Anaíd took her hand; it was freezing cold.

"It's okay, put something warm on and rest."

She extended her wool sweater as a peace offering. Clodia accepted it and put on the sweater with a thankful smile; but she didn't get into bed.

"The shield won't prevent me from going to the bathroom, right? I'm about to wet myself."

Anaíd broke the spell for a moment.

"Okay, you can go, but hurry or the Odish could slip into the room and paralyze me with her eyes."

"Okay." Clodia walked to the bathroom on tiptoe.

Anaíd studied the Odish's movements from the window. She was walking away from the house, toward her car parked on the street. Anaíd sighed, relieved. The Odish was giving up.

When she heard the toilet flushing, Anaíd left her vantage point. She got ready to re-create the shield, but she was taken aback by the sound of hurried steps and the stifled thud of a door closing. What was going on?

She looked out the window with a terrible feeling. She was right—Clodia was running to the car barefoot and in her pajamas. The car's engine was still running, its door open. Anaíd had been deceived. Clodia was smarter than she seemed.

Anaíd shouted but decided to take matters into her own hands. She grabbed her athame and birchwood wand, jumped out the window, slid down the trunk of the cherry tree, and ran after Clodia. Once on the street, she followed her instincts and created an illusion spell. Seconds later, she was sitting at the wheel of Selene's car. This time, she had no trouble driving. She sped after the Odish's white car, which stood out clearly on the winding road. Anaíd kept a safe distance and didn't turn on her headlights.

From the main road, the white car swerved onto a reddish dirt road through the woods that slowly ascended the south wall of the island's majestic volcano, Mount Etna. Anaíd drove riddled with fear—she knew that the smallest hesitation would mean the end of the illusion spell. She tried to convince herself that she was driving Selene's real car and followed the white dot in the distance.

Finally, the white car stopped and its lights went out. Anaíd broke the illusion spell and continued on foot. As the spell vanished, she felt somewhat unprotected, but the forest wasn't a murmur of disquieting sounds anymore. She could now distinguish the voices of the scavengers, those who hunted in the shadows protected by the darkness.

As she walked on, she was lulled by the owl's singing and the bellowing of a young male deer sharpening its antlers on a tree in preparation for the autumn rut.

Anaíd walked toward the light coming from a small shepherd's cottage. Her march was slow and cautious. She had no plans, other than preventing Clodia's death. As she moved forward with confidence, she called Criselda telepathically, in the hope that Valeria would renounce her bloody pride and find a way to rescue Clodia. Criselda replied, warning Anaíd about the danger she faced and urging her to act with caution.

Anaíd decided to wait for Criselda and Valeria, but what she could see through a gap between the door and the jamb was dismal: white as a sheet, Clodia moaned in her sleep, her voice increasingly weak. She was agonizing. The Odish witch stroked Clodia's naked chest and then licked her own lips, from which tiny pink pearls dribbled. It was blood. Anaíd could have tolerated that sight, but what happened next was too much. With her white, elegant, slender fingers, the Odish opened one of Clodia's vacant eyes and felt the eyeball, ready to pull it out.

Anaíd had to stop her.

The stone cottage was furnished with only a wooden table, four chairs, a chest, and a cot by the fireplace. On the floor lay the sweater. Anaíd studied everything carefully and hoped her entrance would have a shocking effect.

One, two, three.

Throwing opening the door, she walked into the small hut and cast a darkness spell to extinguish the oil lamp hanging from a beam.

She didn't want to look the Odish in the eye—if she did, she would be finished. She sought refuge in the darkness and controlled her opponent's movements by positioning herself behind her. This way, the dim reflection of the moon, in its last quarter, illuminated her enemy's body and Anaíd could remain hidden in the darkest part of the room. Anaíd knew she had surprised her for a moment. The Odish paused and dropped Clodia on the floor, looking toward the spot where Anaíd was hiding. Anaíd wasn't going to attack; she needed to buy some time to save Clodia's life.

"Are you hiding from me? Are you afraid of me?"

Anaíd fought hard not to listen to her words. The Odish's voice was like a sweet caress filled with deceit.

The question was a ploy to distract Anaíd, but the Odish wasn't able to take her by surprise—Aurelia's training had prepared Anaíd for this. When she felt the lunge, Anaíd's body unfolded into three. The Odish struck one of Anaíd's illusions with her wand.

"Impressive. I see you are familiar with the snake's art of fighting."

Anaíd didn't respond. She felt the strength of the Odish measuring the range of her protection shield. This witch was very powerful. The intense acrid smell stung Anaíd's senses and grew stronger by the second. The Odish was planning attack strategies. She lunged again, and this time, even though Anaíd jumped to the side and unfolded in two, she couldn't stop her. The Odish's wand reopened the wound caused by the rupture of the bell. Once again, Anaíd felt a lacerating pain in her leg.

Not willing to waste a second, Anaíd took *her* by surprise this time. She charged at the Odish with her athame. It was a spontaneous gesture but it did the trick. Anaíd felt the knife sink into the Odish's hand and heard an object fall to the ground. But she didn't wait to find out what it was or the importance of the wound she'd inflicted. The Odish screamed and her cry echoed in the night. If only she would faint from the pain and allow more time for the other Omars to arrive . . .

The Odish paused; she was panting and holding her hand with rage. Anaíd felt the sound of fabric tearing. She was creating a

260

tourniquet with a piece of her blouse. Anaíd had cut off one of her fingers.

Anaíd could barely move. She knew she didn't have the strength to heal her reopened wound. The only thing Anaíd could do was try to finish off the Odish once and for all. She lunged with all her might, but the witch was expecting her this time. Howling like a wolf, Anaíd charged again, but when her knife came into contact with the Odish's skin, it shattered into a thousand pieces. A splinter pierced Anaíd's arm, and she took a few steps back, perplexed.

They could hear one another's irregular breathing, waiting for the next attack.

"You are a very powerful snake."

Anaíd decided to speak. "I'm not a snake."

Anaíd knew she couldn't listen to her lies or believe her flattering words. Though she could barely move, she must find a way to distract the Odish. The poison, that excruciating poison that had penetrated her body long ago, had been reactivated and was spreading to her extremities. She needed an antidote.

"So, what are you?"

"I'm a wolf. My name is Anaíd, from the Tsinoulis lineage."

"The lineage of Selene Tsinoulis?"

"I'm her daughter."

"Selene's daughter?"

Anaíd noticed the surprise her words had caused in the Odish. She didn't know about her? That was strange. Anaíd's arrival to the island had been announced with great fanfare, and the dolphins weren't exactly discreet.

"Are you really Selene's daughter?"

"And Deméter's granddaughter."

"My name is Salma."

Anaíd was petrified. If Salma discovered her vulnerability, she would destroy her in a few seconds. But for the moment, Anaíd had disconcerted her. *Go, Anaíd!* she said to herself. *This Odish is not made of stone. What are you waiting for? Rub your finger in her wound.*

"And how is it that a powerful witch like Salma doesn't know that Selene's daughter is sleeping by Clodia's side every night?"

Salma didn't reply immediately; she panted. She was confused. Something had escaped her, but if she felt betrayed or insecure she didn't show it. She laughed happily—a fake, hollow laugh that had a calming effect and the ability to lighten the mood. Anaíd felt deceptively comforted. Without realizing it, she had let down her guard, her adrenaline level dropping. Just what Salma wanted.

"Selene, your mother, has betrayed you all. She's abandoned you intentionally."

"That's not true!" said Anaíd, forgetting everything she should have remembered.

In the darkness, Salma relished the moment.

"Selene loves blood as much as I do. She wants to be immortal and beautiful forever."

Anaíd covered her ears, she didn't want to listen, but she'd heard enough. Her legs were weak and Salma was stepping closer—she could feel the burning sensation coming from her, tickling her protection shield, mocking her defenses. The pressure on Anaíd's chest increased, her breathing became irregular.

"Selene doesn't want you, she rejected you; she's forgotten you forever. She regrets having had a daughter and has asked me to take care of you. She wants your blood to be good for something."

Shocked, Anaíd started sobbing and fell to the ground. Salma's claw sank into her chest and snatched away her shield. Anaíd raised her head imploringly and her eyes found Salma's.

Then she felt a sharp pain inside and suddenly everything was black.

. . .

She awoke sometime later. Had an hour gone by? A few minutes? Or seconds? She didn't know. Salma was screaming and fighting with someone. Were the Omars here? What was happening? Anaíd pretended to be unconscious and perked up her ears. She could hear loud voices flying back and forth over her body. Salma was furious.

"Liar! You didn't tell me that Selene's daughter was in Taormina. You isolated her with your spell. Clodia wore that bloody sweater that was supposed to protect Anaíd, that's why I couldn't finish Clodia off."

The answer felt like a slap on Anaíd's face.

"She's mine! She belongs to me!" It was Cristine Olav's warm and maternal voice.

"And what are you going to do with her?"

"That's none of your business, Salma. Leave her alone."

"Have you become so sentimental?"

"You can keep Clodia, but Anaíd is mine."

"You hid her, you prevented all of us from knowing her whereabouts and you protected her like a broody hen."

"I want her for myself alone," insisted Cristine Olav.

Salma's laughter reverberated in the small cottage.

"Ha, ha! You make me laugh! You can't fool me, Cristine. That girl is more than a young Omar."

"That's none of your concern!"

"Oh, no? You are wrong. I've already cursed her."

Salma lifted Anaíd from the floor as if she were a bundle, and poked around her insides with a cold hand.

"Leave her alone!" protested Ms. Olav, grabbing Anaíd's arm and trying to pry her away from Salma.

Anaíd felt her heart shrink as Salma stole her blood, while at the same time Cristine pulled her body toward her. She was going to die. And she would die without knowing if Selene loved her, if Ms. Olav had ever loved her. The pain caused by these feelings of betrayal and lack of affection was stronger than the agony of slowly losing her life. Shouting with all her might, Anaíd suddenly jumped to her feet and broke free from the Odish's grip.

An explosion of rage came from inside of her. Anaíd wished the whole world would tremble with her pain, that the earth would spit out fire and consume Salma and Cristine along with her own suffering.

Why? Why was it that doubting other people's love for her was what hurt her the most?

. . .

And the earth trembled. Once, twice, three times. The tremors became stronger. The dormant Mount Etna was now awake, spitting out fire and lava. The volcano's roaring froze Anaíd's blood. Salma and Cristine were speechless. The earth was shattering and the tiles from the cottage's dilapidated roof were falling everywhere. Anaíd jumped over Clodia's body and rolled under the bed with her. Soon after, the ceiling collapsed just as the figures of two cats swiftly leaped out of the window.

The earth was coughing up lava and fire, and from its bowels emerged a strange, shimmering object—a scepter carved in gold.

The spotted cat stopped and turned into a beautiful woman. She grabbed the glistening object and ran away with it.

Under the rubble, covered in dust and smoke, Anaíd felt a pair of strong arms lift her up, check her pulse, and whisper soothing words into her ear.

"They are alive. They're still alive."

Valeria's voice was the last thing she heard before losing consciousness again.

CHAPTER 25

The Challenge

Selene held on tightly to the balustrade and watched the spectacle that had turned the night sky into a terrifyingly bright display. Mount Etna roared and spewed out fire in a macabre dance, molten lava licking its slopes and sliding down to the valley. The palace, the hill, and the valley shone under the flames, and a thick cloud of black smoke around the volcano's mouth had tinted the horizon.

With every new tremor, the girls screamed until Selene nervously scolded them.

"Silence!"

One of them, the boldest, knelt on the floor and, after crossing herself, brought her hands together and pleaded.

"Please, miss, we are begging you, don't be mad at us. Stop this nightmare."

Selene feigned surprise.

"Do you think I caused this?"

The brave girl—Maria—didn't hide her suspicions.

"Oh yes, miss, we saw you staring at the mountain of fire all night, screaming with rage and pronouncing some strange words. We saw you invoke the earth's entrails with your hands until the Etna woke up from its sleep. Please, miss, make it stop . . ."

Selene stomped on the marble floor with her golden sandal.

"That's ridiculous!"

But a bitter voice contradicted her.

"Actually, it's not a ridiculous suspicion. She's right, Selene. You've awoken the volcano to get rid of me."

Salma's spectral figure stood before Selene, her black dress covered in blood and her gaze full of hate.

"Shut up! We are not alone," objected Selene.

"That's easy to fix," mumbled Salma, producing her athame.

But before Salma could do anything to the girls, an indignant Selene took out her wand and pronounced a lethal spell. The girls collapsed on the floor. Salma applauded.

"I see that you still have strength after what you did."

"I told you to stop your abuses."

"That's why you've intervened? That's why you've protected your daughter?"

Selene opened her eyes wide.

"My daughter?"

"Stop lying!"

Selene was silent for a moment and then went after Salma.

"It was you who challenged me and you've almost had to pay the price."

Salma extended her bleeding hand; she was missing the ring finger.

"I won't forgive you for this."

"I didn't do that."

"It was your little Anaíd, that unattractive and clumsy girl who had no powers . . . The Countess will decide what happens now."

Selene was horrified.

"Are you going to take me to the Dark World again?"

Salma was furious.

"You deceived us. You lied about your daughter."

Selene pointed at Salma.

"And you? What are *you* hiding, Salma? What do you have there?"

Salma recoiled, hiding the shiny object behind her.

"Ask the spirits."

"I will, and the Countess will know."

Fire blazed in Salma's eyes.

"The Countess will decide!"

Selene looked around and sighed for all the riches she was leaving behind.

"Fine, the Countess will decide."

CHAPTER 26

Healing Hands

Anaíd woke up on a heap of fresh hay inside a cave. The air was cold and thick with dampness. She could feel the limestone walls dripping water, and she smelled the familiar scent of wet earth. She looked up. Beautiful stalactites and stalagmites of curious shapes decorated the ceiling and outline of the cave. Beneath her, she could make out the murmur of an underground stream.

Anaíd tried to sit up, but a plump hand stopped her.

"Wait. Don't move yet."

It was good old Criselda.

"What day is it? Where's Clodia?"

Criselda urged her not to talk and checked Anaíd's body thoroughly.

"The wounds have healed, but you'll feel very weak. You've been here a week. Sit up slowly."

Anaíd felt faint for an instant but quickly recovered. She wanted to know what had happened to Clodia.

"Clodia's condition is very serious. Despite the potions, ointments, and the energy from my hands, she might die. Go on, have some broth. You'll feel better."

Anaíd drank from the earthen bowl her aunt offered her and felt invigorated.

"Now, tell me what happened."

Anaíd relived the pain of Salma's attack and her cruel words about her mother.

"Oh, Aunt Criselda, it was horrible!"

And she shared the memories of that night with her aunt. Though it made her anxious, talking about what had happened helped Anaíd exorcise the demons that haunted her at night.

Criselda hugged her with tenderness.

"What Salma said about my mother isn't true, is it?" Anaíd asked.

Criselda ran a hand through her hair, clearly uncomfortable. She was taken aback by Anaíd's unexpected question.

"You were very brave, my dear."

"And powerful," added old Lucrecia.

Lucrecia was sitting in the shadows, watching over a pale body.

"Clodia!"

Anaíd crawled to the makeshift bed Clodia lay in. She was moaning in her sleep and looked as white as death. Old Lucrecia's creased hand grabbed Anaíd's wrist.

"Did you wake the volcano? Was it you?"

Anaíd was suddenly nervous.

"It erupted?"

"The slope and the valley were devastated by lava," said Criselda.

"Mount Etna was sleeping peacefully, but someone roused it from its sleep and it became violent." Lucrecia released Anaíd's wrist, her voice understanding. "It wasn't any of us. Was it you?"

Anaíd hadn't been able to control her rage, but she didn't mean to cause a catastrophe. Had she really unleashed a cataclysm? She'd only felt hatred and the wish to die. That was dangerous, very dangerous. An initiated Omar couldn't cause damage or give in to desperation.

"It wasn't my intention; I'm sorry, I lost control... I just wished the cottage would be destroyed by fire and that everyone inside would perish."

Lucrecia trembled almost imperceptibly. Then her callous hands felt Anaíd's eyes, her mouth, her neck. Lucrecia's fingers paused on the lunar stones hanging from Anaíd's neck.

"There's no doubt about it. You can control the fire."

"So you will do it?" Criselda asked Lucrecia.

Anaíd had no idea what they were talking about.

"I will teach you about the alchemy of fire and how to forge metals. You will forge your own athame with this invincible rock, the lunar stone you've chosen," whispered Lucrecia.

Anaíd was overwhelmed by the honor that old Lucrecia was granting her. She and her future successor within the clan of the snakes were the only holders of that ancient knowledge.

"It will be the last thing I do before I die. Now, give me your hand."

Lucrecia felt the palm of her own hand and placed it upon Anaíd's. Then she looked at Criselda and nodded.

"Do you remember Deméter's song? The one she hummed while she was healing?"

Anaíd remembered it well.

"Put your hands over Clodia, Anaíd," Criselda told her. "You, too, have the Tsinoulises' gift, and you are younger and stronger than me. You might have more luck."

Lucrecia took off Clodia's clothes, and Anaíd saw the small wound through which her life had been seeping out. She placed both hands over the small orifice and murmured Deméter's song. She could smell the nearness of death.

As before, Anaíd felt paralyzed by the glacial cold her body absorbed from Clodia's. As Clodia came back to life, Anaíd lost strength, but she didn't give up. Her fingers, magically prolonged, massaged Clodia's heart and accelerated her heartbeat, making it pump with more strength and conviction. She stopped only when Lucrecia grabbed her arm.

"That's enough, Anaíd, you are becoming ill. You should rest."

Anaíd plopped down on Criselda's lap, but immediately jerked away. Criselda was trying to warm her up with Cristine Olav's bloody sweater.

"That sweater is cursed! Burn it!"

"It is?"

"It has the s-spell of an Odish," Anaíd stuttered.

Criselda put it on her by force. Anaíd was too weak to offer any resistance.

"You are wrong. This sweater has saved your life, and Clodia's. It has a good spell."

The warm wool soothed her like the heat of a lit fireplace.

So . . . Cristine Olav was actually trying to help—like she'd said?

Anaíd was totally confused, but still she fell deeply asleep.

• • •

Clodia and Anaíd had breakfast sitting at the cave's entrance, where a natural canopy of rocks sheltered them from the weather but still allowed them to bask in the warm sunlight.

They'd laid a checkered tablecloth on the gravel and put out two napkins, two pottery mugs, and a jug of milk. They had soft bread, baked by the snakes; butter and goat cheese, a present from the deer clan; and wild blackberry marmalade, the crows' favorite.

Clodia sat next to Anaíd and filled her mug with coffee. Anaíd scooped up some cream with a spoon and dunked it in sugar.

Before relishing one of her favorite pleasures, she invited Clodia to taste it.

"Come on, try it."

"Are you nuts?"

"It's delicious, cream with sugar."

"Exactly, a gazillion calories for my ass."

Anaíd didn't insist. It was Clodia's loss.

"You were skin and bones."

"I was, you've said it. This diet for fattening up cattle is going to make Bruno prefer a cow to me."

Anaíd felt a pang of jealousy. Her relationship with Clodia was friendly now, but they were not close enough for Clodia to confide in her.

"I doubt it. He's crazy for you. Fat, thin, tattooed, or turned into a vampire, he likes you a lot."

Clodia swelled with pride as she took a bite of her bread with butter and marmalade. She hesitated for a moment, chewing slowly.

"And how do you know?"

"I followed you one night to the birthday party. I saw you and Bruno kiss."

"So it's true that you spied on me?" Clodia accused her, her hands on her hips.

Anaíd lowered her head in shame.

"I'm sorry, it had nothing to do with the Odish . . . I followed you because . . ."

"Because?"

"Because . . . I've never been invited to a birthday party."

"What?"

Anaíd shrunk. She brought her hands to her head.

"You heard me."

"But . . . why didn't you tell me?"

"You hated me."

"Well, I had my reasons."

Anaíd didn't understand.

"What reasons? I didn't do anything to you!"

"Oh, no? You were great, the best."

This time Anaíd choked on her piece of bread.

"You are wrong."

But no, Clodia didn't think she was wrong. With the grace of Italians, she counted off on her fingers the reasons to despise Anaíd:

"First, you are the great Deméter's granddaughter. Second, you are the daughter of Selene, the chosen one. Third, you are mysterious. Fourth, you are beautiful. Fifth, you are extremely intelligent. Sixth, you are powerful. Seventh, you are respected. Eighth, you are the apple of my mother's eyes. Ninth, you were initiated before me. And tenth, and most important, all the boys from my group of friends said that your ass was better than mine."

"What?" Anaíd exclaimed, astounded.

Clodia could have been talking about something as foreign as nuclear research. Was Clodia really talking about her? Had she invented a new Anaíd?

"When . . . when did your friends see me?"

"Whenever they came to pick me up or say hello, they elbowed one another and whispered about you."

Anaíd was speechless.

"You are wrong about everything—but I especially disagree with points four, seven, eight, and ten."

"Very funny. Are you going to contradict me now?"

"I'm not beautiful, I'm not the apple of your mother's eyes, and . . . my ass is pitiful."

"Ha!"

"What's so funny?"

"Have you not looked at yourself in the mirror lately? When was the last time you did that?"

Arguing with Clodia was pointless. Sometimes, the best course of action was agreeing with her, as if she were crazy.

"Fine, you are right about everything."

But Clodia faced Anaíd and began slicing the air with her hand.

"Oh, I see! You are just agreeing with me to shut me up; well, I don't believe you. Admit it, if you met someone like you, you would be envious."

Anaíd fell silent. Envy, jealousy. They were familiar feelings.

"I was the one who was jealous of you."

Clodia softened and poured herself more milk. This time, she gave in to the temptation of a spoonful of cream with sugar.

"I'm all ears."

"You're funny and stylish, you have a boyfriend who loves you, a lot of friends, you are Valeria's daughter, and, even though you don't want to admit it, you are stunning."

Clodia puffed up her feathers like a hen. Unlike Anaíd, Clodia basked in her praise and wasn't indifferent to her compliments.

"Really?"

"No, I'm lying."

Clodia got up and kissed her. Anaíd didn't know what to say or do.

"I love you," Clodia whispered.

"You . . . love me?" Anaíd mumbled.

"And I will be your sister forever. I owe you my life."

"You don't owe me anything."

"Oh! Go to hell!" Clodia shot back, making Anaíd sit down.

"You are disgustingly self-sufficient. If I want to owe you my life, I will. It's my right. And, just so you know, we are going to sign a blood pact, whether you like it or not."

And with this, Clodia took out her athame and, in the same swift movement in which she'd chopped the rabbit's neck, made a small incision on her wrist. Then she offered the double-edged knife to Anaíd.

"Come on; do it quickly before I bleed to death."

When she saw the blood, Anaíd turned pale and her legs weakened.

"No, I don't have the guts."

Clodia grabbed Anaíd's wrist and, more delicately this time, made a small cut. Anaíd tried to stay calm to avoid getting dizzy. She offered her bleeding wrist to Clodia, who extended hers, and their bloods mixed in a ritual as ancient as magic.

Then, Clodia grabbed a few napkins to cover their wounds and invited Anaíd to follow her.

"Come with me."

They walked deep into the alcoves of the damp cave, where Paleolithic hunters had performed their ceremonies. Clodia stopped before a narrow tunnel and crawled a few feet forward. She pointed her flashlight at one of the side walls and showed Anaíd the faded drawing of a bison. Next to it, dozens of superimposed images of red hands decorated the walls and ceiling.

"Get some of my blood in your hand; I will do the same with yours."

They placed their red palms on the curved wall of the cave and pressed for a few minutes, leaving their marks forever.

"Now you're stuck with me. Wherever you go, our lives will be tied. These hands will be a reminder of our union."

The sound of slow, heavy footsteps came from one of the galleries on the side.

"Anaíd? Clodia? Are you there?" It was Lucrecia.

Anaíd was about to reply, but Clodia put a finger on her lips, motioning for her to keep quiet. They slipped away on tiptoe.

"Where are we going?"

"We'll hide for a while. I'm sure Lucrecia wants to lock you in the depths of hell to teach you that boring stuff about the alchemy of fire and the forging of metals."

Anaíd felt bad about avoiding Lucrecia, but she truly preferred to spend time with her new friend.

"And what are we going to do?"

"This is our schedule of activities for the morning: I'll teach you how to put on makeup, do your hair, and walk with sex appeal. If you don't learn how to move that butt of yours, I'm warning you, I'll switch it with a spell. You decide."

Anaíd didn't think twice; Clodia's invitation was very tempting.

Lucrecia had waited a hundred and one years. She could easily wait a few more hours.

. . .

"What are you doing?" complained Anaíd, her face made up and her hair half-done.

Clodia was rummaging in her bag.

"I'm looking for your toiletry bag; I need a thin comb and a pair of hairpins."

"Wait, don't turn it upside down!"

But it was too late; Clodia was already emptying it out on the ground.

"What do you carry in your purse, girl? The *Encyclopedia Britannica*?"

The ground was covered with books and paper, but there was no trace of a comb or brush.

"I don't need a comb."

"Ha! That's what you think. Your hair has gotten really long, and it's disgustingly dirty and tangled. We need to condition it and comb it."

Anaíd brought one hand to her head and ran her fingers through her hair, trying to loosen up a knot. It was impossible. She had run out of the special shampoo prescribed by Karen, and now her hair was a mess. She'd be better off cutting it.

"Let's put this away and leave the hair conditioning for another day. Lucrecia is waiting for me."

Anaíd began to clear the mess. Putting all the books, socks, and panties back in the bag was a lot more amusing than watching them fall to the ground had been. And she was doing that, lost in thought, when a piece of paper slipped through her hands and a sixth sense made her pause. All of a sudden, she knew that the piece of paper was extremely important. She hadn't noticed it in her purse before, but she knew that it would have meaning now. The paper was hot, and it emanated an acrid stench. It was an e-mail from Selene's computer, and it had been printed, the date was at the bottom, the day after Selene's disappearance. The e-mail she was holding was dated a week before and it read:

Dearest Selene,

In your previous e-mail, you said that the best time to meet and spend a good amount of time together would be this summer. I'm dying to move the date forward, but I will contain my curiosity and impatience. We will meet, then, this summer.

You won't regret it. By my side, you'll be able to enjoy anything you feel like doing or having, and no one will refuse your wishes. If you want to, you'll be able to have an eternal vacation.

Yours always,
S

Anaíd couldn't take her eyes off that winding and treacherous *S*. *S* for snake. *S* for Salma. How could she have been so blind?

THE PROPHECY OF OM

She will see the light in the frozen hell,
Where the oceans blend with the firmament,
And will grow up in the earth's backbone,
Where the high peaks graze the stars.

She will feed from the she-bear,
Grow under the warm mantle of the female seal,
Absorb the she-wolf's knowledge,
And, finally, she'll be obliged to the shrewd female fox.

The chosen one, daughter of the earth, will emerge from the ground,
Who will love her and shelter her in her womb.
A prisoner of its warmth, she will remain blind and deaf,
Cradled by dark mothers,
And wrapped in their sweet lies.

CHAPTER 27

―――――

The Scepter of Power

In the deep caverns of the Dark World, a place neither time nor color can liven up, the voice of the Countess thundered.

"Is it true, Selene?"

Selene raised her head challengingly.

"Yes, I have a daughter. Salma was aware of it."

"She lied to me," protested Salma. "She said Anaíd was adopted and didn't have any powers; that she was a mere mortal."

"She didn't have any powers, I didn't lie to you," Selene defended herself.

Salma showed the Countess her injured hand. She was missing the ring finger.

"That girl is very powerful; she can fight like a snake and she's fearless. Selene has kept things from us."

The Countess rummaged in Selene's conscience with her tentacles but was confronted by a wall of resolution that impressed her.

"Are you resisting my stare?"

"Tell me what you want to know and I will respond," said Selene.

"Why didn't you initiate her?" repeated the Countess.

"I've told you a thousand times," insisted Selene, "Anaíd didn't have the abilities to be initiated; she was clumsy and insecure."

"That's not true."

"This subject is exhausting; we are here for something more interesting."

But the Countess wasn't willing to change the subject.

"Perhaps, but Anaíd seems very interesting to me. And Salma's wound is of interest to her."

Salma didn't want to change the subject either.

"I want her for myself," said Salma.

"You've heard her," said the Countess. "What do you say, Selene?"

Selene was quiet for a moment and then addressed the Countess in a distant and disdainful tone.

"Salma has consumed so much blood that her power might jeopardize your authority."

Salma was furious.

"Are you threatening me?"

"Yes, I'm accusing you of treason, and if the Countess opened her eyes, she'd realize that you are hiding even more things from her."

The Countess stirred in her corner in the shadows.

"You are learning, Selene, you are learning very fast. You accuse, you are insensitive; you love money, power, and blood. And you look younger—you, too, could jeopardize my power."

But Selene smiled.

"I doubt it, Countess. Without me, you are all doomed to disappearing."

"That's not true," shouted Salma. "She's lying; she's trying to make us believe she is essential. She wants to find out our secrets to rule our destinies. We don't need her."

"Are you sure, Salma? Have you wondered how the chosen one will help the Odish defeat the Omars?" insinuated Selene.

The Countess drank in her words.

"How, Selene?"

Selene pointed at Salma.

"You know it very well, Salma. The chosen one will destroy her enemies with the scepter of power. You will be fed by the energy and magic of the witches who are eliminated."

Salma refused to talk about this.

"I don't believe in the prophecy."

"The alignment is drawing near," said the Countess, "all the signs indicate it."

Salma turned pale.

"Let's destroy Selene. If the alignment hasn't occurred and she's dead, the prophecy won't come true."

"It *is* coming true!" shouted Selene with authority. She pointed at Salma accusingly. "You have the scepter."

"Indeed, it is coming true," repeated the Countess, agreeing with Selene. She stood before Salma. "Give it to me, Salma."

Salma fell silent. The shadow of the Countess grew bigger and bigger, until it was a dark and threatening cloud.

"Give me the scepter of power."

Salma refused.

"It's mine, it came to me."

The Countess's shadow enveloped Salma and covered her with darkness.

"It doesn't belong to you, Salma, give it to me."

The struggle lasted an absurd amount of time in a place where there is no time. Then the scepter rolled toward Selene's feet and all she had to do was bend down and pick it up.

"It has come to me, it belongs to me."

Surprised, the Countess watched the scene from the shadows.

"You know what your job is, Selene. You must destroy the Omars."

Salma, exhausted and defeated, lay panting on the floor.

"She won't do it; she will use it for her own purposes."

"Shut up, Salma," ordered the Countess.

Selene stroked the golden scepter and read the inscriptions carved on it. *The scepter of O.* Her hands trembled slightly. She could feel its immense power.

"The time hasn't arrived yet, Selene."

"What time?"

"The time of the alignment. The scepter won't rule until the alignment has occurred; then you'll have to pass the first test."

Selene was surprised.

"A test? Don't you have enough evidence?"

"We do, of your condition, but we want proof of your loyalty. You will eliminate Anaíd and Criselda."

Selene furrowed her brow.

"Why?"

"They are looking for you—to destroy you."

Selene took a step back.

"That's not true."

"It is, Selene. If you don't want to eliminate them first, they'll kill you. Once the Tsinoulis lineage is finished, you'll be nothing more than a lonely wolf, far from your pack."

Selene was silent for a moment. She stroked the scepter, brandished it above her head, steamed it up with her breath, and polished it with her light gown.

"It's beautiful," she said frivolously.

"Extremely beautiful . . . Now give it to me."

"No!" Selene shouted, holding it tightly.

"Don't force me to take it away from you, like I did with Salma," roared the Countess.

But Selene turned around and left the cavern with the scepter in her hand.

"I'm not Salma; I'm the chosen one!"

And she lost herself in the forests of the Dark World.

CHAPTER 28

THE LONELINESS OF THE FRONT RUNNER

Lucrecia forgave Anaíd for not showing up sometimes. She'd been an attentive disciple who treated Lucrecia with respect and was grateful for her teachings. Perhaps, Lucrecia thought, she'd made Anaíd work too hard, without taking into account that a teenager should enjoy life's pleasures. The snake's many years had made her forget about things the girls' laughter had brought back to her memory.

She was glad that Anaíd and Clodia had hit it off. During their long recovery, they had become best of friends. Next to the young dolphin, Anaíd shone with her own light; she had blossomed. Anaíd was much more beautiful and charming than when Lucrecia first met her a month before. She and Clodia shared secrets, breakfast, bubble gum, and their chatter lasted until well after midnight. Lucrecia knew that a good friend was the best gift for a lonely witch.

Anaíd looked sad and a bit crestfallen when she appeared for her last alchemy class. Lucrecia didn't think much of it; it was normal for a young girl to go through emotional ups and downs. After all, danger and uncertainty awaited her, and she could sense it. It was natural for Anaíd to doubt her strength. Lucrecia thought that perhaps it would be best to leave her alone and let her lick her own wounds. An initiated witch had the support of her tribe and the other clans, but she had to learn how to overcome the most difficult times by herself.

Lucrecia sat on the ground of the deep cavern in front of her young disciple. A little more effort and she would finish her task; at over a hundred years old, she deserved to be able to rest forever. She handed Anaíd her beautiful double-edged athame.

"So, Anaíd, you chose the moon's stone and it chose you. When you forged your talisman with it, you were unaware of the secrets you know now. The moon measures the time, tides, crops, and blood. But the moon doesn't give strength to the witches' actions; its light is cold and indirect. The fire, wise and ardent, feeds the earth and nourishes it with life. Now, you know how to use the fire's power and make it obey you. Your athame is the most powerful knife the snake witches have ever forged. It is the result of blending the earth's magma and your teardrops carved of lunar rock. Speak to your athame—it's yourself, your hand, the prolongation of your strength and power. Along with the wand, the athame is an Omar's most valuable treasure."

Anaíd looked at the polished blade of her knife. It was the result of her perseverance and her good judgment in choosing the lunar stone. She was proud of her work, but that didn't alleviate her sadness.

Her mentor stood up and gave Anaíd one last order.

"Now you'll become one with your athame."

And Lucrecia walked away slowly through the galleries, leaving Anaíd immersed in her sadness, staring at her shimmering black treasure.

As part of her learning, Anaíd had learned to meditate and retreat into that hell of fire and smoke that was the cave now. She could spend long hours in silence, surrounded by darkness. She wasn't afraid of being alone. However, she decided to light an oil lamp to better appreciate her work of art.

Under the flickering flame, she noticed that she was not alone. A young intruder, wearing an odd tunic and makeup, gazed at her athame with her same curiosity. Anaíd was now an expert on these chance encounters.

"Hello."

At first, the intruder didn't even acknowledge her words.

"I'm saying hello to you—the one in the mask and tunic."

"Me? Are you talking to me?"

"Yes. Why not?"

"I am just a miserable soul doomed to roam the earth for my crimes."

Anaíd sighed, resigned. He had the airs of a poet.

"I'm Anaíd Tsinoulis."

"Marco Tulio, to serve you and cheer up your evenings with my humble art."

"What kind of art is that?"

"The art of interpreting comedies."

"An actor?"

"A comedian."

"Wow, had I known before, you could have kept me company. And what was your downfall, Marco Tulio?"

"Must I remember it?"

"If you don't want to . . ."

"I forgot my lines in the midst of a performance of *Mostellaria*, Plautus's comedy."

"Oh . . . Did you die of embarrassment?"

"I hid in the caverns to avoid being lynched by the audience."

"And they killed you?"

"I slipped and fell down a cliff. I still carry their curse on my shoulders, me and my battered honor."

"Poor Marco Tulio."

"It was my fault. The night before, I was tempted and had some magnificent wine brought from Campagna. What a night in the Blue Lion Tavern of Taormina!"

"It no longer exists, I'm afraid."

"I thought so. It's been a long time . . ."

"Do you regret it?"

"Yes, always. There's nothing worse than developing absolute amnesia just as you appear before an audience eager to hear laughter, jokes, and witty dialogue. It's excruciating! Horrifying! Indescribable!"

"I can help you," said Anaíd.

"Remember my lines? I've been trying to for two thousand years, but to no avail."

"No, to forget them; to break free from your curse."

"You'd save my honor?"

"I'm offering you peace."

"In exchange for what?" asked the drunken comedian with caution.

"You need to answer my question: is it true that I can reach Selene through the stone quarries?"

"Selene, the she-wolf?"

Anaíd nodded, and the spirit was lost in thought for a moment.

"The stone quarries connect the two worlds, but to reach Selene you must go back to where she vanished and follow the path of the sun."

"What does that mean?"

"Can you set me free or not?"

"Of course," lied Anaíd.

"Are you an Odish?"

"How else would I be able to see you?"

"They all think you are an Omar. They are talking about you right now."

"Who?"

"The matriarchs."

"Can you hear them?"

The comedian brought his ear to one of the cavities in the rock. He nodded.

"Come closer. Can you hear them?" He motioned her over.

Anaíd perked up her ears. It was hard to decipher their words. Marco Tulio must have more experience in this kind of scheme.

"What are they saying?"

"Criselda refuses to use her athame against Selene. She believes that the knife wasn't conceived to hurt or kill another Omar. She's suggesting that they prepare a lethal potion."

Anaíd's heart sank. She felt sick.

"It can't be. You must be wrong."

"Listen for yourself."

White as a sheet, Anaíd focused on the words that had become lost in the cave's secret tunnels.

"Anaíd must not know it or suspect it," insisted Criselda.

"Without her, we won't be able to reach Selene," said Valeria.

"The possibility that she is not one of them is getting smaller and smaller, but we shouldn't accuse her before finding out the truth," old Lucrecia objected.

"I made an oath to kill Selene and I will fulfill it, but the alignment is near and we must hurry. Anaíd has already recovered; we can begin our search tomorrow," said Criselda.

Anaíd had heard enough.

She was the victim of a terrible lie. The betrayal predicted by the oracle during her initiation was coming true. Wolfs, snakes, crows, dolphins, and deer were sending her to find Selene so that Criselda, her own aunt, could kill her.

Holding her head with her hands, Anaíd let herself fall to the ground.

Criselda too?

Could she trust anyone?

They wouldn't give Selene a chance to defend herself?

And most horrible was that she herself was also beginning to doubt her mother's integrity.

The comedian's spirit grew impatient.

"What about your promise?"

"I'll set you free. Did you say I have to go back to the place where Selene disappeared and follow the path of the sun?"

"Yes."

Anaíd got over the pain, took out her wand, and traced the signs for the spell in the air.

"Marco Tulio, by the power granted to me in my initiation, and in the memory of the she-wolf, I permit you to break the chains of your curse and rest among the dead forever."

Marco Tulio smiled gratefully and began to dissolve into thousands of particles.

Anaíd bid him farewell.

"Send my love to my grandmother Deméter."

Marco Tulio tried to delay his evaporation for a moment.

"Why didn't you ask me before? The spirits can summon the dead," he shouted, before disappearing completely.

Anaíd grasped the meaning of his words too late.

"Wait, don't go!"

But Marco Tulio no longer existed.

So the spirits could summon the dead. That meant that she could communicate with Deméter.

She desperately needed her grandmother's knowledge and serenity, but she also needed the clairvoyance death makes possible. The living beings around her couldn't tell truth from deception. And neither could she.

What was true?

What was a lie?

"Any spirits out there?" shouted Anaíd.

But only the echo of her voice came back to her, multiplying like a virus.

She was alone, more alone than ever.

. . .

The face of Cornelia, the matriarch of the crow clan, was stamped with sadness. She enjoyed walking in the countryside at dusk and greeting the flocks of black crows with shimmering feathers flying over the wheat fields. Sometimes, she walked up to the cliff by herself and gazed at the ocean her late daughter, Julilla, had loved so much.

That afternoon, Anaíd found her looking at the hectic coming and going of cranes, hoopoes, swallows, and storks, who migrated south toward African lands, announcing the arrival of fall.

Cornelia received Anaíd with affection. Anaíd reminded her of her daughter. Perhaps it was the disturbing seriousness of her eyes, as blue as Julilla's on the day of her initiation, afraid of what the future might bring.

Cornelia had few occasions to converse with young girls. They usually shied away because of her solemn appearance. Since the death of her daughter, she'd worn black, like her ancestors and the birds of her clan. Cornelia decided to adopt the mourning tradition because her sorrow would last forever. That was the sentiment of the women and mothers from her land, and she, a witch but still mortal, agreed with it.

"Tell me, what can I do for you?" she asked Anaíd.

Anaíd knew that Cornelia wouldn't deny her anything.

"I want to know the secret of the birds' flight."

Cornelia could tell that Anaíd was concealing something; she could hear the urgency in her words.

"Does Criselda know about this?"

"Yes, of course."

"It's dangerous."

"I don't care."

"In order to share that secret with you, I need the approval of the matriarchs. I think I should speak to Criselda first."

Anaíd took her hands and stared imploringly at Cornelia's black eyes.

"I can't wait; it must be done now and in secret."

Cornelia felt the warmth of Anaíd's hands in her own. She was young, full of life, and carried an enormous responsibility on her shoulders.

"Help me, please, I need you. I know it, and you know it too."

Cornelia was aware of this but was trying to avoid her fate.

"Be careful, young one. What you want to do is dangerous."

But Anaíd, with the conviction of the daring, honed her intuition.

"Tell me, Cornelia, why have you come here? Why do you gaze at the migrating birds flying over the island?"

Cornelia didn't want to think about the answer.

"And you?"

Anaíd put her cards on the table. She had nothing to lose.

"I asked myself what I should do, and my steps brought me

here. When I saw you looking at the birds, I understood that you were the sign I'd been waiting for; that you would teach me how to fly like them so I could find Selene. This is the path I must take."

Cornelia sighed. Fate wanted to involve her in the prophecy. She couldn't avoid it.

"Are you ready?"

Anaíd sure was. She had never been more ready in her whole life.

Cornelia flapped her dark arms with the elegance of a swan, and Anaíd imitated her.

"Pick a bird, the one you like the most, and watch it. Feel the flailing of its wings and its weightless body."

Anaíd's eyes landed on a beautiful fish eagle flying over the lake, its wings spread out as it caught a pike with its talons.

Cornelia followed Anaíd's gaze and shuddered. Anaíd had chosen the eagle, the most powerful bird of prey.

"Repeat the flying spell after me."

And they both moved their arms in unison, reciting the beautiful chant of the bird. Their bodies became light as feathers, and their arms turned into wings. Together, they soared into the air.

Anaíd flew over the water, over and over again, her long hair waving in the wind, her face furrowed and streaked with tears. As she followed her instructor, she relished her dominion of the air.

By sunset, she had mastered flying at low level, gliding with the wind currents, and crisscrossing the sky majestically. Squealing like an eagle, she bid Cornelia farewell, and headed north, in the opposite direction of the migrating birds. But Anaíd wasn't concerned, for she wasn't a bird—she was a witch with wings.

Cornelia wished Anaíd luck as she watched her fly away and understood, for the first time, that there was a reason for the misfortune of outliving her own daughter.

Holding Anaíd's hand, she had entered the territory of the prophecy.

CHAPTER 29

THE PATH OF THE SUN

Anaíd was exhausted. She had flown nonstop for days and nights, pausing only for tiny sips of water. Her body had lost a great deal of weight. Her clothes were crumpled and soaked, her hair tangled, and her skin cracked by the wind.

As Anaíd flew over Urt's bell tower, she was filled with nostalgia. She had once thought she'd never hear its low-pitched chimes again.

It was after midnight when she reached her house. But it was locked. She needed help—and food—so she flew to Elena's cozy house, where there was always a stew in the kitchen and an extra bed ready. There, she banged on the shutters with all her might, eager to lie on a couch and have some hot soup, but the crying of a baby stopped her.

Was she crazy?

She couldn't show up at Elena's window looking like a winged witch.

Elena had seven children and a husband. Actually, she might have eight children by now.

Anaíd descended slowly and landed on the patio. The door to the barn was ajar, but she couldn't walk. Somehow, she made it to the pile of hay next to the mare and lay down, exhausted.

Slowly, very slowly, her wings turned to arms again and her body regained its weight. However, fatigue kept her in a state of lethargy for hours.

In a dream, a dark-skinned boy caressed her face and moistened her lips with a piece of wet cloth. Then he placed his lips on hers for an instant, but it was enough time for Anaíd to feel fire on her skin and the aniseed taste of his tongue.

"Roc!" she exclaimed, surprised, when she opened her eyes.

Roc jumped to his feet, mortified.

"You know me?"

Anaíd laughed a genuine laugh.

"We swam naked in the pool a million times when we were kids."

Roc was disconcerted, and Anaíd was really enjoying it. Strangely, she was not embarrassed at all.

"You and I? I can't remember . . ."

"Look at me carefully."

Anaíd moved the strands of hair covering her face, and Roc recognized her blue eyes. His surprise was immense.

"Anaíd! What happened to you?"

Anaíd was about to reply but held herself.

"I've taken a long trip. I need food and clothes. Is your mother home?"

Roc nodded and hurried out.

"Wait!"

The boy paused for a moment, and Anaíd looked at him inquisitively.

"Did you give me water while I slept?"

Roc nodded and lowered his head, but Anaíd didn't say anything that would embarrass him.

"Thank you."

A broad smile lit up Roc's face. He had candid eyes the color of molasses and black, curly hair. He was very handsome.

When he was gone, Anaíd shuddered. Had he kissed her without knowing who she was? Did she look so different?

Elena confirmed it.

"Anaíd? You're Anaíd?"

A chubby baby with rosy cheeks eagerly sucked from Elena's nipple.

"Another boy?"

"Isn't he beautiful? He has such a sweet face that he looks like a girl. I wanted to name him Rosario."

Anaíd cracked up.

"Don't do that to him. He would curse you and cursed spirits can be quite wicked."

"No, I named him Ross . . ."

Ross nursed placidly, oblivious to everything around him. Anaíd sighed.

"I'm home again."

"My beautiful girl, you've grown so much . . . You are taller than me now! And let me see those legs—they are longer than Selene's! Your hair is a mess, though, I'll have to wash it."

Anaíd let herself be loved.

"It's been a week since I last had a bite to eat."

Elena was horrified.

"Why didn't you tell me before? Roc! Bring a plate of stew! Quickly!"

What would she have done without Elena's stew? It was rejuvenating, capable of returning the strength to a bear after hibernation, Anaíd thought while she savored the bacon, cabbage, chickpeas, and broth. Her stomach was grateful for it.

Anaíd ate and slept, slept and ate. Then she agreed to take a bath, but . . . she didn't have any clothes to wear. Elena's were too big for her.

It was Roc who gauged her size with an expert eye.

"The same as Marion's."

And he soon came back with a super-trendy outfit.

"I told her I needed it for a costume party. She loved the idea."

Her hair clean and dry, Anaíd squeezed into Marion's underwear, tight jeans, and top.

Roc showed his approval with a whistle.

"I hope that Marion doesn't see you; her clothes look better on you."

Anaíd would have liked to look at herself in the mirror, but there was no time to lose.

Elena was waiting for Anaíd in the library, piling up books. She seemed annoyed; Anaíd could sense her irritation from the door. When she saw her arrive, Elena looked sideways and Anaíd could tell that she was hiding something from her.

Everything had gone well until that moment, and that worried Anaíd too. The easy roads are always the trickiest. So Anaíd, toughened after a thousand battles, decided to play Elena's game and act dumb.

"Hold on a second, I'm almost done," said Elena, without looking up from the books.

Anaíd sat on a peeling wooden chair where she'd spent so many long afternoons reading as a child. She saw Elena close her notebook, raise her head, and suddenly cover her mouth to suppress a scream.

Anaíd looked nervously behind her.

"What's wrong?"

Elena was behaving very oddly. She brought a hand to her chest and breathed heavily.

"Oh, nothing. I'm sorry, since your mother's disappearance, I get very nervous and now, when I saw you . . ."

"Did I scare you?" asked Anaíd, looking at her clothes. She had never worn anything so brazen and revealing.

"Yes . . . when I saw you . . . it was as if . . . You look like Selene. Have you looked at yourself in the mirror lately?"

Anaíd hadn't. She never looked at herself in mirrors, and it had probably been a month since she'd seen her reflection anywhere.

"I've summoned a coven for tonight," said Elena in a secretive tone. "Gaya and Karen are dying to hear your story."

Anaíd nodded and glanced at her watch.

"I have to stop by my house to check if there's any of Selene's ointment left," she said. "Do I need anything else? This will be my first coven with the clan."

"Your athame, your bowl, and your wand."

Anaíd jotted that down on the back of her hand and stood up quickly. Elena stopped her for a moment.

"Come over for dinner tonight, Anaíd. We'll be waiting for you. We'll fly to the clearing together."

"I'll be here," Anaíd lied.

And she left, grateful for the fact that Elena couldn't read her mind. Until that moment, she had avoided all her direct questions about her return to Urt. She'd answered vaguely, fearing that Elena might call Criselda. Or vice versa.

But that had already happened.

Only a day had gone by, but Elena had already been notified of her escape and must have been instructed to keep Anaíd there until Criselda arrived. Or to send another Omar with her, who would be responsible for the difficult task of eliminating Selene. Would it be Elena herself? Her dear friend Karen? Or her hated enemy, Gaya? The mere thought of it turned Anaíd's stomach.

Anaíd stood paralyzed in front of the door to her house. Shit, the keys. She'd left them in Taormina. Where would she find another set of keys to her house? Anaíd studied the doors and windows carefully, but it would be impossible to get inside. She realized she had been living in a real fortress. She sat under the porch lamenting her bad luck.

Aunt Criselda hadn't told her who had locked the door the day she left the house at four in the morning with only what she was wearing.

An hour later, Karen showed up with the set of keys sent by Elena. Anaíd was moved by the gesture and let herself by kissed, hugged, and complimented. But she tried to ignore Karen's many questions and realized that she, too, was looking at Anaíd strangely. Karen insisted on coming into the house with her. Inside, she turned on the lights and pointed around the hall.

"I made sure the house stayed clean and locked. I knew you would come back."

"Who?"

"You and Criselda . . . and Selene, of course."

"Thanks, Karen. My mother always considered you her best friend."

From the corner of her eye, Anaíd noticed the effect her words had had on Karen.

"Anaíd, I . . . love Selene very much."

"I do too."

"But . . . sometimes . . . the people we love the most change, or . . . we realize they're not who we thought they were."

Anaíd was growing nervous.

"I've noticed that," she agreed.

But Karen couldn't wait. She put her hands on Anaíd's shoulders.

"Anaíd, your mother prevented you from growing and developing your powers."

"What do you mean?"

"I never prescribed the medication she made you take, which inhibited your powers and growth hormones."

Somehow, this time she knew that Karen was telling the truth. Anaíd was upset. She had forbidden herself to let anything or anyone hurt her again, but Karen had taken her off guard.

"You are wrong."

"No, Anaíd, I'm not wrong. We don't know why, but she did it."

Anaíd was fighting her desire to cry and find comfort in Karen's arms. She couldn't afford to be weak now. She bit her lips with rage until they bled.

How could Selene have tortured her for so many years, making her believe that her delay was due to natural causes? Why would Selene deprive her of her powers when she knew she had them?

No. She didn't want to think. Thinking about it confused her, and she needed her mind open, willing. She couldn't hold any grudges. Anaíd needed to love her mother deeply to be able to reach her. If she didn't trust the chosen one, who would be able to help her?

"And you should also know that when you were gone, someone paid off the mortgage on your house. An incredible amount of money, Anaíd."

Karen wrung her hands nervously. She felt guilty. Unloading her burden on Anaíd had been a way of releasing her own pain.

"I'm sorry, Anaíd, but I had to tell you."

But Karen didn't seem to have rid herself of any burden. She left the house crestfallen, now also carrying Anaíd's sorrow on her shoulders.

Anaíd swallowed her tears and entered Selene's room. She needed to hold on to something in order to feel her mother's love. She opened her drawers and closets, anxiously searching for proof of that love.

She found it in an old shoebox on which Selene had written "Anaíd, my girl" in her pointy handwriting.

Inside was a small mother-of-pearl box containing her baby teeth; a pair of tiny patent-leather shoes, probably the first ones Anaíd ever wore; and a silver chain with a locket.

With trembling fingers, she fumbled for the locket's clasp and opened it. And as she stared at it, fascinated, her worries dissipated.

On one of the locket's faces was a picture of Anaíd as a child; on the other, a lock of Selene's red hair. When she closed it, her image and her mother's hair came together and remained in close contact.

Anaíd breathed, relieved, and hung the locket around her neck, very near her heart and the leather bag containing her athame and her wand.

She checked her watch. She couldn't wait until nighttime; she needed to communicate with the spirits before it was too late.

• • •

Anaíd's bedroom was pitch-dark, but she urged the spirits to come out. She called them, begged for their presence, but to no avail. Finally, she heard a raspy answer—the knight and the lady apologized for not being able to appear before her. Cristine Olav had erased their faces. Irritated, Anaíd undid the spell.

"I order you to return, with voice and a face, to the world of the spirits where your curse condemned you to remain," she murmured, waving her birchwood wand.

The lady and the knight appeared before her utterly astonished. Their surprise was genuine.

"Oh, precious young one, are you really the same?"

"Was your power able to undo the Odish spell?"

But Anaíd had no time for their adulation.

"I came to fulfill an oath and let you rest, as you've requested, but before that I need you to summon Deméter."

The lady and knight smiled at each other and disappeared. Anaíd waited for them patiently and was happy to see them actually come back.

"Deméter will be waiting for you in the cave at dusk, before the last ray of sun disappears from the forest."

Anaíd was annoyed. "I thought that she would materialize here, with you."

"Beautiful young one, it is the dead who choose their meeting points, not the other way around."

"It's not easy to make a date with them."

"Some of them refuse; they don't want to come back."

Anaíd hushed them with an abrupt gesture. "Fine, I will grant you your wish once I've spoken with Deméter."

"But that is not fair, beautiful young one . . ."

"Please precious young one, fulfill it now . . ."

Anaíd, impassive, considered that they should reflect on their last betrayal.

"Oh, yes? And who told Cristine Olav about my plans?"

Then she disappeared from the room, leaving the spirits deep in thought.

Anaíd reached the cave at the time indicated by Deméter. She nervously studied every corner and shuddered whenever she saw the dancing shadows cast innocently by the oil lamp. She thought she saw the figure of her grandmother in each one of the grotesque silhouettes projected by the stalactites and stalagmites.

But Deméter appeared under an unsuspected guise.

The wolf, the great she-wolf of gray fur and wise eyes, emerged from the depths of the cavern and greeted her with a howl.

Anaíd recognized her and tried to hug her, but the she-wolf stepped aside and spoke in the wolves' tongue.

"They are waiting for you, Anaíd, and there's not time to lose. I will protect you."

"From whom?"

"It doesn't matter. They know you will try to do it, so don't look back. I will be here, protecting you. Are you sure you want to try?"

"Yes."

"You must follow the path of the sun. You will ride the last ray of the sunset to enter the Dark World. Don't be afraid, I will tell you how."

Anaíd wrung her hands in distress.

"I need to know if my mother has betrayed us."

But the she-wolf didn't respond to her question.

"You will return, with or without Selene, riding the first ray of the sunrise. Remember that well because, if you don't, you will be trapped in the Dark World forever."

"How will I know if Selene is one of us?"

"Don't expect to be certain before you take any risks. You'll have to make decisions on your own and the choices will be difficult. Now follow me, and remember, don't look back."

Anaíd got to her feet and ran behind the old she-wolf, who entered the deep forest expertly, picking the quickest shortcuts. Anaíd could feel a threatening presence closing in on her, surrounding her; she could feel a pair of sharp, burning eyes filtering through the oak leaves, a misleading whisper calling her, inviting her to stop, and she felt a strong desire to turn around, but she didn't. They reached the clearing as the last rays of sun were fading.

"Now! Ride!" ordered the she-wolf.

A thundering roar resonated behind her. Anaíd paused; the she-wolf was fighting, grunting, and howling; defending herself and Anaíd from someone. Anaíd hesitated—she wanted to help her grandmother and confront the danger face-to-face—but she remembered Deméter's warning and the fact that she was a spirit, and didn't turn around.

"Now!" shouted Deméter.

And following the she-wolf's order, Anaíd jumped onto the sunbeam that was cutting through the air. Her long hair glistening in the sun, she rode the last sunbeam and plunged into the darkness.

TREATISE OF DOLS

The goal of this treatise is to develop the theory that the chosen one might belong to the clan of the she-wolf.

Our tradition, now in the collective unconscious, is teeming with allusions to the alleged perversity and aggressiveness of the wolf, and consequently, the she-wolf. The animal has often been considered a "creature of the darkness," even linked to the devil.

It is not surprising that a predator like the wolf, one of the only creatures capable of confronting us in the natural environment, and who acts in an organized and effective way, awakes in us the ancestral fear of being hunted. However, in the battle between man and wolf, the wolf's attacks are infinitely fewer compared to ours. Proof of it is the current state of their species.

In the myths of Romulus and Remus, or Gargoris and Habis, human babies were suckled by female wolves. Native Americans view the wolf as an honorable rival, whom they respect and admire. In Chinese characters, the wolf is literally represented as a "distinguished dog," perhaps due to its almond-shaped eyes.

The wolf is one of the most common animal motifs in ceremonial glasses, urns, and plates used by the ancient Iberians. These motifs usually reflect the diabolical nature of this animal (slightly slanted eyes, pointy ears, stretched lower lip revealing its sharp teeth and fangs). In the whole Mediterranean region, the wolf has been related to beliefs about the spirit world. There are areas in pre-Roman Spain where the wolf was represented as a totemic animal in coins, which was later replaced by the Roman she-wolf. Also, the myth of the werewolf has been part of old cultural traditions for centuries. The werewolf has appeared with different names in numerous stories and legends, especially in the western part of the peninsula. Considering the aforementioned, I will try to locate the possible geographical area where, according to Om, the chosen one will grow up, along with the clan that will share its knowledge with her. In these pages, I will rule out the possibility that it is the Alps or the Apennine Mountains, and I will try to defend Rivana's theory about the Pyrenees. I will also prove the greater possibility that she belongs to the clan of the she-wolf, as compared to a not-yet-discarded hypothesis that maintains she belongs to the clan of the female bear or fox.

CHAPTER 30

———

THE DARK WORLD

At first, Anaíd didn't notice anything different. Was she still in the same spot? In the forest's clearing, the oak trees stood tall around her, and far away, among the treetops, she could make out the familiar mountain peaks.

But the light wasn't the same.

At first, she attributed this to the sunset, but soon she realized that the light in this place wasn't changing. It was always the same—dull and devoid of contrast. She could barely distinguish any colors. In fact, there were no colors. Anaíd rubbed her eyes. Was she in a parallel world? Was this where Selene now lived? It didn't look like a particularly sinister place. It reminded her of rainy fall afternoons, when the clouds filter the sun, casting a spectral light.

Suddenly she heard a laugh. Then another one. And another one. Thousands of laughs resonated around her. An army of childish laughs. Threatening. Irreverent.

Anaíd nervously got to her feet. Who was laughing?

"Is anybody there?" she asked.

"I'm *there*. And you?"

"I'm *there* too."

"Where are you?"

"I'm *there*."

"I don't know where I am."

And again, mocking laughter. But Anaíd wasn't intimidated. There must be someone hiding behind every voice; it was a matter of finding out who it was. She walked deep into the woods and searched with her eyes open, removing the fallen leaves from the ground, rummaging in the oaks' roots, and picking up stones. They were everywhere; hundreds and thousands of the forest's goblins, unashamed and minute, barely a few inches tall, coming out to provoke her like ants.

Well, she wouldn't let them bother her.

"I know who you are. Don't hide."

"What a smart girl."

"More than smart, super smart."

"Are you smart?"

"Beware, I don't trust the clever."

Anaíd stamped her foot impatiently. If every remark would generate such stupid comments, she'd rather keep quiet. She decided to try one more time. She swiftly crouched down and caught a playful man, who fit in the palm of her hand. When she closed her hand, she felt him kick, bang with tiny fists, and even bite furiously. Finally, he calmed down.

"I'm looking for Selene," Anaíd whispered to him softly.

The words she pronounced in such secrecy immediately spread around the forest at the speed of light.

"She's looking for Selene."

"The beautiful girl is looking for Selene."

"How smart is the girl looking for Selene?"

"She arrived on rays of sun and wants to find Selene."

"Where is Selene?"

"In the lake."

"In the cottage."

"In the cave."

Anaíd took a few breaths.

"Stop!" she shouted angrily.

Nobody did, however, and the infinite stupid comments about Selene's whereabouts continued until a robin spoke to her from the branches of a tree.

"Beware of the Countess, child."

"The Countess? Who's the Countess?" Anaíd asked.

Once again, hundreds of insipid comments were uttered around her.

"The girl doesn't know who the Countess is."

"If the Countess finds the girl, she will know who the Countess is."

"Selene does know the Countess."

"Is the Countess asleep?"

"Oh, dear! And if the girl wakes the Countess up?"

Anaíd was disappointed. She couldn't stay there, surrounded by mocking goblins. So she began to walk in one direction. If she was in a parallel word to the real world, as she assumed, she would find her way home. So she took the old trail she knew so well. The goblin she held in her hand kicked furiously, but Anaíd was also furious and didn't care at all.

Finally, after a long walk, she realized that she had made the wrong assumption.

The trail ended abruptly, and before her was a steep wall of rocks. There, where the first traces of civilization should be, the Dark World ended.

"Fine," she told herself, "I will go back to the clearing and walk toward the lake."

She turned around but soon got lost. Anaíd knew the forest like the back of her hand. But here the river changed direction randomly. She noticed this when she walked past the same spot three times. It was hopeless. She was walking in circles. Even if she walked straight, the river seemed to walk as well and kept crossing her path.

It was then that she understood the difference between the Dark World and the real world. Here, nothing was predictable. The sky's dome didn't even exist. The sky was a grayish stain above her head, with no sun to guide her.

She would never find Selene.

She would never be able to go back to her own world.

She sat on a rock and started sobbing inconsolably. All the tears she had swallowed now flowed like a spring, rolling down her cheeks and soaking the ground. In desperation, she opened her fist and let the goblin go. But the goblin didn't move. He was looking blankly at the spot where Anaíd's salty tears were falling. A smooth-skinned fish, buried long ago, had emerged from the ground and was now rolling on the wet soil.

"Oh, yes! This is wonderful! Please keep crying. Your tears are salty and delicious! It's about time; I've been waiting for this moment since the ocean withdrew."

The goblin was indignant.

"Go back underground, ugly creature."

"I don't feel like it."

Then, the goblin turned to Anaíd.

"Stop crying, clever girl."

Anaíd didn't care about anything, and continued sobbing.

"Fine. I will take you to Selene," the goblin mumbled.

Anaíd stopped abruptly.

"Really?"

"And you are going to believe him?" the strange fish complained. "Selene is dead. You will never find her."

Anaíd felt like crying again, but she realized that the strange, wicked fish loved tears, so she decided to provoke him.

"You are lying! Let's go."

And she grabbed the goblin, who stuck out his tongue at the fish.

"Ha! Serves you right!"

Anaíd felt much better. Crying had helped her calm down. She still didn't trust the miniature man, however.

"Where are we going?"

"The lake, but I wouldn't go there if I were you."

"Why?"

"You're not going to cry again?"

"No, please tell me."

"Selene wants to make you disappear."

"I don't believe you!" she yelled at the goblin. She needed to find her bearings.

Was she walking north? South? East?

"Meow."

Anaíd froze. She thought . . .

"Meow."

No doubt; it was Apollo, her beloved kitten.

"It's me, Apollo! Anaíd!" she called, ignoring the mocking replies to her words.

The cat appeared before her. He looked exactly the same as when he had fallen down the abyss. As if not even a minute had passed. Apollo walked over to Anaíd and licked her affectionately. Anaíd hugged him, and they rolled on the ground together. Then, recovered from her excitement, Anaíd meowed Selene's name, and Apollo invited her to follow him.

Anaíd walked behind the kitten and decided to check her watch. How odd. She couldn't figure out how long she'd spent in this strange world. Her watch marked midnight, but . . . had five hours gone by since she disappeared from the clearing? She wasn't sleepy, or hungry, or thirsty. She didn't feel tired. This was certainly a peculiar world. They would get out of here as soon as she found Selene. The first rays of sun appeared around seven in the morning. She should be back in the clearing by that time.

Apollo walked playfully in front of her, then suddenly stopped by a bend in the river, distracted by a small stone that had landed at his feet. A flirtatious female voice addressed him.

"Come on, kitty, pick up the pebble and bring it back to me."

"It's not a dog," said another voice. "It's a cat."

"Well, I'd prefer a dog, but there aren't any around. Apollo can bring me the stone in his mouth. Right, Apollo?"

The voices sounded reasonable to Anaíd. She took a few steps forward and saw the long-haired young women bathing in the river.

"Anaíd!"

"Hello, Anaíd."

"Are you looking for Selene?"

"Is Selene waiting for you?"

Anaíd was astounded. How did the two beautiful women know her name?"

"How do you know so many things?" she asked them.

"We heard the voices in the forest."

"We always hear about everything that's happening."

"The voices spoke about you and Selene."

"Do you know Selene?"

Anaíd didn't know who to reply to. The Anjanas whispered to each other.

"She doesn't know it," said one.

"Is she her friend or her enemy?" asked the other one, in a childish voice.

"She's my mother," Anaíd finally replied.

Silence and then laughter. The Anjanas spoke to each other as if Anaíd wasn't there.

"I told you."

"She's old."

"And she thinks she's beautiful."

Suddenly, an Anjana tilted her head to the side with a seductive smile.

"Look at me, Anaíd. Am I beautiful?"

The other one swayed her long hair and demanded Anaíd's attention too.

"She has wrinkles. Look at me, Anaíd."

Anaíd looked at them, one at a time. They were young and slender. They wore translucent gauze gowns and their hair was threaded with flowers.

"The two of you are very beautiful."

"More than Selene?"

"You are different; she's not like you."

"I told you, she's not an Anjana. And you? Are you an Anjana?"

"I'm a witch."

When they heard this, they immediately fell silent, exchanged a nervous glance, and dove into the river's waters.

"Wait. I'm an Omar, not an Odish. I won't hurt you."

But the Anjanas were no longer there.

Anaíd set off behind Apollo again. She followed the river's course and gradually ascended until she'd entered the wide glacial valley.

Apollo meowed to show her the stunning landscape—the lake

surrounded by high peaks. Despite her sadness, brought on by the permanent twilight, Anaíd's heart swelled with pride. This was her lake.

. . .

In that very moment, in the world without time and contrasts, a new presence caused a commotion among the raucous green men of the forest.

"Are you looking for Selene too?"

"Are you clever?"

"As clever as Anaíd?"

"You didn't come on the sun."

"How did you get here?"

A dry voice urged them to stop.

"Shut up! She's *my* guest. Her name is Criselda and I brought her here. I don't want to hear another word . . . Understood?"

The little men stopped talking. They feared her and obeyed her blindly. It was Salma.

Criselda glanced around cautiously and checked her watch.

"So? Where's Selene?"

Salma gestured vaguely toward their surroundings.

"The Dark World is unpredictable. She will come to us."

But Criselda was agitated.

"We can't wait. Selene is dangerous and the girl is looking for her."

"You want to move quicker than the girl? She can defend herself, look at my hand."

Criselda glanced at Salma's hand from the corner of her eye but stuck to her guns.

"That was our deal. I will take care of Selene, but you'll forget about Anaíd."

Salma remained quiet. Her silence seemed to acknowledge the pact.

"But there's something else," she added.

Criselda sighed.

"I thought so. It was you who came to me. I'm sure you didn't do it out of kindness. What do you want, Salma?"

"The scepter of power will be mine."

Criselda placed her hands on her hips.

"That's absurd. The scepter of power can be used only by the chosen one."

Salma rubbed her hands.

"I don't fully believe in the prophecy, but I can feel the scepter's power."

Criselda wasn't willing to budge.

"The deal was very clear. Everything must stay as it is now. If the chosen one dies before the alignment occurs, neither of us will be destroyed."

"Of course," Salma quickly agreed.

"In that case," Criselda pointed out, "the scepter must disappear."

All of a sudden, Salma brought a hand to her mouth and gestured for Criselda to stop talking.

The Countess's voice thundered through a crack in the cave.

"Salma, I know you are there with an Omar. Have you brought her for me? Is she young?"

Salma motioned for Criselda to be quiet, then took out her athame and brandished it fearlessly.

"By the power of the Dark World's shadows, I order you, Countess, to sleep until the scepter of the Queen Mother O cleanses your memory and you awake on her command."

And as Salma uttered the spell with the power of all the blood

317

she had recently consumed, the trunks of the ancient oaks bent, their branches creaked, and a strong wind erupted, almost blowing the plump Criselda away. Criselda clung desperately to the trees' roots, closed her eyes, and hoped that Salma's powerful spell and betrayal wouldn't kill her, too.

The hardest part was still ahead of her.

CHAPTER 31

—

THE CHOSEN ONE

On the banks of the lake, dozens of beautiful women combed their hair and gazed at their reflections in the water.

Anaíd's heart froze. Something told her that one of them was her mother.

But which one? She couldn't distinguish the bright crimson of her hair. The strange light tinted the colors, making contrasts unnoticeable. Anaíd began her search slowly.

"Mom? Has anyone seen Selene?" she whispered.

The Anjanas complained about Selene's aloofness but didn't help Anaíd. They made vague gestures and resumed their never-ending bath... Then, after turning a corner and walking by a willow, Anaíd saw her.

Selene was on her knees by the bank, combing her long hair. With her gaze lost, she sang, or hummed, an old song. It was a song Anaíd remembered from her childhood. It was her mother.

"Mother!" shouted Anaíd, throwing herself into her arms.

But Selene didn't open them. On the contrary, she shrank back, folding her arms in fear.

"It's me, Mom; Anaíd, please!" She begged her mother to recognize her.

Selene had crazed, vacant eyes; like those of someone who's roamed many worlds and doesn't know the way back home. She was staring at the bottom of the lake.

"I dropped it and I can't get it back. Nobody will help me; I want someone to help me."

Anaíd followed her mother's gaze and saw a sort of golden branch at the bottom of the lake, half-hidden in the mire and marsh plants. The lake was deep and its waters so cold that nobody who dared dive in would survive. No, it would be impossible to recover the object Selene wanted.

"I've come to get you; we have to go," Anaíd whispered, taking her mother's hand.

"No! I won't leave without my scepter."

She bent over the lake again, turning her back to Anaíd. The Anjanas laughed.

"Selene wants the scepter so she can be the most beautiful of all."

"And the most powerful."

"To eliminate the Tsinoulises."

"Shut up!" roared Selene with hatred.

Anaíd shuddered. Her mother's voice was different from what she remembered. There was no trace of tenderness. It had a metallic sound, like coins clinking in a purse.

"Mother," Anaíd said with difficulty.

It was hard, but she wasn't willing to give up so quickly.

"What do you want?"

"I want you to come home. I love you."

Selene turned around quickly, like a snake about to attack. Her face was only a millimeter from Anaíd's.

"If you love me, if you really love me, get my scepter back."

Anaíd looked at the bottom of the lake. She slowly stripped off her clothes until her whole outfit lay on the ground.

320

"Don't do it, silly girl, she will destroy you."

"Don't give the scepter back to her. That's all she wants."

But this time, it was Anaíd who ordered them to shut up.

Then she turned to Selene.

"If I get your scepter, will you come with me?"

Selene looked as if she couldn't even see Anaíd. Despite her demented look, she nodded.

Anaíd took a deep breath and dove cleanly into the lake from a rock. The waters became murky and swallowed her body.

Suddenly, Selene extended her arms toward the lake. She couldn't see the bottom. She couldn't see the golden branch that had captured her mind.

"Anaíd, come back! Anaíd, Anaíd . . ."

A hint of fear flickered in her eyes and horror began to take over her conscience.

The Anjanas laughed, indifferent to her suffering.

"The lake has swallowed Anaíd!"

"The lake has taken its victim."

"The lake never returns its prey."

"They are kept prisoners by the marsh plants, their hair caught in the branches."

"They never return from the cold waters."

Selene was gradually recovering her memory. It was impossible to estimate how long ago Anaíd had jumped into the water, but she wasn't coming back to the surface. Selene grabbed the clothes Anaíd had left on the ground and brought them to her face. She smelled them, like any other wolf would do, and howled with pain. Suddenly, she heard a bubbling sound on the surface of the lake. A huge trout with shrewd eyes was holding the scepter in its mouth. Selene extended her hand with uncertainty and took it. The trout leaped out of the lake and landed on Selene's lap, fluttering in agony. It was suffocating and Selene didn't know how to help. It was Anaíd.

"My beautiful girl, my dear Anaíd...Come back, please, Mom will sing you a song and cradle you in her arms."

And Selene caressed her, rocked her, and hummed to her. The trout's convulsions slowly came to an end, her fins turned into long, thin arms and legs, and her scales transformed into Anaíd's white-blue skin.

"Anaíd?"

"It's me," she murmured, exhausted.

Selene hugged Anaíd tenderly. The vague memories from her previous life were slowly returning to her.

"Anaíd, my child."

"Mom!" said Anaíd, shivering with cold. She cuddled against her mother's warm chest.

And the loving embrace finished melting the icebergs of indifference that had taken over Selene's heart.

"What are you doing here? How did you get here?"

Anaíd checked her watch. There was no time to lose.

"I rode the last sunbeam. We must take the first one back. Let's go."

But Selene wasn't listening; her eyes had paused on the scepter she had dropped on the rocks. She grabbed it, dried it with her gown, and waved it.

"The prophecy."

Anaíd didn't understand.

"The prophecy is coming true," Selene muttered again.

She rummaged in her daughter's leather bag and took out the athame made of lunar stone.

"She will ride the sun and brandish the moon," she exclaimed.

And Anaíd began to slowly understand—too slowly. Selene opened the locket Anaíd carried around her neck and smiled when she saw the picture of her daughter as a child.

"My child. I didn't even want to bring your image to this place, but how I've longed to have you by my side . . ."

Anaíd was shaking.

"Was coming here your choice?" she asked Selene.

"Yes."

"And you didn't fight against the Odish?"

"No. I wanted only to draw them away from you."

There was so much information to process that Anaíd was afraid she wouldn't be able to understand.

"Why?"

"To distract them; I made them believe I was being tempted, so they focused their attention on me and moved away from the real chosen one."

"So you are not the chosen one?"

Selene gazed at her with conviction.

"Haven't you realized yet . . . ?"

Anaíd shivered with cold and fear.

"You are the chosen one, sweetheart."

"No, that's not possible," Anaíd said seriously. She was paralyzed by fear.

And Selene melodically recited the prophecy of O:

And the chosen one, Om's descendant, will arrive one day.

She'll have fire in her hair,
Wings and scales on her skin,
A howl in her throat,
And death in her eyes.

She will ride the sun
And brandish the moon.

Anaíd listened in silence. This couldn't be true; Selene was wrong.

"Anaíd, you can see the spirits of the dead and understand and speak the language of animals. You are the chosen one. I've known it since you were little. A comet announced your birth."

But Anaíd couldn't understand; she didn't have fire in her hair. Unless . . . A suspicion suddenly crossed her mind. Selene guessed what she was thinking and opened the locket Anaíd carried around her neck.

"That red lock of hair is yours, Anaíd. I cut it off when you were a baby."

"That's not true! You are lying!" Anaíd refused to believe it.

"I've always dyed your hair, and mine," Selene insisted. "I've switched their colors. By now your roots should be red again."

Anaíd began to understand Elena's astonishment when she saw her with her hair clean.

"So you . . . deceived them on purpose?"

"Deméter and I decided to protect you and mislead them, making them think I was the chosen one. The comet the Odish detected appeared fifteen years ago, when you were born."

Anaíd felt guilty.

"You let yourself be caught for me?"

"Anaíd, look at your watch. Time doesn't pass here. You must go back; I'll guard your exit. Put on your clothes."

"I've come to get you and we both need to escape," Anaíd insisted as she got dressed. She wasn't willing to renounce her mother so easily.

Selene was heartbroken.

"I can't, Anaíd. No Omar has ever been able to leave this place. They live forever as prisoners by the lake. They lose memory and hope. I let myself be caught to avoid suffering. I didn't think you'd get here. They wanted me to kill you."

"Me?"

"The Countess is suspicious. That's why I took the scepter, that's why I threw it in the lake. But Salma is very dangerous and won't forgive you for cutting off her finger."

"I don't want to leave you."

"Get away, Anaíd, and hide until you are ready to rule with the scepter of power. The alignment hasn't occurred yet, you still have time."

The scepter shone brightly. Anaíd was about to take it when Selene spoke.

"Don't touch it!" she warned.

"Why?"

"I don't know, it's O's scepter, so powerful that it made Salma rebel against the Countess and it made me go mad."

"Fine, I won't touch it, but you have to come with me. Someone has to carry it. You can take it."

"No, Anaíd, I will stay here and remain beautiful forever. When you feel sad, look for me in the lake; I'll be under the water, smiling."

But Anaíd stood firm. "If you don't come with me, I'll stay under the water too. I'll comb my hair, smile, and look around with crazy eyes."

Selene grew desperate.

"No. You've been on a long journey by yourself. I never thought fate would bring you to this sad world, but I do know that you shouldn't stay here. Your place is in the real world, with the Omars. You are the chosen one, Anaíd, you must fulfill the prophecy. Do you hear me?"

"I've come to get you," Anaíd insisted stubbornly, "and I won't leave without you."

Selene knew that Anaíd was as determined as her mother.

"Okay. I'll try to escape with you," she said, standing up.

Anaíd checked her watch. It was four thirty and the sun rose at seven. Would they make it?

. . .

Returning to the real world was easier with Selene, who quickly guided Anaíd to the clearing, skillfully dodging the Anjanas' provocations and the goblins' insolent shouts. Selene was one more inhabitant of that unusual and ridiculous world, but she was calm and lucid and Anaíd was happy to learn that the horrible suspicions around her mother were not true.

Unlike the she-wolf, who never abandons her pack, Selene had actually acted like a cunning fox, pushing hunters away from her litter and astutely provoking them with her calls. Selene had betrayed the spirit of her clan and deceived the Odish. All of them, Omar and Odish, had believed she was the chosen one. Selene had expertly played the part, making everyone turn their eyes to her. The small, ungainly Anaíd—a witch without powers whom it wasn't worth initiating—hid behind her provocative, red-haired shadow.

But she hadn't had enough time to finish tying the loose ends of her plan. The Odish had abducted her before she could safely deliver Anaíd into Valeria's hands, and she'd believed that her strategy, planned years before with the help of Deméter, had failed.

However, despite Selene's disappearance, Anaíd's destiny was inevitable.

During the journey back, Selene felt hopeful again. She'd been so uncertain about the future that she had forgotten about her own life. Her daughter had made her remember and laugh, suffer, and fear. That's why when they were near the clearing, a feeling of anxiety invaded her.

"They know you are here. They are waiting for us. They'll try to stop you," she murmured.

Anaíd could feel danger looming as well. It was six o'clock. They had only one hour to get back. How long was one hour in a place without time? The best she could do was follow her watch.

"Anaíd, darling, I knew you would come."

Anaíd and Selene were taken aback. The sweet and charming Cristine Olav was blocking their way.

"You don't know how happy I am to see you are safe and sound, and as beautiful as I imagined you in dreams. I never thought you'd be able to outshine Selene the impostor, but you have. You are taller than your mother now, Anaíd; slimmer, younger, more beautiful, and you have the power of the chosen one."

Turning pale, Selene covered Anaíd's ears.

"Don't listen to her; don't believe a word she says."

Cristine's clear laughter resonated in the forest.

"Haven't you explained anything to her, Selene? You know I love her; I love her as much as you do. I don't mean her any harm. Haven't you told her the truth?"

Selene stood between the two.

"Let us keep going if you truly love her."

"Oh, no, Anaíd is as much mine as she is yours, Selene. You deceived me once, but you won't do it again."

Selene stood tall as a lioness and marched toward Ms. Olav. Fire came out of her eyes, and Anaíd felt sorry for the sweet and fragile woman.

"Step aside," Selene thundered.

But Ms. Olav's fragility was only a guise. Her sweet voice

concealed a power infinitely superior to Selene's. The power granted by thousands of years of immortality.

"No dear, I won't step aside or let you leave. We'll share her, you and I, like a family. Remember, I comforted you in my arms, Anaíd? Didn't I make you happy? I've treated you like a daughter. Did I ever hurt you? I protected you in Taormina; I watched over you and sheltered you from Salma. I was in your closet in the form of a cat. Tell Selene, she doesn't believe me."

Anaíd was confused. Ms. Olav disconcerted her. She was telling the truth. And she seemed to have met her mother before. How did they know each other? What rights was Cristine Olav claiming?

Selene pushed her.

"Don't listen to her, Anaíd, she's lying. Run, the sun is about to come out. Get out of here. Get out of this trap."

Anaíd hesitated for a few seconds; then she looked into Ms. Olav's eyes with confidence.

"I believe you, but please let us go."

Ms. Olav blinked. Anaíd saw a tiny tear form in her eye. Was it possible? Cristine's lips quivered, a reflex of her emotions.

"You believe me?"

Selene took her by the hand.

"Enough, Anaíd, don't look her in the eye, don't—"

But Anaíd ignored her mother; she continued to stand before Cristine Olav with her bare hands.

"Please, let us go."

"Is that what you want, Anaíd?"

"Yes."

"Fine, you can go."

"Both of us?"

"If that's what you really want."

328

Following an impulse, Anaíd hugged Cristine Olav and let the Odish's slender arms envelope her. Before saying good-bye, Anaíd kissed her on the cheek and felt her warmth and affection.

Then, to her astonishment, Ms. Olav turned into an elegant white cat and disappeared.

· · ·

Anaíd and Selene reached the clearing a few minutes before seven. But they were not alone.

Criselda and Salma were waiting for them.

Salma met them with a smile.

"Welcome. We thought you would never make it."

Was it really good old Criselda standing next to Salma? What did this mean? What had happened?

Anaíd and Selene glanced at them, one at a time, trying to figure out which one was more dangerous and unpredictable.

"Carry out your sacred mission, old Omar."

Criselda took out her athame. She looked at Selene and then at Anaíd.

"I won't do it in front of the girl. I want her to leave. I will fulfill my task once she's back in the real world."

Anaíd refused.

"I won't leave without my mother."

And Salma produced her hand, which was missing a finger.

"I will deal with the girl. There's something unsettled between us. You take care of the chosen one, the alignment hasn't occurred yet. You can sacrifice her; she's of no use to you or us. She made me think she was drinking a baby's blood, but then returned it alive."

Criselda noticed the light filtering through the clearing and looked pleadingly at Anaíd. Selene caught her look too.

"Ride the sunbeam!" she cried.

And with surprising strength and agility, Criselda lunged at Salma with her athame.

Selene screamed. Anaíd didn't quite understand what was happening. Criselda's strange reaction had thrown her off balance. Instead of fulfilling her oath and eliminating Selene, Criselda had attacked Salma. Anaíd decided to help her and unsheathed her athame. But it was too late.

Criselda had fallen, dead or unconscious.

Salma looked at her, surprised.

"I will never understand you Omars; you are willing to sacrifice yourselves for one another so stupidly."

"There are many things you don't understand, Salma." Selene provoked her. "Maybe you are the stupid one. I have the scepter. Move aside or I'll kill you."

Anaíd saw the glimmer of the first rays of sun in the dark, murky sky. Selene saw it too.

"Go, quickly!" ordered Selene.

Salma walked toward Selene with her wand extended, and she would have hurt her like she hurt Criselda, had it not been for Anaíd, who unfolded herself into multiple illusions and stabbed her with her lunar athame. This time, the knife didn't shatter. The invincible weapon she'd forged in the depths of the earth returned Salma's spell of destruction back onto herself. Anaíd cut Salma's shoulder so badly that the Odish released her wand with a scream.

Salma's pain unleashed a tempest. Anaíd and Selene were blinded by lightning and surrounded by an enormous shadow. Salma's power was manifesting itself fully. They could feel her claws oppressing them, suffocating them, squeezing their hearts dry. Selene wrapped Anaíd in her arms to protect her, and Anaíd felt the scepter touch her hand, luring her like a magnet. Without hesitating, she took it away from her mother and brandished it powerfully over her head and against Salma.

"Scepter! Destroy the immortal and return her to the beginning of time!"

And all Anaíd could remember was chaos and confusion. There was a terrible explosion, and Selene's strong arms dragging her toward the sunbeam, forcing her to ride it by herself. Criselda's voice urged Selene and Apollo to go. Selene and Anaíd embraced on the first rays of the dawn, leaving a world without contrasts, without time, and riding toward light and clarity.

Upon touching the ground, Apollo meowed at the new day's sun.

CHAPTER 32

THE WEIGHT OF THE PROPHECY

Anaíd held on to Selene, sobbing. She felt like a small child in her mother's arms.

"Did I really destroy her?"

"Yes, sweetheart. Salma disintegrated."

"So . . ."

Selene trembled as she pointed to the sky.

"The planetary alignment has occurred. It's amazing. Do you see them? They are aligned, one behind the other: Mercury, Venus, Mars, Jupiter, Saturn, and with us, the earth, the moon, and the sun . . . You can rule now."

Anaíd held her breath as she watched the phenomenon. It was extraordinary and truly beautiful.

She looked away from the sky.

"What will happen to Aunt Criselda?"

Selene stroked her hair and smiled.

"Have you looked at yourself in a mirror lately?"

Anaíd wiped her tears and shook her head. The sun's light shone on the top of her head.

"Fire in her hair . . . ," murmured Selene, moved.

"Really? Is it red?"

"When was the last time you used your special shampoo?"

"A month and a half ago, maybe two."

"We'll have to dye it again immediately."

Anaíd was suddenly aware of her new responsibility.

"Elena realized when she saw me, and I think Karen did too. That's why they told Criselda; that's why Criselda agreed to play Salma's game."

"It's possible."

Anaíd had one doubt. "Why did Salma need Criselda to eliminate you?"

Selene didn't hesitate. "To defend herself before the Countess. The Countess wouldn't have allowed Salma to destroy the chosen one. She needs her to survive. The Countess is running out of strength and only the chosen one holds the key to her immortality."

"What is it?"

"The scepter of power, which will bring about the end of the Omars."

Anaíd was very anxious. She stared at the shimmering scepter in her hands.

"I don't know how I did it. I just said the words the scepter told me."

Selene thought about this.

"Deméter and I kept the secret of the real chosen one fervently. Nobody knows the truth; though Valeria might sense it."

"No, she was convinced that you were the chosen one," Anaíd disagreed. "Actually, they all thought you were the chosen one, except for Gaya."

Selene chuckled maliciously and stood up.

"Gaya will be very happy to know she was right!"

Anaíd got on her feet too.

"I'm not ready."

"I know, Anaíd, that's why we'll have to keep the secret and hide until the time comes for you to rule."

"Was your hair dark when you were a child?"

"Yes."

"So how did you deceive Criselda and the others?"

"When you were born, your grandmother and I moved to the Pyrenees, where nobody knew us. Deméter spread the rumor that she was hiding me, the chosen one, and had dyed my hair since childhood, but it didn't matter anymore because the Odish had already found me."

Anaíd sighed and filled her lungs with clean, fresh morning air. She took in the colors of fall and their tones—ochers, yellows, and coppers; reds, oranges, and purples. What a beautiful world this was! Even the feeling of hunger was wonderful. How amazing it was to be thirsty, and how magnificent to feel tired.

"Poor Aunt Criselda."

"I survived. You can survive in the nothingness."

"But you are stronger than her."

Selene gazed at Anaíd, astonished.

"Do you really think that?"

Anaíd nodded.

"Aunt Criselda is a disaster, she has no idea about—"

Selene laughed sincerely.

"Didn't she tell you?"

"What?"

"Criselda is Deméter's successor. She's kept the tribes united. She has watched over you and protected you."

Anaíd was surprised.

"But it looked like . . ."

"Don't rely on appearances. The Omars are never who they seem."

"Neither are the Odish," said Anaíd, thinking of Ms. Olav. But Selene started running.

"One, two, three! The last one will cook breakfast!"

"Wait!" shouted Anaíd. "You have to tell me about Max!"

. . .

The department store was packed. Anaíd had never been as happy as that afternoon shopping with her mother. They had decided to empty the new items section.

"Can I really buy this sweater? How come we have so much money?"

Selene looked to one side then the other discreetly.

"It's an open secret. I was an Odish for a while and that was my pay."

"But if we spend it all at once, we will be poor again."

"I like to splurge, Anaíd, that's why it was so easy to convince them that they were tempting me. I love diamond rings, caviar, and champagne."

"Weren't you afraid?"

"Yes, often."

"What was your worst moment?"

"Making Salma believe that I was bleeding a baby."

"That's horrible!"

"Yes, but I have to say that there were some good things about it. I can guarantee that we'll never go hungry!"

They left the store with so much stuff that they could barely carry the bags. At the door, they bumped into Marion.

"Marion!" It was Anaíd who recognized her.

Marion didn't pay attention at first.

"Anaíd?"

Anaíd kissed her naturally, as if they were old friends.

"Thanks for the clothes you lent me. They fit perfectly."

Marion was self-conscious.

"You are welcome. I . . . Is it true that you are leaving?"

"Yes, we are going away."

"Where?"

"North," said Anaíd.

"No, south," corrected Selene.

Anaíd shrugged.

"We haven't decided yet."

Selene laughed and showed Marion the new clothes.

"Just in case, we've bought a bit of everything."

"Oh, how fun," said Marion, clearly impressed.

Anaíd tried to make her feel comfortable.

"Yes, we did have a lot of fun."

Marion prolonged the meeting with an unexpected invitation.

"Would you like to come out with us on Saturday?"

Anaíd thought about it for second.

"I'd like to, but I have other plans . . . Anyway, I'll have a party before I leave."

"A party?" Selene was surprised.

"Yes, it will be my birthday party. And you are invited, Marion."

"Oh, thank you, I . . . I'm sorry you weren't here for mine."

"Don't worry, everyone will be at my party, and I will introduce you to my best friend. Her name is Clodia."

"Clodia, cool."

"Yes, and she is even cooler; she can chop a rabbit's neck in a single blow. It's amazing."

Marion turned pale.

Anaíd kissed her good-bye.

"Don't worry, I said a *rabbit's* neck."

Marion smiled timidly and turned around. Selene walked up to Anaíd on the street and whispered in her ear.

"Look at you, you've lied three times."

"Not one!"

"What do you mean?"

"I have a date with Aunt Criselda at the lake this Saturday. I plan to celebrate my birthday, and Clodia, my best friend, will be my guest of honor, and you'll see her cut a rabbit's neck."

Selene was impressed.

"Wow, I guess I've missed a lot of things."

"Lots," agreed Anaíd.

MEMOIRS OF LETO

I walk back and forth the road of life. I stop at the fountains to drink fresh water and rest for a moment. I converse with the other travelers and eagerly await their responses. Their words are the only light that guides my steps.

Knowing that she, the chosen one, will also have to travel a long path of pain and blood, renunciation, loneliness and regrets, worries me.

Like me, she will suffer from the dirt on the road, the harsh cold, and the burning sun. But that won't stop her.

I wish I could save her from the bitter pang of disappointment, but I can't. The chosen one will embark on her own journey and hurt her feet on the stones that were laid out for her.

I can't help her chew the impending sorrow or sweeten the tears that haven't been shed yet.

For they belong to her.
They are her destiny.

CHAPTER 33

———

AN UNCERTAIN FUTURE

The cold waters of the lake softly rippled in the wind. Anaíd walked restlessly around the edge, without taking her eyes off the bottom. Her image, the image in the lake, was reflected back at her, making her feel strange and proud at the same time. She thought she saw her mother in that slender young woman of long hair and feline movements. But she was hoping to see another face—the dear face of Criselda, who remained imprisoned in the Dark World.

Finally, she saw it.

"There she is!" Anaíd gestured with excitement.

Selene knelt down next to her. The two watched Criselda comb her long and beautiful hair on the shore. She looked younger, more serene, absent.

"Can she see us?" Anaíd asked.

Selene nodded.

"She knows we are looking at her. See?"

And Criselda smiled sweetly. She seemed at peace.

"Is she happy?"

Selene held Anaíd in her arms.

"You are the chosen one and you are alive. That's enough for her."

"And I'm already a woman."

"She doesn't know that, but she can sense it. Look at her, tell her with your eyes."

Anaíd smiled back at Criselda, and her smile contained the promise of her return. She would never forget her.

Anaíd sighed.

"I'm afraid."

"It's natural," Selene reassured her. "Power causes vertigo."

"Do you promise not to leave me alone?"

"It will be you who leaves me."

"Me?"

"It's the law of life, Anaíd."

"Did that happen to you?"

"Of course."

"Was that when you met Cristine Olav?"

Selene turned pale.

"That's a long story."

"Will you tell me someday?"

Selene remained silent, deep in thought.

"Someday."

Suddenly, Anaíd brought her hands to her head.

"Oh, no!"

Selene grew worried.

"What's the matter?"

Anaíd started walking back home.

"I forgot to fulfill a promise."

"A promise?"

"I promised the treacherous lady and the cowardly knight that I would set them free."

"What?"

"What you've heard."

"But—"

"It's a long story," Anaíd cut her off.

Selene understood and winked at her knowingly.

"Will you tell me someday?"

Anaíd paused and pretended to think.

"Someday."

Maite Carranza

Maite Carranza studied Anthropology and worked as a teacher. In 1992, she began to write full time. She has received several awards, including the EDEBÉ children's literature prize and has written more than forty books for young readers. Maite lives in Barcelona, Spain.

Noël Baca Castex

Nöel Baca Castex, the translator, was born in Argentina. After receiving a degree in Spanish/English, she worked in publishing for ten years. Nöel is now a full-time translator and lives in New Jersey, America.

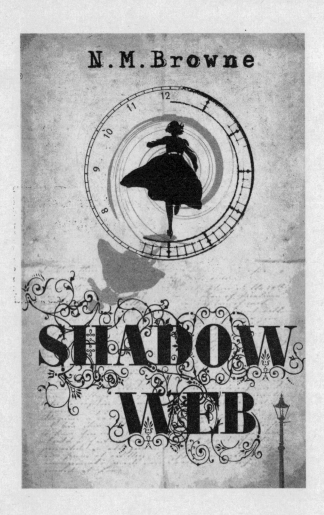